DARK DISCOVERIES

Winter 2014, Issue Number 26, *www.DarkDiscoveries.com*

I0683850

Publisher
JournalStone Publishing, LLC

Editor-in-Chief
James R. Beach

Assistant Editors
Aaron J. French (Managing Editor)
Kenneth Heard (Reviews Editor)
Lacey Friedly (Senior Submissions Editor)

**Art Director,
Layout, and Design**
Cyrus Wraith Walker

Contributors

Norman Partridge
Gary A. Braunbeck
David Liss
Hank Schwaeble
Gemma Files
Joel B. Kirkpatrick
Leah Jung
Steve Holetz

Nick Freeman
Aaron J. French
Rocky Wood
James R. Beach
Yvonne Navarro
Robert Morrish
Richard Dansky
Amy Shane

Michael R. Collings
Jonathan Maberry and David F. Kramer

Special Thanks
David Liss
Chelsie Aryn
Joe Bob Briggs
Quentin Tarantino

**Contributing
Artists/Photographers**
(Cover Image) Nicovision
Other Photographers (See Captions)

DARK DISCOVERIES
(ISSN 1548-6842) is published (Qtrly) by
JournalStone Publications, 1261 Peachwood
Court, San Bruno, CA 94066

Christopher C. Payne
JournalStone Publications
1261 Peachwood Court, San Bruno, CA 94066,
U.S.A.
christophercpayne@journalstone.com

Please make check or money order payable to:
JournalStone Publishing and send to the address above.
Credit/Debit cards via Paypal at:
christophercpayne@journalstone.com. Advertising
rates available. Discounts for bulk and standing retail
orders.

FICTION

INTERVIEWS

FEATURES

HELLNOTES REVIEWS

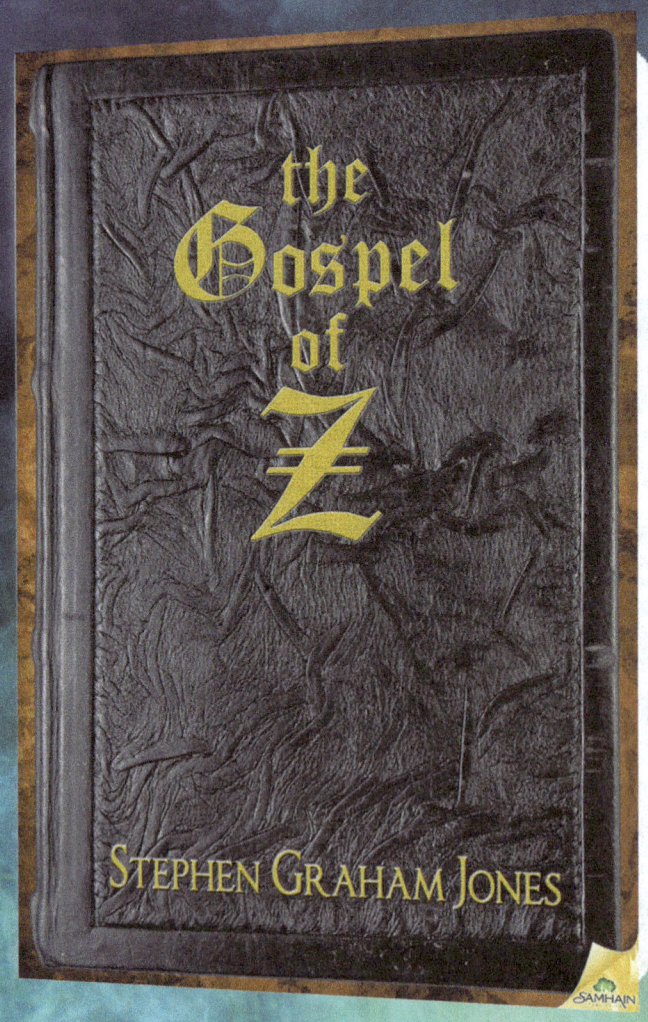

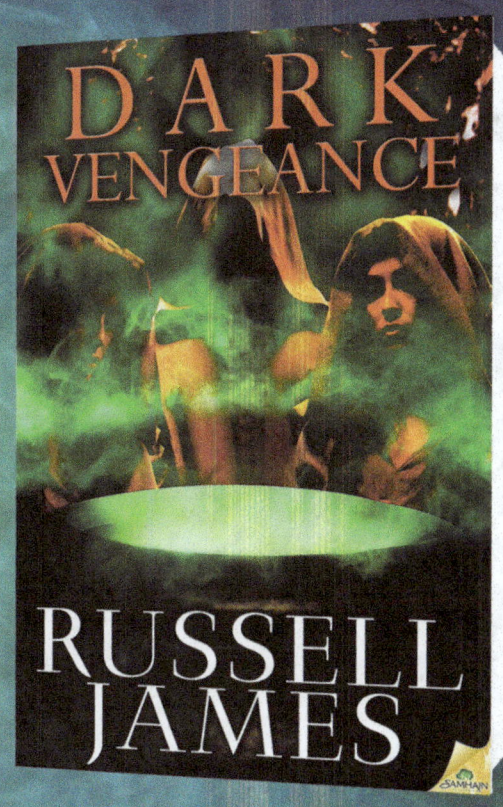

$\mathcal{U}$pdates from the Dark Beach

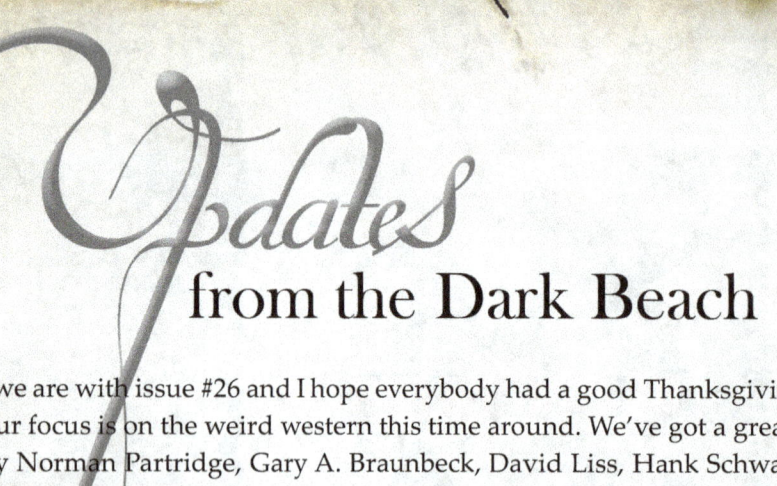

Here we are with issue #26 and I hope everybody had a good Thanksgiving, Christmas and New Years. Our focus is on the weird western this time around. We've got a great issue with brand new fiction by Norman Partridge, Gary A. Braunbeck, David Liss, Hank Schwaeble and Gemma Files. Interviews with Quentin Tarantino (on Django Unchained), Drive-In champion Joe Bob Briggs, David Liss and our lovely cover model Chelsie Aryn. We've also got articles by Rocky Wood on Stephen King and his western influence, the 50th anniversary of spaghetti westerns and cult director Alejandro Jodorowsky. And of course our usual lineup of great columnists (like Robert Morrish, Yvonne Navarro, Jonathan Maberry, etc.), reviews of new books & movies and more!

On the topic of anniversaries, it's one for Dark Discoveries as well. Hard to believe, but it's been 10 years of continuous publication for the magazine. In January of 2004, I officially launched Dark Discoveries Publications and issue #1 debuted at the start of March. I hired my first designer, David Emrich, around August of 2003, started soliciting submissions and asking stores to carry it (Matt Schwartz of Shocklines was the first, and also by advertising he helped get other people to buy ad space too). I hardly knew anyone in the publishing and writing world, but with lots of support, encouragement, and help from people, DD took off. Through trial and error, ups and downs, successes and failures and most importantly not quitting when it got tough, somehow Dark Discoveries survived.

Jason V Brock came on in late 2008 to help me turn it from a small press publication into a more professional one and broaden our content to help grab more readers and attention. Our themed-issue direction came from Jason and he helped me with a lot of advice on the business end as DD was growing. Cyrus Wraith Walker took over the design/layout after Jason left to start his own magazine, Nameless, and to continue his book line in early 2012, and Aaron J. French also came on that spring to help with editing in the transition. JournalStone Publishing owner Christopher Payne was the final piece and took over publication of Dark Discoveries in August of 2012 to help move us into that next level of a pro-magazine completely.

We've had some amazing contributors over the years and many heroes of mine have appeared in these pages like Ray Bradbury, Richard Matheson, Stephen King, William F. Nolan, Bruce Campbell, Elvira, Dan O'Bannon, Joe R. Lansdale, Richard Laymon, Jack Ketchum, George Clayton Johnson, Thomas Ligotti, Adrienne King, F. Paul Wilson, Ramsey Campbell, Al Feldstein and many, many others. Thanks to everybody who helped out with Dark Discoveries over the years (too numerous to mention but you know who you are) and especially to our readers, subscribers and advertisers who have supported DD. Here's to many more years to come!

And on that note, there is a little more transition happening with Dark Discoveries. I want to also congratulate my assistant Aaron J. French on his moving into the Editor-in-Chief position starting with issue #27. I am stepping down to free myself up to work on some book projects that got put on the back burner and also assist a couple other publisher friends who need help (and honestly I need a little break from it. You don't get vacations in the small press—not when you're running one at least!). Aaron has done an excellent job and both Chris Payne and I feel he is ready to step it up. Aaron is a sharp guy and has been a big part of our continued growth and shaping the issues. I will still be helping as a "Creative Consultant" and with some editing, though, so not to worry. Dark Discoveries was and always will be my baby, but the baby has finally grown up.

Lastly a popular star of Spaghetti Westerns, Giuliano Gemma, passed away this year leaving a big legacy. Giuliano was the first Italian lead to break through in 1965. Prior to him, the popular trend was to use an American actor such as Clint Eastwood. Director Duccio Tessari cast Gemma as his main man in A Pistol For Ringo (Una Pistola Per Ringo) – which spawned no less than 11 sequels (some in name only) – and The Return of Ringo in 1966.

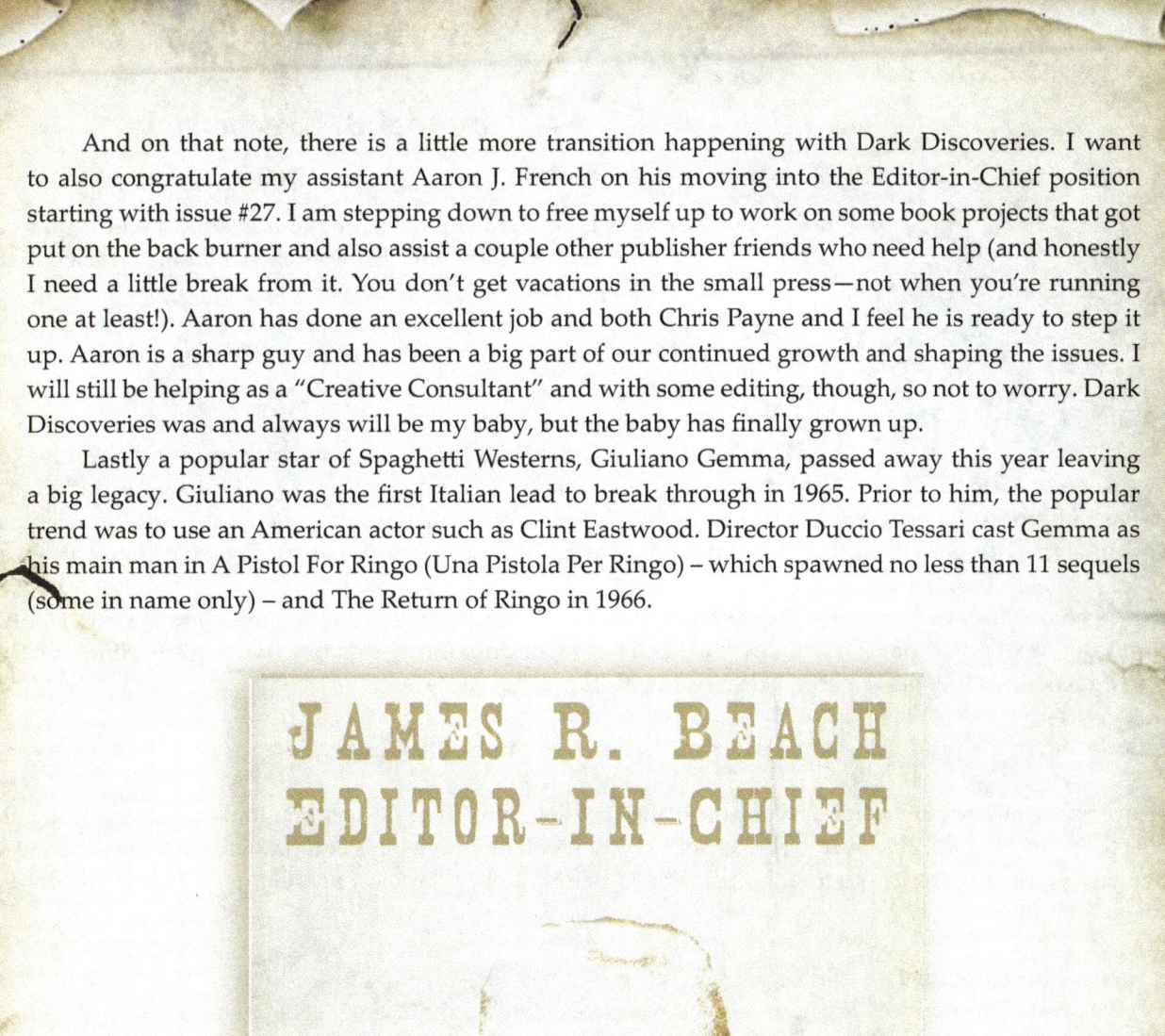

JAMES R. BEACH
EDITOR-IN-CHIEF

WANTED
DEAD OR ALIVE

A Conversation with David Liss

by Joel B. Kirkpatrick

Photo by John Davenport

Pursuing a doctorate is an undertaking that will batter any student who sets their sights upon that goal. It is almost a given that at some point in the task they will throw their hands up in disgust and vow never to go back to it—PhD be damned! The rigors of composing that kind of product loom as too impossible to be completed.

Hardly any of those abused students thrash out a fiction novel instead, submerging themselves in one arduous writing task in order to avoid another. David Liss did.

David took a wild turn in his planned career and never looked back. Now, living in San Antonio as a satisfied best-selling author, and with seven published works, two future novels in progress, at least four collaborations, half a dozen short fictions and a novella—and also writing for comic books—David Liss has earned more than a literary degree. He has earned acclaim.

JBK: It has been eighteen months since the publication of your last novel *The Twelfth Enchantment*. That usually means a writer is deep into the next novel. We know you have been working during that time writing storylines for Dynamite Entertainment comics. How far along is your next novel, *The Day of Atonement*?

DL: It is done and in the production pipeline. It is scheduled to come out in fall of 2014.

JBK: You are also a member of a collaborative group, the Candlelight Writers Group, and JournalStone will be publishing your collective novel *Century* next year. This is not your first collaborative project (another will be mentioned in just a bit). Have you worked with the other authors involved before: Robert Jackson Bennett, Joe McKinney, Rhodi Hawk, and Hank Schwaeble?

DL: No, we have been friends for a while now, and our group has been meeting for about three years, but this is the first time we have done a joint project. It's been a great experience. I loved writing my section, but I also really enjoyed the sessions we had hammering out ideas. Getting five writers together to brainstorm a concept is my idea of a good time.

JBK: You also recently contributed to JournalStone's *Out of Tune*, a project edited by Jonathan Maberry, to be published May 2014. What did you write for that anthology?

DL: Jonathan allowed us to choose from a wide range of folk ballads. I picked "Sweet William's Ghost," which appealed to me because it's about the living haunting the dead. There's something fascinating in that setup.

JBK: A character with a history, and characters *within* history are your bread-and-butter themes. Yet, it was writer's block with a dissertation—British Literature, no less—that drove you to write for your own pleasure. You came into fiction truly by accident, agreed?

DL: I would probably frame it a little differently. It wasn't writer's block with my dissertation that drove me to write my first novel, but rather my realization that I did not want to stay on the academic track. I'd always wanted to write fiction, but I had convinced myself that making a living as a writer was for "other people." But at a certain point I felt like I was at a crossroads and had to make a real decision about what I wanted to do with my life. I thought that I could apply the analytical thinking skills I'd learned in grad school toward

figuring out what makes a novel tick. I also decided that someone had to get published, so why not me? Essentially I took a big chunk of my dissertation research and figured out how I could turn it into a story that would be enjoyable to write and, hopefully, to read.

JBK: The product of that failed dissertation was the very well received *A Conspiracy of Paper* (Balantine, 2000). It earned you an Edgar Award for First Novel. You have a great love of that book's era, the early Eighteenth Century.

DL: It was really the last time when a man could wear a wig and stocks and not look silly doing it.

I joke, though I really do love the 18th century aesthetic. But my fascination with the period comes from it being simultaneously remarkably similar and shockingly different than our own. If you go back further, say to the renaissance, people saw the world and themselves so differently as to be unrecognizable to us. Once you get to the 19th century, people are basically us, just with inferior technology. I often think that looking at 18th century culture is like looking in a fun house mirror: you see yourself reflected back, but grotesquely distorted.

JBK: You have said that the period was "*...vibrant, brutal, colorful and more exciting than I would have believed.*" That statement speaks to a lot of reading and research on your part. What writers did you turn to for the best look at the realities of the time?

DL: When I was working on my dissertation, I spent a lot of time reading contemporary newspapers, magazines, social-issue pamphlets, how-to books, and a variety of other primary sources that give a fairly good sense of life in the period. There are also extremely popular writers, now forgotten, like Ned Ward, whose book *The London Spy* provides an amazing and disgusting look at early 18th century culture. According to Ward, there's almost nowhere you can go in London, including bathhouses, where someone won't try to smear shit on you. It's all very strange, but this was the 4th most popular book in 18th century England, after *The Pilgrim's Progress*, Shakespeare, and the Bible.

On the less grotesque side, my favorite 18th century writing is certainly Henry Fielding, but I look to a lot of other figures to learn about the social nuances of the period, especially Tobias Smollett, Frances Burney, Eliza Haywood, and many others less well known.

JBK: It is a rare author who garners a coveted award with

their first published book. You earned a Barry Award, Edgar Award, Macavity Award in each of their First Novel categories. Here was definitive proof that you're a skilled writer. Weren't you eager to complete your doctorate suddenly?

DL: No, I was thrilled that I was suddenly expected to write more novels. I walked away and never looked back.

JBK: You have only refrained a single time from crafting historical characters, in *The Ethical Assassin*. Your character in that book, Lem Altick, is an about-to-be-surprised encyclopedia salesman—a previous-life job you know fairly well. We can guess you could fill three or four novels with the strange stories of that sort of occupation.

DL: I spent a summer as a door-to-door encyclopedia salesman, and I always knew it was something I would have to write about one day. The experience was so strange and twisted, and the people so freakish, that even now I'm not quite sure I believe my own memories. But I don't think I need to write any more on the subject. Everything I had to say pretty much made it into that book.

JBK: Which is most important to you: that the setting be factually accurate; or the story be strong enough to carry the reader past any horseplay with realism? Do you ever receive reader responses about the accuracy of your books?

DL: For me, the story comes first, but not at the expense of accuracy. The research is meant to give depth to the story, rather than have a story that's a vehicle for relating my research. I know there are some writers of historical fiction whose main goal is to convey the history in a lively way, but my first goal is always to tell the best story I can.

In terms of mistakes, there has never been a historical novel written free of anachronisms. Historical fiction, after all, is an act of translation, and that means sometimes nuances have to be sacrificed in order to serve the larger meaning. That said, most of the time when I hear from readers who think they've found mistakes in my books, they have done less research than I have and aren't correct. Still, it is often more important to seem right than to be right.

JBK: Has your research ever revealed facts of an era that by their discovery forced you to change the plot of your books?

DL: Nothing drastic, though research has often led me to adjust character or plot, or sometimes something as subtle as a detail of internal design within a house can help me see new depth to a character. The bottom line for historical fiction is the more you know about a period, the better you can understand your characters. So, yes. New information has often changed how I view a story, but I've never had to make huge changes in plot.

JBK: One fact of history you seem to have ignored was that London in the mid-1700s was not particularly harsh to its Jewish Community. You paint a darker, meaner image of the place than actually existed.

DL: I would say just the opposite is true. I've toned down the vehement anti-Jewish sentiments of the period in order to keep the stories from seeming like a screed. This is a great example of how a writer must sometimes alter facts in order to create a more accurate sense of history. If in *A Conspiracy of Paper* I represented English anti-Semitism accurately, it would be nonstop and relentless, and the reader would become frustrated with the kinds of encounters repeated over and over again.

Additionally, 18th century bigotry is not the same thing, from an ideological standpoint, as contemporary bigotry. We live in a world in which the dominant philosophical position is that all people should have equal rights, and to adopt another position is to willingly choose an anti-social stance. In the 18th century, it was a perfectly moral position to believe your people were better than others, and to believe those not of your country or religion to be inferior and contemptible. In other words, for an 18th century man to adopt a position of hating Jews or Catholics or the French or Italians was not to align with an anti-social discourse, as would be the case for someone today joining, say, a white power movement. Thus to rail against 18th century bigotry is to suggest a kind of immorality that was foreign to the period.

JBK: As a definitively *modern* American writer you take advantage of the modern reader by framing your stories to meet so many tastes. They encompass all the proper elements of crime, mystery, thriller, historical—an in the case of *The Twelfth Enchantment*—elements of romance and fantasy. It this out of pure artistic freedom, or does the modern reading market demand such diversity?

DL: I'm lucky enough, for the most part, to be able to write what I want and to get away with it. At times, I've resisted a great deal of pressure to write sequels that did not interest me. I work in different genres because I enjoy those genres. I have, on a couple of occasions, bowed to pressure and written a book that I didn't want to write. I've always been happy with the final product, but I've enjoyed the experience a lot less.

JBK: What style of novel has always flirted with your imagination, but never found its way onto paper? Are there any forms of writing you don't believe you do well enough to publish?

DL: There are certain kinds of writing I don't have a feel for, and so they seem difficult to approach. For example, the kind of complex thriller with a huge cast of perspective characters has always seemed outside my reach, not because I can't figure out how to do it, but because I don't know that I would be interested in doing it. I tend to stay away from writing styles that don't hold my interest, but I don't think I've ever genuinely wanted to tell a story but felt too intimidated by genre or form to make the attempt.

JBK: Aren't you also working on a young adult space opera, titled *Randoms*? Are you at all intimidated by the youth market?

DL: The youth market is huge and vibrant and exciting. That said, I don't really enjoy most of the science fiction that's out there for the young adult market, which is often depressing and bleak. When I was a teenager, I was attracted to optimistic science fiction. I liked the idea of the future being cool and exciting, not miserable and oppressive, so in many ways *Randoms* is an attempt to write a science fiction novel with a much different vibe than the dominant dystopian portion of the market.

JBK: Beer Soup. Have you tried it yet?

DL: I often want to try the disgusting foods my historical characters eat, but that one I've taken a pass on.

JBK: Many of your readers may think you invented the notion of brewing coffee with red wine, but it was the proper thing to do in the setting of *The Coffee Trader*, wasn't it?

DL: The idea of mixing milk with coffee was unpopular in the period, and water wasn't commonly used as a household beverage. Beer was generally the drink of choice for quenching thirst, but beer and coffee were not seen to mix. Wine and coffee, to the 17th century mind, were much more compatible because they were both dark and strong.

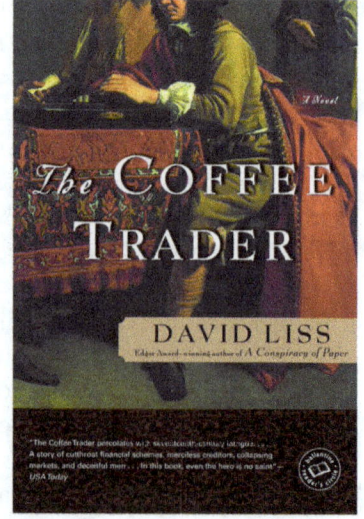

JBK: But mixing coffee with milk causes leprosy...?

Was that a serious belief of the era?

DL: Absolutely. I took that directly out of a 17th century medical text. Medicine of the period was largely a collection of precedent, supposition, guesswork and lies.

JBK: You once told Barbara Peters on her webcast *The Criminal Calendar*, "…I like to write books about things that people don't think they will find interesting, but then they do." Then you go on to laugh that you are not particularly interested in finance.

DL: I think I was saying that I'm not particularly interested in following modern markets in great detail. I am, however, interested in historical markets and how they emerge. People think historical finance must be boring, but really it's about people trying to control huge amounts of wealth and power, and that's always interesting. That said, in order to understand the material, I've had to wade through a lot of dry reading.

JBK: Your stories are actually studies in emerging economics. Worldwide economics, rather than the collection of kingdoms and empires. You've noted that economic history seems to keep repeating itself, even with the difference in modern information flow and number of players. In your mind, what is the greatest engine of the globe, money or politics?

DL: I think it's always wrong to see money and politics as separate, especially in today's world of hyper capitalism. The two are so intertwined that they are essentially different aspects of the same thing. It's like asking whether the head or the torso is the most important part of a horse.

JBK: Tell us about Jeffery Deaver's *The Copper Bracelet* and your collaboration with fifteen other authors to create a single story. Who contacted you and suggested your involvement?

DL: That project came out of International Thriller Writers, an organization I've been part of since its inception. Many of the original members were part of *The Copper Bracelet*. Honestly, I don't remember how it happened, but I suspect one of the people I know emailed me and asked if I wanted to do it, and I said yes.

JBK: Did you have access to all the chapters previous to yours, or did you only have a timeline and premise from which to work? Did you make a conscious effort to write in a similar style as the other writers, or is the finished book really a quilt of different styles?

DL: I read through all the previous chapters. For the most part, we were free to go where we wanted, but the editor

of the project made some requests. I think at that point the story had become a little sprawling, and I was asked if I could help focus its direction, which I did my best to do. I do feel like I tried to write in a way that was stylistically in sync with what had come before me.

JBK: You once admitted that your writing process begins with an opening scene, which you then allow to evolve as it wishes. Are your characters also malleable creations, changing as their situations change?

DL: I don't see these things as happening on their own, of course, but you do a different kind of thinking when you are writing than when you are *planning* to write, so I often get ideas or insights while at the keyboard. If they seem interesting or compelling, I run with them.

JBK: Collaborating with the artists of Dynamite Comics has placed you in the enviable category of a novelist reworking seriously iconic characters. *The Spider*—Richard Wentworth; *The Black Panther* (Marvel Comics); and just this last year, Moriarty himself. Who has the control in these emerging narratives, you or the character?

DL: When dealing with characters who have a long history, you have to have a lot of respect for what has come before you. The people who own the characters also have to agree with whatever I decide to do, which I understand. That said, when I write stories about those established characters, I want to tell a story that I enjoy telling, so I usually take as much freedom as I can get away with.

JBK: Your modern treatment of the iconic pulp character The Spider for Dynamite is a real departure from novel writing. Comic books are more closely parallel to screenplay writing. How did these types of projects come about?

DL: I originally started writing comics when I was contacted by an editor at Marvel, who had read my novels and wanted me to work with him. I've always loved comics, so it was a no-brainer. I've been working in comics for about four or five years now, and it's simply another part of my creative and professional life.

JBK: *The Spider* was a project that you accepted with very little prior back-reading or character knowledge—though you were well aware of his mythos and mystique. Are characters of that sort intimidating, and are you more eager now to delve into the preexisting material?

DL: It's always a little intimidating to approach a character who has been around for almost a century. When writing any character who's been around for a while—The Spider, The Shadow, Black Panther, etc.—you have to do a ton of research, but that's all part of the game. But once I absorb that research, I tend not to continue going back. Though, with The Spider, I've tried to incorporate elements of the original pulps in my modern retelling, and I have gone back to read some of those novels during my time on that series.

JBK: New readers may not be aware that you explore horrific elements in your short fiction. *The Double Dealer, What Maisie Knew, Watchlist*, and *A Bad Season for Necromancy* are published stories that could be termed "horrific." Have none of them produced the seed for a horror novel, or is that something you plan to do?

DL: I don't know that I have any plans for a full-length horror novel, though I'm very attracted to the novella form these days, and I am planning on writing some horror novellas over the next year.

JBK: Will your character Benjamin Weaver reappear in any future works? He has appeared in three of your novels thus far. Have you played his story out to the end?

DL: I have no plans for more Benjamin Weaver novels, but a much older version of the character will appear, in a minor role, in my forthcoming book, *The Day of Atonement.*

JBK: You mentioned once that you share your work with your wife. Does she function as a beta-reader on projects?

DL: She read the manuscript of my first novel very carefully, but since then I've found it not great for our marriage for her to read early drafts. Because she's an academic, she's used to a particular kind of close reading that isn't really what I'm looking for, and she has a hard time turning it off, so it takes her a very long time to read early drafts, and she comes back with a ton of notes. I'm usually looking for a quick read with broad comments, so I have a network of friends who are early readers.

JBK: It has been several years since you mentioned film developments for *A Conspiracy of Paper* and *The Coffee Trader*. Where are those projects currently? Are you cynical about the film industry actually bringing them to the silver screen?

DL: I am always cynical about the film industry. Various projects are in various stages of development, but until I'm in the theater, eating popcorn, I'm not going to believe any of them will actually happen.

JBK: It's well established now that you will take a major turn in your objectives when it suites you. After producing major fiction works and succeeding with them, you are now settling into the world of pulp fiction, with hardly a visible tremble. Would you admit you're having the most fun of your career?

DL: Absolutely. I am still writing historical fiction, and I still love it, but I'm also doing comics, horror, dark fantasy and space opera. Every day I feel incredibly lucky that I get to work within the genres that I love.

Dead Man's Pecker

By David Liss

The wife had just about run out of energy for her screams, and the daughters weren't doing much more than whimpering, so things had quieted down nicely, which was to my satisfaction. I don't much care for excessive noise. That little cabin, located just outside Llano, Texas, had become my very own, for the Swiss fellow who'd built it was lying dead on the floor, and he was in no position to contest my claim.

I'd heard he'd settled there a year or two back, with his wife and three daughters. It was on an isolated plot of land, so upon hearing of it, I was tempted to have a look for myself, and found the discourse to be entirely correct. I should add that I had not thought it absolutely necessary for anyone to die, for I am not coldblooded in that particular way, but things went bad almost from the start.

The eldest girl, a real pretty thing with yellow hair, maybe fifteen years old, got herself away, and her ma got to screaming, which led her to becoming gutshot. Next thing you know, the Swiss husband, with his big beard and silly trousers, is lying on the floor bleeding from the general vicinity of what used to be his head. The wife was bleeding something fierce, but alive. The two daughters I still held on to were unhurt as of yet, but I wasn't liking anyone's attitude and could not speak to the future.

The wife was real pretty, not yet thirty-five, also with yellow hair and a nice shape to her under her frumpy Swiss dress. Not bad for a woman who has squeezed out three little ones. Of the remaining daughters, one was about thirteen, the other maybe eleven. That girl who'd got away was on foot, and we were far enough from town, so I figured I had three, four hours to have some fun.

The wife was likely to die soon, which was its own sort of pleasure. Any man can kill a woman in the middle of doing his business. There's nothing to it. You can strangle or stab her or even shoot her in the head. I've done such things, and they're not so satisfying because they're common. But if you can time it right so she's alive and fighting you at the beginning, and stone dead at the end, well, that's something special. That's something to savor.

I strode from one end of that cabin to the other, taking stock of my domain. The dead husband lying there in a pool of his sticky Swiss blood in the middle of the floor over by the stove. The girls, all tied up and weeping, red in the face from where I'd slapped them. The mama didn't need to be tied up. She was lying on the bed, pressing a wad of rags to her bloody middle. These were good and soaked with blood, and they couldn't absorb another drop, but she was pressing it there all the same. I guess she was what you'd call an optimist.

The cabin had stunk of leather and soot when I'd first come in, and now the stink of blood and piss filled the air too, but I did not let these things trouble me. Despite these odors, it was, I like to think, a near perfect moment—as close to untainted as anything in this mortal world can be. They were mine for the taking. What I had right then was undeniable and absolute. I stood before them like some new god, and they could worship me or die, whichever they saw fit.

That's when I heard the horses outside, and a gunshot fired into the air. Whoever it was, they weren't trying to sneak up on me. They wanted me to know they was there. I guess cause they had me surrounded and so figured there

was nothing I could do, but figuring that was a mistake, because there was always something I can do. That's how I got to be who I am: The Hailstorm Kid, they called me, on account of me raining down lead without mercy, and in a matter of a half year I'd become the most feared outlaw in Texas. The mere mention of my name made girls faint and men piss themselves and women experience sexual titillation. A reputation like that does not come cheap, and it can't be earned by half measures.

"Gordon, you come on out of there," I heard someone call, his voice fuzzy from distance. "You'll be walking out of that cabin or we'll be dragging you from it. The choice is yours."

I had worked very hard, and with a singularity of purpose, to become The Hailstorm Kid, so I did not much care to be addressed by my given name. This particular lawman knew as much.

"We got a dozen men surrounding the cabin," this lawman shouted. "Think about it, Gordon. If you make us come in there, you're going to die. Right here, and right now."

It did seem a likely outcome, I admit, but this I knew, that this lawman out there wouldn't want guns to start firing and for me to be lying dead here in this Llano cabin, my bullet-ridden body glorious amongst the carcasses of insignificant Swissers. This particular lawman would have to report what he'd done to his ma and pa, on account of him being my own brother. I knew his voice the moment he spoke, and I knew a situation like this was just a matter of time. My very own older brother, a Texas Ranger, had made it his particular mission to track me from El Paso to Nacogdoches and then back to Llano. He'd always been out to get me, and this was no different than it always was.

With my back to the wall, I turned my head to the window. "John!" I called out. "I got me one dead, two living, and one almost dead in here. We can make it four dead if you like, or you can get on your horses and ride away. Your call. I might end up before a judge, but it won't be until I've killed everyone in this cabin."

"They're *Swiss*," my brother called back. "There's no one of import who cares for their safety. They care that you're running loose."

His point, I knew, was a good one, but I also knew John. It was one thing for him to say it was of no concern if the Swiss lived or died, but it was another to watch me kill a little girl. I figured I had to show him I meant business.

The wife wasn't going to last long enough for this business to get resolved, so I figured I should expend her first. I propped her up and moved her to the window and put one in her head. Simple as that. Used to be harder, but it wasn't anything to it these days. Just something I did because I could and there wasn't anyone to stop me and no damn good reason to stop. Killing the Swiss mama or not killing her. What's the damn difference? To her? To me? I don't see that there is one.

After I shot her in her pretty head and the girls got done screaming and they'd settled into mournful wailing, I heard nothing but quiet from the lawmen outside.

"John," I called, "I got two more in here, both of them girls, youngest one not even twelve years old, I'm guessing. Got some nice buds on her too. You want that kind of blood on your hands?"

"I reckon it'll be on your hands, Gordon," John called back, and this was what I would describe as being typical of him. He was always trying to be clever with me, to show me he was smarter, to turn things around. This was how it was when we were boys. He would trick me and make me look the fool somehow or other, and he would laugh, and pa would laugh too, which is not right. That is not appropriate for a boy's father in my estimation.

I wasn't prepared to let John outsmart me this time. This wasn't some stupid game we played as children, and I couldn't let him win on account of it being too humiliating to be taken down by him. "That's how most people'll see it," I shouted, "but what about you? Late at night, lying in bed. You still see it that way, or will you think you just as good as pulled the trigger yourself."

"That reputation you built for yourself gives me no choice, Gordon," John called. "I got no reason to think those girls'll do any better with us here or gone, so I may as well put an end to what you've been doing. Fifteen people, Gordon. Can't let it go on."

"Seventeen," I called back. "Counting these here Swiss. And I can add two more to the tally without much trouble."

He didn't say anything for a long time, and I got to thinking about how this probably was not going to end so well for me after all. Best situation, I figured, was getting to jail in Llano and then trying to get out. Shooting my way past Gordon and his posse was not a likely outcome. Maybe if I did end up in jail, someone would tell the truth about what I done, because that's what bothered me most. They just said I was a killer and a thief, but they didn't say what I done to those women. They didn't tell the truth, because the truth was too indelicate for them, so they ignored it. That made me mad. You make yourself a god among men, and you want folks to acknowledge who you are. Why, a banker in Ft. Worth had put a $500 bounty on my pecker. I likely had the most valuable manly part in the whole United States, but no one knew it because the newspapers would not write about such matters.

"Give yourself up," John shouted, "and I'll make sure you get a newspaper man from San Antonio to write it all up. Hell, I'll even make sure he talks to you in person while you're in jail."

I hated how John seemed to know what was running through my head like that. It made me real mad that I wasn't surprising him, but that wasn't reason enough to get killed. Newspaper man and jailbreak seemed like the chance I had to take, so I fired two shots, putting down

the two younger girls, because it didn't make things any worse for me, but I knew it would make things worse for John. I was always thinking like that. Planning. It was why I was going to beat him in the end.

I threw my guns out the window and came out, showing my hands, all nice and slow, looking about as cheerful as I could manage. A couple of John's men grabbed me by my arms and forced them behind my back. They were tying my wrists and not being gentle about it either, and John stood there, with his big old hat shading his eyes and one of those stupid thin cigars he liked dangling out the corner of his mouth. It smelled like boiling beans, and I didn't care for the odor, though it smelled better than the cabin. Above that cigar and the cigar stink rested his ridiculously oversized mustache which made him look like a ninny, but I wasn't about to tell him. Better he should look like a ninny and not know it. He stood there, glaring at me, sneering like the brute he was, puffing on his damn stinky cigar and looking as mean as a snake.

John was three years older than me, and he used to beat me something fierce when we were boys. He used to bend back my arm until I cried. He was a real cruel one, and now that cruelty was on full display.

The girl who had run away—Anna, she was called—was off to the side, weeping on some other lawman's shoulder. She knew better, I guess, than to weep on John's, as he was uncaring. Then she came over and looked at me. Her tears dried, just like that, which means they probably weren't real to begin with, and that Swiss girl just spat in my face like I was dirt. John, of course, let her do it because that's the sort of brother he is.

***

I sat in that jail in Llano for a few hours, mainly just resting on account of being taken by lawmen is more tiring than most people think. Before leaving me be, John had given me a few punches to the gut and some slaps to the face. He said it was for the Swiss, but I'd never known him to care too much about foreigners, and I think he did it for himself.

That jail cell was right hot, and the air was as still as a tomb's. It stank nearly as bad as the Swissers' cabin too, and that turned my stomach. Even so, when they gave me some bread and dried beef, I ate it to keep up my strength. I hadn't seen a way out of that cell yet, and I figured I had to be ready for it when it came. There was always a chance, maybe only one, but at least one. That's the way the world was set up, and the men who rose to greatness were those who saw the chance and took it. I knew for a fact, an irrefutable fact, that I was one such a man. There were eighteen corpses who would tell you so themselves. All I needed was for the chance to reveal itself. I wasn't going to miss it.

After three days in that hot and stifling and piss-stinking cell, John came swaggering in with one of those cigars wedged between his teeth. He was followed by another man, this one much older, dressed in a fancy suit like you'd see a man wear in a place like Chicago, a city I have visited on two separate occasions. This man was tall and kind of expansive in his gut. He had some gray hair remaining on a fringe along the back of his head, and a long gray beard so he looked like maybe he was a Swiss himself. I don't have anything in particular against Swiss, by the way. This was only an observation.

"His morphology in no way appears atypical," the bearded man said, and he sounded not like a Swiss at all, but like an easterner, all clipped and proper. "A slight distending of the frontal brow, but in no way outside normal parameters."

John puffed on that bean-stink, trying, I knew, to look thoughtful. "You're saying there's nothing wrong with him?"

"His behavior dictates otherwise," the old fellow said. "I simply note that the shape of his head does not, upon first glance, give me any insights into his pathology."

I sat up on my bunk and leaned forward, meeting this geezer's eye. I didn't much like being discussed as if I weren't there. "Hey, old timer. You the newspaper man?"

"There's been a change of plans," my brother said. "There ain't going to be a newspaper man."

I hated when John broke his promises to me. He was always doing that, even when we were boys, saying he would give me something if I did a favor for him, and then I'd do that favor, and I wouldn't get anything for my pains. I felt like a fool for having trusted him, but I also figured that even without the promise of getting my story told, I would still have turned myself in on account of there not being another way out.

"You gave me your word," I said.

"When a man acts as you've done," John told me, "I don't have to honor my word. I just have to put an end to his killing. That's what the doc here is for."

"I don't need no doctoring," I said, now feeling a bit uneasy, as I did not love the thought of John giving a sawbones unfettered access to my person.

The old fellow narrowed his little eyes at me. "I am not here to tend to your hurts, I assure you. My name is Doctor Theodore Howard Williams, and your brother had agreed to let me attempt a procedure on you which will help us learn a great deal about the mind of a ruthless killer such as yourself."

"Is this before or after my trial?" I asked.

"This will be in lieu of the trial," said Doctor Theodore Howard Williams.

"The particular procedure the doc has in mind requires that you be dead," my brother explained. Then he grinned at me. His little cigar bobbed up and down like a drowning man upon the ocean, his big old mustache twitching like a caterpillar on fire. John thought this was the best joke in the world. He was a cold one.

***

Doctor Theodore Howard Williams was a cold one himself, as it turned out. He stood there in front of my jail cell, holding up all kinds of jagged little knives and a hand drill and a curious little machine. This was no bigger than an egg, and of the same shape as one, but unlike an egg it had all kinds of wires and gears, which turned all on their own, like it had been wound up somehow, though I didn't see a key. It was a marvel of a thing, and the doc said he'd invented it himself. He said he was going to cut a hole in my head, take out the part of my brain that made me do all those killings, and put that machine in there instead.

"What good is a machine in a man's head?" I asked.

"Once I activate it," the doctor explained, "you will be, of course, dead, and completely unaware of yourself, but it is my hope that you will remain animate, and, I believe, responsive to suggestion. You will be the test case, you understand, so I cannot say for certain, but I believe I am quite right. This procedure will transform you into a useful member of society. You can perform tasks that are too dangerous for ordinary men, working within mines or upon railroads."

"I don't want to work in no mine," I said.

"You won't know you're doing it, I assure you."

I looked over at my brother, and I fear some actual desperation may have been upon my face, for what this man with three first names was proposing was odious to me. I had to believe that, despite his lifelong habit of being unkind to me, some sort of brotherly devotion would thaw his cold heart. He would come to see that what I needed was not to be killed and mutilated and turned into a miner. What I needed was a newspaper man and a means of escape.

"I don't want to do this," I told John, not hiding the concern in my voice. "I want to talk to someone from the newspaper. You promised me someone from San Antonio, and cutting me up wasn't part of the bargain. This isn't what I want."

"Honestly, Gordon," John said, giving his head a sad little shake. "No one cares what you want."

"And how exactly do you plan on getting me to lie still for this head-cracking?" I asked. "Because if you come in here, it's all over for you. I mean, you get close to me, and I will destroy you, and then I'll take those fancy tools from the doctor and I'll cut a hole in him, and then I'll stick my five-hundred-dollar pecker in that hole just to show how I feel about working in mines, which is something distasteful to me."

It was at that point that John shot me in my chest, which turned out how they planned to get me to lie still.

***

When I opened my eyes, I was lying on a table that had been wheeled into the jail cell. Doctor Theodore Howard Williams was leaning over me, holding a candle up to my eyes, squinting through his spectacles. My brother stood beside him, his hand all covered with blood, as though he had been messing around inside my head.

"Interesting," he said. "I did not anticipate pupil dilation."

"I did everything just like you said," my brother told him.

"Of that I have no doubt," the doctor replied. "But this procedure was experimental. Some of the outcomes are uncertain."

I lay there, all still and otherwise immobile, waiting for my brother to leave, which he did after not so very long. Then the doctor raised the candle to my eyes once more.

"Get that damn light out of my face, doc," I said.

He staggered backwards, as though I was made of fire. I sat up and saw I wasn't wearing any clothes, and that I had a hole in my chest where John had shot me. It didn't hurt, and it wasn't bleeding. It was just a red hole near my heart. I stuck my finger in there and wiggled it around, and it didn't feel bad to do it. It didn't feel like much of anything. It was a curious sensation, though, like cold, but without any temperature at all, and when I pulled my finger out it was covered with congealed blood, which I wiped on a cloth by the table.

I hopped off the table and took a few steps toward the doctor. He backed away, all nice and terrified.

"You killed me?" I asked.

"Your brother shot you, yes," the doctor replied.

And here I was, walking around, like it was nothing. I wasn't wearing a stitch of clothing, and I looked down to find my most-wanted pecker all shriveled and, to be honest, somewhat blue in color, which I did not relish looking upon. I gave it a few shakes to see if I could stir up some action, but it was as dead as a slice of bacon, and this development alarmed me.

"My pecker don't work," I said to the doctor. "Can you fix it?"

He looked scared, but also thoughtful, like this was a puzzle for him to solve. I could see now the doc was that sort of man, and so maybe he could be useful. After a moment of deep thought, he proved my hunch correct. He adjusted the spectacles and squinted at my blue, lifeless pecker. "I suppose I could modify one of my surplus engines to operate a pneumatic pump that would enable tumescence."

"You best get to work on it," I told him, sticking my face in his like I was apt to bite his nose off. "Like your life depends on it, which it does, as I intend to kill you if you don't do as I ask."

I stepped out of the cell, which they had not troubled to lock, on account of them thinking I wasn't going to know who I was when they brought me back to life. This was a mistake, as I knew who I was and a great deal more. I found a mirror on the table with a bunch of the doctor's butchery tools, and I knew enough to look at it and see that they'd carved a big old slice out of my temple, and it was stitched up something ugly, which hindered my looks, as they had always been of the admirable variety. It was too bad, for I enjoyed having a handsome face, but on the other hand, they'd arranged it so I could not be killed, as I was already dead. This was the way out I'd hoped for. Ordinary men would not have remembered who they were, like the doc said should have happened to me, but I was destined for better things. I was, once again, like a new god.

"Get that pecker fix going," I said to the doc. "Then I'll have just about everything I need."

I stepped out into the main room of the jailhouse. I didn't bother with clothes. I couldn't feel if I was hot or cold, so there wasn't much point. I liked that people would be made to gaze upon my nakedness, as befits a god. It would be like my calling card. I would stroll around any town I wanted, or even take a train, and I would be naked as I wanted, and what could they do to stop me? If they tried to make me put on some pants, I'd just kill them. If they tried to kill me, they couldn't as I was dead already.

In the front room, my brother was sitting there talking to the sheriff, and they both looked up in surprise. I can't say I shared the surprise, since the stink of his cigar announced that I would find him there. He, however, hadn't expected to see me standing there naked and all deified and such. The sheriff wasn't much on quick thinking, and before he could get his gun out of his holster I had already reached down and yanked it away from him. Then I killed him, a shot right in the head.

I turned the gun to John. "I ain't putting on no pants," I told him.

John was holding up his hands, all gentle and easy, still puffing on that thing sticking out the corner of his mouth. "No one says you have to, Gordon. You just take it easy, now."

"I will take it easy," I said. "I'll take it real easy on account of what you done to me."

"I didn't have no choice," he said. "You can see that, I hope. There you were, riding round killing folks and violating women. You had to be stopped."

"You didn't have to do this to me," I said.

"You're right, Gordon. I didn't have to do that."

I think I surprised him because I hugged him then. I couldn't remember ever hugging my brother before, but I hugged him now because he had made it so I never had to worry about getting killed ever again. After all these years, he'd finally done something nice for me.

I pushed him away real quick, before he could reach for his gun. True, I could not die, but I did not particularly want to have too many more bullet wounds disfiguring my form.

"I think this is the best thing anyone has ever done for me," I said. "I don't have a care in the world now, and I won't ever have one again. I am now truly, truly free."

John smiled at me, but I think maybe he was forcing it because he was kind of grimacing like he was in some kind of pain.

Then he pulled his gun from his holster. I don't know what he was planning. Maybe he thought if he shot me enough times, it would stop me. Maybe he would go for the head. I wondered if someone shot away that egg-shaped machine in my head if that would put an end to me. Maybe John meant to try. So he reached for his gun, but I had it out of his hand before he could even wrap his finger around the trigger.

"Holy Jesus!" I shouted. "You see how fast that was?" And it was. I moved like lighting. You'd think being dead would make a man slower, but it turned out it was just the opposite. I was probably the fastest man alive. Or, I suppose, the fastest man in the world as such a description would be more accurate.

"What have I done?" John asked, looking like a man who had gambled away all he owned in the world. John was looking like a man who had lost it all, and that cheered me mightily, because I'd never seen him look so before, and I had certainly never been the cause of such a countenance.

I laughed. Then I looked down at my shriveled blue pecker and stopped laughing, because that part of the transformation was without humor.

"What do you plan to do, Gordon?" my brother was asking. "Where will you go?"

I didn't want to tell him about my idea of riding a train naked, on account of him probably thinking it would be a silly plan, so I had to think of something else, something more meaningful.

"Soon as the doc gets my pecker working," I said, "I think I'll go kill that Swiss girl. Anna was her name, as I recollect. She's got to pay for running off and fetching the law on me. Not to mention she spat in my face, which was unkind."

I did not mind telling him this plan, as no one would be able to stop me, except maybe shooting me in the head. Maybe even no one could do that, as I was so fast. Still, I did not tell him of this concern for obvious reasons.

***

John seemed to know how things were now. All my life, he'd been faster and stronger, and he'd believed he was smarter. He never let me forget his superior skills. That was done now. I made him fetch me some coffee, and that didn't go over so good. I tried to drink it, but I didn't seem too able to swallow right, and it ended up dribbling out

my mouth in an unsightly cascade. Same with water. And then whiskey.

"Well, hell," I said. "I guess I can't get drunk."

"No point in living then, near as I can see," John said. "You may as well have the doc take out that machine from that head of yours."

I winked at him, cause I was onto his trying to pull one over on me, on account of what the doctor had done, making me smarter and all. "That's real clever," I told him, "but not clever enough. I guess I'll miss getting drunk and eating a good piece of beef and all that, but I imagine there're other pleasures that await me, maybe some I can't yet imagine."

"Maybe you'd like to encounter such pleasures while wearing a pair of trousers, so the world don't have to look at that worthless pecker of yours," John suggested.

"It's still worth five hundred dollars," I told him with a grin. I said no more, because I chose to be magnanimous about his jealousy.

A few hours later, Doctor Theodore Howard Williams came out from the back and announced that he had a fix for my woes. He held up a machine about the size of an egg with little moving gears on it—being true to his word that he'd made some changes to one of his brain gizmos—but linked to that were a couple of tubes, one of which had a little plunger type thing at the end. There was also a big piece of copper wire which linked to a metallic nipple-type thing.

"This is the best I could do on short notice," he said. "It may cause some additional engorgement, but as your pain receptors are non-functional, I don't believe it will be a problem."

I hopped off the desk where I was sitting. "Let's get going!" I cried.

The doc then turned to John. "Perhaps it would be best if you come in and observe these proceedings." He spoke all strange and slow, like he was reading from a playbook.

I knew then what was going on, and I was not about to be fooled. "So you can get me to lie still and distract me and then maybe shoot me in my egg-shaped gizmo? No, sir. I won't have it. I see my brother, or anyone else, in there with me, I'll kill you right quick, doc. You best believe it. You treat me right, though, you'll have my gratitude. *Undying* gratitude, you might say." I waited for them to laugh, but I guess I could have waited all day, cause neither of them cracked a smile.

So we went back to the jail cell, and I made the Doctor Theodore Howard Williams lock the door so no one could surprise me. I got down on that table and he went to work, with his cutting and inserting and laying of wire. It was a funny thing, because I looked down and saw all these gashes in my flesh, over near the groin area, where a man is usually loath to have gashes of this nature, but I didn't so much as flinch. It was like I was this new thing, and so I didn't have the feelings or responses or concerns of being an old thing. I thought that maybe John wouldn't find it so easy to change his way of thinking as I did, and I guessed that this was why I'd come out on top in the end. He had his ways, and those were the ways the world said were better. My ways were sometimes frowned upon, but they seemed to have served me alright.

It took a hell of a long time for the doctor to do his business. He would work for a few hours and then declare he needed a rest, telling me to lie still. A few hours later, he came back and repeated the whole thing. That happened twice, but at last the doc finished and began to sew me up. I imagined that those wounds were never going to heal. They were going to look like that forever, and I didn't much care for it, but as there wasn't much to be done, I decided it was better to think of them as badges of honor, of my newfangled divinity, than marks of disfigurement. As soon as this idea entered my mind, I felt better.

I got off the table and decided I had to test out this machine before I let Doctor Theodore Howard Williams go anywhere. Operation of the machine, he said, was simple, gesturing to the metal nipple which now stuck out on my left hip bone. Flip it upward in a suggestive direction, and the pecker gets inflated. Flick it down, and it gets deflated. Easy as that.

Needless to say, I wasted no time in testing it. I won't go into too much detail about this, as there might be ladies reading this account, and I don't want to offend no ladies, nor their delicate sensibilities. Suffice to say that the extra engorgement he spoke of was on full display, and I did not mind at all. I also discovered that I couldn't feel anything like I used to, and *that* I did mind, but the doc said there was no helping it, and I believed him, since if I could not feel pain, why should I feel pleasure? This, I decided, was as it should be. There were new pleasures to be discovered, as I observed before, though I had not yet found them.

I pressed the button that deflated me, and I strode out of that there jail cell like a man with nothing to fear, because that's what I was. John was out there, sitting with his feet up on the desk, drinking a cup of coffee, which I guessed was supposed to mock me since I could not. But I wasn't about to let him get to me. I was a bigger man than that.

"I'm leaving here," I told him. "And you don't try to stop me."

"I won't," he said, sipping at his tin cup.

"You tried to do me wrong, but I emerged victorious."

"And naked," he said.

"You may think you are mocking me, but my nudity is a sign of my triumph over this world and its ways."

"I understand that, Gordon," he said, puffing thoughtfully on his stinker. "I do. I see now it was wrong of me to kill you and permit that machine to be inserted in your head. It was unkind. But now that you have changed into something vastly superior to mortal man, I am begging you not to use these powers of yours for evil. Imagine what a benefit to mankind you might become were you to step off the path of iniquity and instead join the march of the righteous."

I just laughed at him, because I understood why he wished to turn me from all the killing I now intended. "You done this to me," I said. "You made me what I am, and now the whole world will blame you what you've done as I embark upon my campaign of naked terror. You're only saying such because of your embarrassment."

He looked away, and he blushed, and I knew I had the right of it.

"See you some other time, John," I said. I twirled my pistol, which had been his pistol until lately, upon my fingers, and stepped out into the street. As I did so, people stopped and gaped at me, naked god that I was, with my marks of honor upon my head and my groin and my chest. They gazed, astonished, and I flipped skyward my pecker switch, and that astonished them even more. Perhaps these were the new pleasures of which I had speculated.

There were some horses tied up over by the whore house, and I figured I could help myself to any of them I liked. The horses shied away from me, I guess not being used to a being of my particular divine nature. I tried talking to one to sooth it, and to see if maybe communication with beasts was one of my new abilities. It was not, but I was determined, and I knew no mere beast could defeat me. I was about to hop onto the animal, when I heard the sound of a pistol being cocked in my direction.

I saw a man of the unwashed and drunken variety standing near the entrance of the whorehouse. He wore filthy trousers and a filthier shirt, and his suspenders were askew. His weapon was pointed at me, and it was clear he meant to stop me from taking what I chose to take.

"Get away from my horse, you naked fool," he said to me.

I grinned at him, eager to explore my new divinity. "If that's what you want, you'd best be prepared to make me get away," I told him, and this was very fair, I thought.

He was prepared, and he fired his gun, but I was already out of range, having used my godlike speed to evade the bullet. I then ripped the weapon from his hands, struck him across the mouth with the barrel, relishing the sound of his breaking teeth and, perhaps, jaw. I then shot him to demonstrate my contempt for poor hygiene.

I approached his horse once more, which vocalized its discomfort and skittered away. As I was faster than an ordinary man, I got on top of that animal before he could stop me, and he settled down soon enough. I waved to the crowd, whose mood by now had turned from shock to admiration. I turned off my pecker inflator and rode out to the Swissers' cabin to finish what I already started.

It took little more than a hour before I could make out the cabin through the patch of mountain cedar. I dismounted and the horse ran from me as quickly as it could, but I did not mind. There would be others.

I then approached closer, and the front of the little building came into view though I think the girl, Anna, must have heard me coming, and she was no longer so inclined to trust strangers after our last encounter. She stood outside, a shotgun in hand, watching me approach.

A firearm, as I have demonstrated, was not going to offer much of a difficulty to a being of my superior nature. I therefore strode toward her, confident and, I feel certain, intimidating. I thought about turning on the old pecker, but I figured the sight of me, in my new godlike form, was enough of a shock for now. I'd save some surprises for later.

"I got unfinished business with you," I told her. "You run away and brought my brother down upon me. You spat upon me. There's got to be a reckoning."

She raised her gun and fired, but I moved about thirty feet to the right before she knew it, and I listened to that shot whiz past. I was faster than a gun, and nothing could stop me. Another one of those pleasures, I reckoned.

Anna fired again, but she missed just the same way, and I barked out a laugh. I was liking this. I was indeed. The girl was now fumbling with shells, trying to reload, but she kept dropping them and her hands were shaking something fierce. I took another step toward her, and she panicked. She turned and ran into the cabin.

This would do her no good, on account of there not being another way out. I moved closer, being careful to listen for any sign she was about to shoot. I wasn't afraid of a shotgun blast, not at any distance, but I didn't want all that shot in me if I could help it.

I peered through the window, and saw her cowering in the corner, still trying to load. This was going to be more fun than even I had thought. I threw open the door, and strode toward her, taking the gun from her hands in a quick yank.

"I came here before to do some business," I said, "and I mean to finish that business."

She stood up, trying to look brave, but she didn't fool me. There were no half dozen law men to bind my hands and keep her safe. She was mine for the taking, and I flipped my pecker switch to emphasize this point, but she only twisted her mouth in disgust, which I did not like.

I looked about the cabin, seeking the right place for violating her as she deserved, and I was shocked to see a bunch of dead bodies lying there. Her mama and her papa and her two sisters, dead as when I'd left them, still on the floor.

"What's wrong with you girl?" I asked. "Don't Swissers bury their dead?"

"I sent them off to the undertaker," she said, her voice trembling, "but the man made me bring them back."

At first I thought it was because the undertaker didn't want to bury Swiss, or because she had no money, but then I thought more about what she said. He didn't sent her away, he made her take them back.

"Who made you?" I asked.

"The ranger," she said. "He told me you were going to come after me, and that this was the only way to stop you. It didn't sit well with me, but he said I had no choice. I had to bring them here and let him do something to them."

"Why did the ranger want these bodies here?" I said. "Tell me now. He's my brother, so that makes this family business. You best come clean."

"He had to do something to them," she said. "He wanted to put something inside their heads. At first, I did not like to think of it, but when he explained, I knew it was something I had to see with my own eyes."

I sensed movement behind me, and I turned around. They were all up, they were all on their feet, the mama and the papa and the two girls. And they all had scars, just like the one I had, on their temples. They stood, staring at me, mostly grinning, though the husband hadn't much of a jaw left. But I could tell he was grinning on the inside, because there were four of them, and they had me outnumbered but good.

"Goddamit," I said, and I was right angry, because John had bested me yet again. He had tricked me into going into the jail cell and having my pecker machine put in while he came out and inserted egg-shaped things into the heads of the Swiss. That's why the damn doctor had taken so long—so John could turn these Swissers into gods like me.

"This ain't right," I said. "I've been deceived."

The mama said something to me in Swiss, and the others laughed, and that made me even angrier, because I hate to be left out of a joke. And then they started moving toward me, faster than you would believe. I tried to turn away, to run, but they were as fast as I was, and the little girls somehow got ahead of me, blocking the exit. They pushed me back, and the mama and papa grabbed me, and that's when I knew I was right trapped. One of the little girls started pulling on my left arm. Pulling and pulling until I felt an unpleasant pop and the arm came loose and I had to turn away, because it was not something I liked to look on.

I struggled with my right arm, now not trying to free myself, but what I wanted more than anything was to press that button and turn the juice off, because I had something down there that was presenting itself as a target to these angry Swissers, and I did not like to think on it.

That's when I noticed the smell, that awful smell like boiled beans, and I looked up and there he was, my own brother, standing at the door and puffing away, his grin nearly hidden by that damn fool mustache, and in his hand he held a long knife with a serrated blade that he flapped back and forth like it was some kind of a fan.

"The doc wants the head intact," he said. "Wants to

see if it can live without a body, but otherwise, do as you like."

"John!" I cried. "This is not right. You can't let them tear me apart."

He shrugged, like it was nothing. "You made your own choices, Gordon. You gave me no choice."

I stared at him in dismay. I wanted to tell him that there likely had to be some other choice than this, but I could not find the words.

Then John walked toward me, still waving about that serrated knife, still puffing on his cigar. "Time to earn that five hundred dollars," he said, and I turned away, because what came next was going to be extremely unpleasant. I did not want to see what he would do to me, and I did not want to see him enjoy it. That would be the final indignity. At least, that's what I hoped.

☙ ☙ ☙

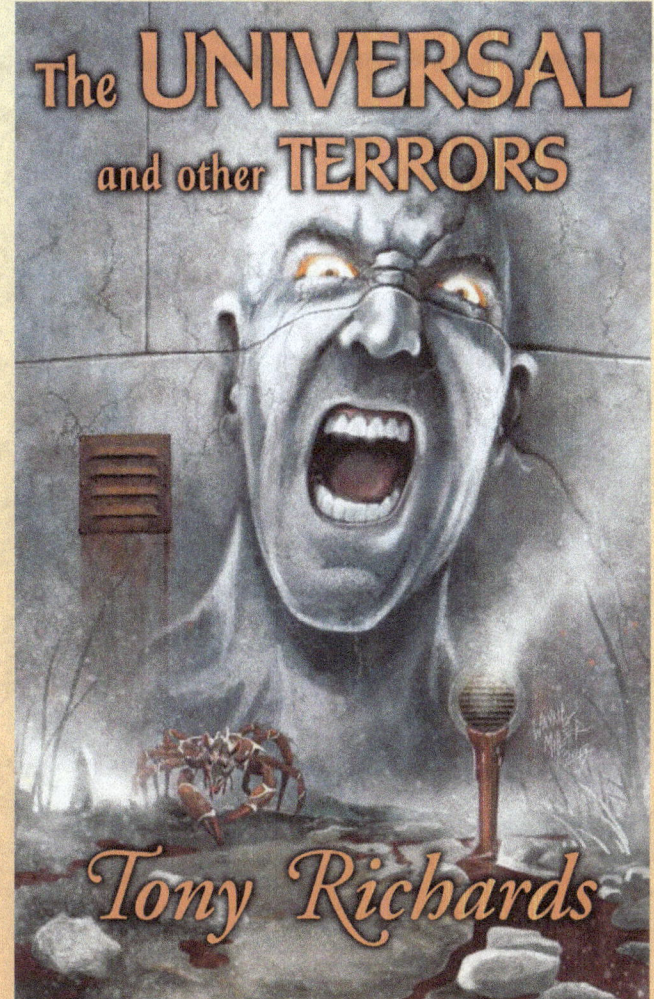

DOUBLE X CHROMOSOME:

By Yvonne Navarro

I HEAR VOICES IN MY HEAD

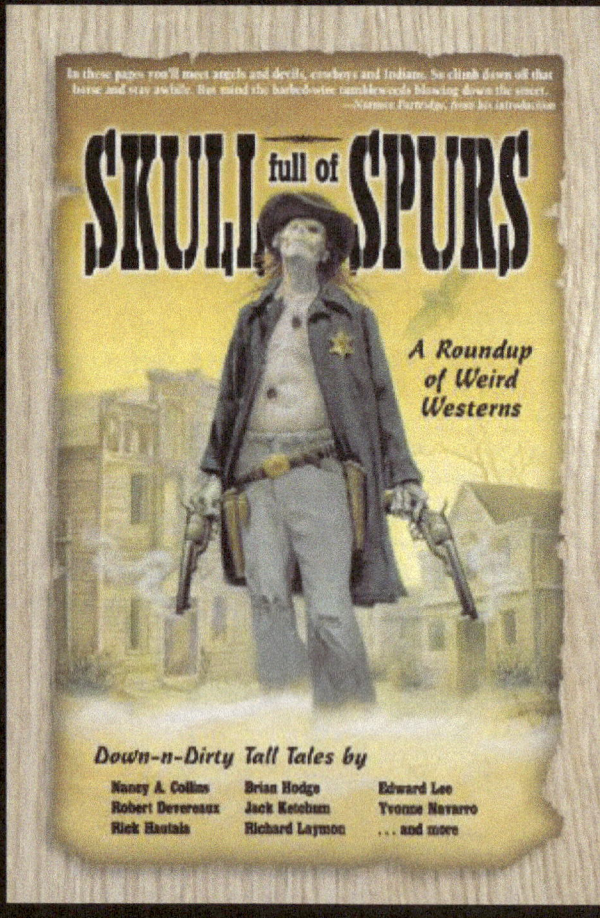

When I think of western horror, I think of none other than Joe Lansdale HisOwnSelf (how he sometimes refers to himself). That's in fiction, of course, but there's lots of fine material elsewhere. Take comics: DC started its *Weird Western Tales* in the early seventies, and one of the most famous comic characters in that series was Jonah Hex. Jonah Hex was taken to the big screen in 2010 in a decent adaptation with more action than characterization. There are lots of films, too, including the infamous Nicolas Cage in the *Ghost Rider* films, the unforgettable *From Dusk til Dawn* (George Clooney and Quentin Tarantino), or the grand and great *Tremors films* (Kevin Bacon and Fred Ward). My favorite? *Cowboys and Aliens*. The old west, a very well-aging, gravelly-voiced Harrison Ford, aliens, and Daniel Craig—is there anything better?

Eye candy aside, I'm a fiction writer at heart, so I always end up coming back to the words. There are untold numbers of stories that take place in haunted woods and castles and hundred-year-old houses. No offense, but I don't find the thought of Sasquatch all that scary. Maybe it's the beef jerky commercials about messing with Sasquatch (and my husband ripping the pocket on my sweatshirt after telling me I was "messing with Sasquatch" when I was hitting him on the head with a sock) very frightening. This is a creature that seems to hide rather than hunt. The goblins, ghosts and ghouls that otherwise pop out of dark forests have been doing so since the beginning of time. They may never exactly get old, but they do seem somewhat predictable.

But the west… oh, yeah. Nowhere else in the world but in the good old USA. Desert, mountains, strange rock formations, scorpions, coyotes, Indians, cowboys, angry spirits, peyote, razor-tipped tumbleweeds, the elements, choking dust storms, blinding monsoons, death by sun and thirst, tarantulas and tarantula wasps, snow, mountain lions and bears in the high desert, bizarre insects, and ruins. The list of the wondrous and potentially terrifying goes on. And on.

Now add aliens, ghosts, monsters, and give it a good *shake*.

Check these out:

Stephen King's *Dark Tower* saga
Dead in the West by Joe Lansdale
Dead Man's Hand: Five Tales of the Weird West by Nancy A. Collins
The Crossings by Jack Ketchum

And countless others, including books by Robert E. Howard, Louis L'Amour, Emma Bull, and others (note I'm focusing on weird western here, rather than just western western). As far as I'm concerned, Joe Lansdale is THE MAN for weird westerns. There's a reason he's written his own stories and books and provided the introduction to a whole bunch of others.

About fifteen years ago I was asked if I wanted to contribute to a weird western anthology called *Skull Full of Spurs*. I did, and I wrote a story called "Divine Justice," about two down-on-their-luck men traveling through the desert and who come across an angel with a broken wing. One of the men just wants to shoot it, but finally they put the injured being in their wagon and head off to parts unknown. Everything goes along merrily until you factor in the minds and changing motives of men and what's expected of angels and by whom. After accepting the anthology invitation, I might've wondered what I was getting myself into since I'd never written anything even vaguely western. I'd never even put a male character in a cowboy hat, boots and chaps, or a female into a bonnet and lace-trimmed, checkered dress. But that was okay. See, back when I was a baby horror writer and attended my first horror convention in Nashville, I went to a reading by a writer I knew nothing about. To this day, I can hear that guy's voice in my head—my audio memory can instantly recreate his Texas accent and my visual memory fills in exactly what he looked like as he turned each page of his manuscript. That writer was Joe Lansdale, and the story he read to a standing-room-only audience was "The Night They Missed the Horror Show" (published in *Silver Scream* edited by David J. Schow in 1988).

That was in the eighties and Joe Lansdale has since become a good friend of mine who's helped me in more ways than I'm going to go into here. But prime among those times is that reading—it was his voice and western accent, his style, that kept me on track when I wrote "Divine Justice," kept me grounded smack in an Arizona desert rather than let me slide back to inner-city Chicago, where I grew up. Now I live in Arizona, having fulfilled a dream that blossomed before I even met Joe, but back then I had almost zero experience with desert anything other than a few vacations.

There's no particular reason to my rhyme here (is there ever?), other than to say don't ever let someone tell you that you can't write about a particular subject or location if you've never been there. At the time I wrote the novelization for *Species*, staring Natasha Henstridge and a bunch of other well-known Hollywood folks, I'd never been to Los Angeles, plus it was well before the time of Internet surfing at the touch of a few key strokes. You know that Beatles song, *With a Little Help from my Friends*? It's a prime example of how to tackle something you can't do yourself. I had a couple of friends who lived in LA literally run a treasure hunt for me, telling me what was at which intersection, what types of vegetation and flowers were where, what was around certain key locations, and more. It worked like the proverbial charm.

Just like hearing voices in my head does. Joe Lansdale's, to be exact.

🌻🌻🌻

Yvonne's "Divine Justice" was published in *Skull Full of Spurs*, edited by Jason Bovberg and Kirk Whitham and published in May of 2000.

Comments? Questions? Suggestions? Yvonne Navarro can be reached via her website, www.yvonnenavarro.com/ Facebook, www.facebook.com/yvonne.navarro.001 or at her Dark Discoveries email: yvonne@journalstone.com.

Photo Courtesy of Weston Ochse

PEARRY TEO'S
BEDLAM STORIES
THE PREQUEL TO THE BESTSELLING SERIES
PROJECT
ALICE
DOWNLOAD FOR FREE AT WWW.BEDLAMSTORIES.COM

Stephen King in the Old West

By Rocky Wood

Photo Courtesy of Rocky Wood

These were days when my imagination was so clear I could smell the dust and hear the creak of leather.

— Stephen King, on writing *The Dark Tower Cycle*

This article summarizes the use of Old West/Wild West imagery in Stephen King's fiction. For these purposes the Old West/Wild West is loosely defined as the second half of the 19th century in areas around the expanding frontier of the United States. A similar period in Mexican history, ranging for a century to about 1920, mostly in the north of that country, has also profoundly influenced King's Dark Tower Mythos. This imagery has been popularized and mythologized by Hollywood, the TV series of the 1950s and 1960s and, of course, by the "western" literary genre.

Such imagery includes the plains and the desert, horses as the major mode of transport, cowboys, ranches, range wars, disputes and wars with Native Americans, the US Cavalry, gangs of bandits, gunslingers, posses and lawmen (those last four interchangeable at times), the lawless frontier, wagon trains, saloons, whores, expanding settlement, stagecoaches, railways, small time mining—often by individuals or small teams, and rugged individualism (the lone drifter is practically a western staple), amongst others.

In "Old Mexico" the images are added to by isolated family haciendas, poor rural towns at the prey of lawless thugs, dry landscapes, and Revolution (Pancho Villa, Zapata, et al); as well as the Spanish language, a small landholding aristocracy, a largely incompetent or corrupt military, and the Robin Hood like figure of Zorro!

Stephen King has never published a novel or short story in the western genre but perhaps the most important character in his entire canon is a gunslinger. Indeed, King's entire *The Dark Tower* Cycle is imbued with themes literally derived from a spaghetti western. But more of that later.

According to various sources the legendary film director Sam Peckinpah died while pre-producing King's script, *The Shotgunners*. Peckinpah made *Straw Dogs* and *The Wild Bunch*; wrote for many TV western series including *Bonanza* and was famed for the violence portrayed in his later films, long before the emergence of Quentin Tarantino. *The Shotgunners* is clearly the forerunner of King's novel *The Regulators*, the Richard Bachman credited companion volume to King's *Desperation*. While the premise is the same in both novel and script, the characters are completely different. It seems the screenplay developed into *The Regulators* novel. If Peckinpah was indeed working on pre-production for this screenplay when he died in 1984, it was over a decade until it appeared reworked as *The Regulators* in 1996. Bachman/King's dedication in the book, "Thinking of Jim Thompson and Sam Peckinpah: legendary shadows" would seem to confirm the story.

The premise for both *The Shotgunners* and *The Regulators* is attacks in the present day that originate as beyond the grave revenge by six men hanged for robbery in 1874. The companion novel to *The Regulators*, *Desperation*

contains important scenes set in the period when cheap Chinese labor was prominent in the mining business and the building of railroads.

It is not widely known that King has attempted two western novels; or that he published a satirical western in the tone of movies such as *Blazing Saddles* or *Evil Roy Slade*.

George D X McArdle is a busted novel King attempted in the 1980s—a delightful, humorous western. It opens with a scene following a shootout involving three members of a gang who have just robbed the Kingston Stage. A wounded Pete Crager is found by one George D X McArdle and his troop of "girls"—McArdle plans on becoming the world's first progressive whoremaster! The partially completed manuscript covers the adventures of the two men before they met—a series of increasingly improbable but entertaining vignettes. The "present day" of the story is 1873, near Gordon's Stream in the state of Missouri. King offers a range of western imagery—from brothels, to carnivals and a medicine show (Professor D X McArdle's Pandaemonium Magic Show) to duels and bartending; and from the Civil War (which appears quite rarely in King's fiction) to crooked preachers, detailed back stories for each of the prospective prostitutes, and "the meanest railroad dick west of the Mississippi."

STEPHEN KING

WRITING AS
RICHARD BACHMAN

THE REGULATORS

The undertone of the story is certainly one of humor, not quite satire, but close to it. One is left wondering if King was simply having fun and realized the end result was likely to be uncommercial and certainly not what the average King fan would have expected.

In a 1989 public speech King said, "A few years ago, I did try very hard to write a western, because it's a form I like. I wrote about 160 pages and the only scene that really had any power was when this old guy got drunk outside this farmhouse and fell into the pigsty, and the pigs ate him. That one scene has some real drive and punch. This is what turned on my lights, for reasons I don't understand." I recently asked King if this was the same busted novel as *George D X McArdle* and he replied that they were two *separate* western novels.

Slade, one of King's earliest published works, is best described as western satire. It was published as a serial in *The Maine Summer Campus* in 1970, a student newspaper of the University of Maine at Orono.

The story was spread over eight chapters, most ending in typical cliff-hangers. In Chapter One we read, "It was almost dark when Slade rode into Dead Steer Springs." We are regaled with his description, "…tall in the saddle, a grim faced man dressed all in black. Even the handles of his two sinister .45s, which rode low on his hips, were black." There had been whispered legends about his dress "…since the early 1870s, when the name of Slade began to strike fear into the stoutest of western hearts." In one version, the black color was mourning dress for his "Illinois sweetheart, Miss Polly Peachtree of Paduka," killed when a Montgolfier balloon crashed into her barn while she milked the cows. Others had it that he was "the Grim Reaper's agent in the American southwest—the devil's handyman. And there were some who thought he was queerer than a three-dollar bill. No one, however, advanced this last idea to his face."

And so it goes, with King lampooning multiple western genre elements—salons, piano players, "fancy dan" cheating gamblers, hired gunmen, undertakers ("Slade was a peace-loving man at heart, and what was more peace-loving than a dead body"), range wars, Chinese cooks, bordellos, and back-shooting (all mixed in with humorous pokes at Nixon's administration in a style reminiscent of Philip Roth's *Our Gang*, published in

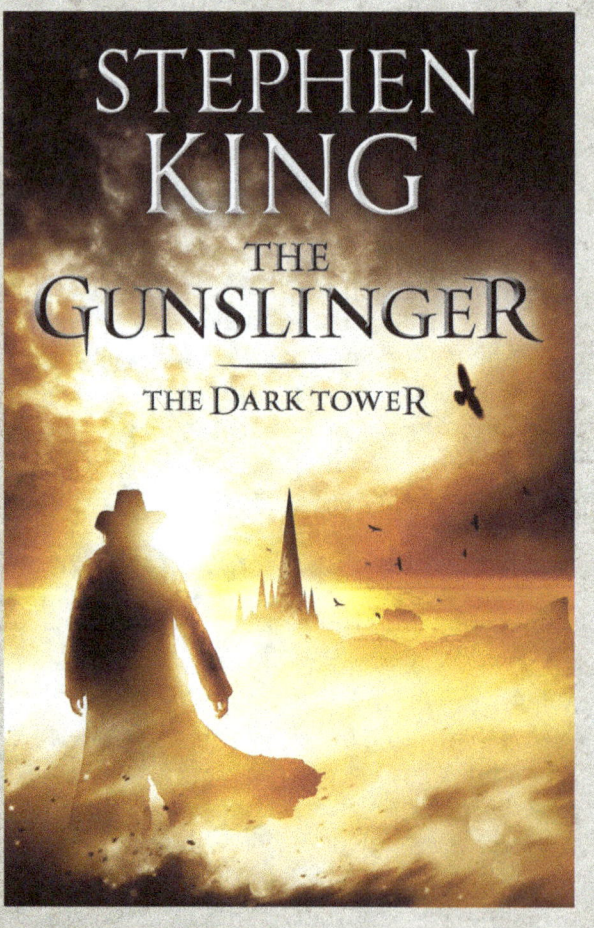

1971). The story itself does not matter much; King's great fun with the satire does.

King expert and academic Michael Collings has this to say about the tale: "*Slade* is as derivative as King's early extant tales; the difference is that he is now aware of the fact … Everything—every movement, every line of dialogue, every locale and every character—functions strictly according to stereotypes, yet King gives them new life by blending them with both parody and burlesque." Notably, King apparently began *The Dark Tower* the same summer he wrote *Slade*.

King relates something of the origins of his magnum opus, *The Dark Tower* Cycle, in the Revised Edition of *The Gunslinger*. The introduction, *On Being Nineteen (and a Few Other Things)*, reveals that from as early as his reading of J.R.R. Tolkien's classic, *The Lord of the Rings* in 1966 and 1967 King had determined to write something as sweeping, "but I wanted to write my own kind of story."

"Then (in 1970), in an almost completely empty movie theater … I saw a film directed by Sergio Leone. It was called *The Good, The Bad and the Ugly*, and before the film was half over, I realized what I wanted to write was a novel that contained Tolkien's sense of quest and magic but set against Leone's almost absurdly majestic western backdrop … And, in my enthusiasm … I wanted to write not just a *long* book, but *the longest popular novel in history*. I did not succeed in doing that, but I feel I had a decent rip…" What King did create is a lengthy dark fantasy with heavy science fiction, horror and western elements. To date there are eight novels and one novella in the Dark Tower Cycle proper, with many other links and stories in King's canon.

As an aside, King had this to say in his *King's Garbage Truck* column for the July 18, 1969 issue of *The Maine Campus*: "Best Lousy Movie: *The Good, the Bad, and the Ugly* (1967), mostly for Clint Eastwood's cigar, which would have given a lesser man cancer of the lip two Italian westerns before. Also for director Sergio Leone, who has a talent for finding more ugly extras than anyone on the face of the earth—and zeroing his wide-screen lens in on their beard-speckled faces for long, loving, drooly close-ups." Apart from indicating that King had seen the movie before the 1970 date he later reported, this is again King in satirical mode.

Of course the most obvious clue to a western inspiration for the Cycle is the title of the first novel, which describes the protagonist. The first appearance of a Dark Tower story was *The Gunslinger* in *The Magazine of Fantasy and Science Fiction* for October 1978. However, King had been working on his magnum opus since 1970, taking Robert Browning's 1855 epic poem *Childe Roland To The Dark Tower Came* as an inspiration. The various parts that would become the first novel, *The Dark Tower: The Gunslinger*, each initially appeared in *The Magazine of Fantasy and Science Fiction*, before being combined into the novel, first published in 1982. A mass-market edition of *The Dark Tower: The Gunslinger* was not published until 1988 and it was only from that point that King's wider fan base *may* have begun to appreciate the importance of the Cycle to his overall fictional output.

King slowly added to "The Dark Tower Cycle" with these novels: *The Dark Tower II: The Drawing of the Three* (1987); *The Dark Tower III: The Wastelands* (1991); *The Dark Tower IV: Wizard and Glass* (1996); *The Dark Tower V: Wolves of the Calla* (2003); *The Dark Tower VI: Song of Susannah* (2004); *The Dark Tower VII: The Dark Tower* (2004); and *The Wind Through the Keyhole* (2012). His novella, *The Little Sisters of Eluria* (1998) is part of the Cycle; and major and minor links to his multiverse appear in dozens of novels and short stories, particularly in the collection, *Hearts in Atlantis* (1999).

The protagonist of *The Dark Tower* Cycle is Roland Deschain, the last of his world's Gunslingers, a knight/warrior. Long before we meet him the high culture to which Roland was to have been heir had been extinguished in a civil war, which ended the centuries during which "Mid World" was ruled by the descendants of Arthur Eld. Eld, Mid World's answer to our King Arthur, lived 700 years before Roland. He set in place a code known as the Way of the Eld, to which the gunslingers adhered. Excalibur was Arthur Eld's sword and, at some point, the barrels of Roland's inherited guns were forged from the blade.

As a result of his training Roland is incredibly proficient with his pistols—in the town of Tull, for instance, he slaughtered the entire population within minutes. Tull itself is a stereotypical western town—located just north of a desert, the buildings are sand-colored, it is situated on a "coach road" and the only businesses in town are a livery, a tailor, a barber, a dry goods emporium and Sheb's Bar, which has batwing doors, a sawdust floor, a piano player (who Roland shoots), card games and the obligatory spittoons!

The gunslinger autocracy had ruled over the baronies of Mid World, including the Barony of New Canaan and its capital Gilead, which was the last to fall in the civil war. At the stage of this world's history covered by the main storyline of the Dark Tower Cycle battles and skirmishes are largely fought with pistols and rifles, as in the American West; although machines and technology left over from a previous civilization (created by the Great Old Ones) are sometimes deployed. Travel was largely by horse, although there were some decaying railway lines still sporadically operating.

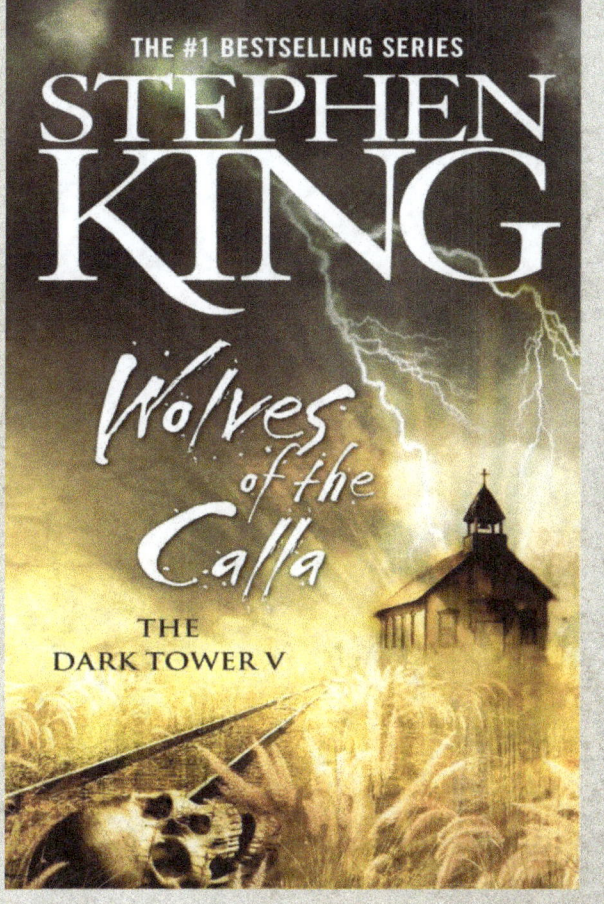

THE #1 BESTSELLING SERIES

STEPHEN KING

Wolves of the Calla

THE DARK TOWER V

There are many aspects of Roland's world that reflect "Old Mexico" or perhaps the Old American Southwest. There are a series of Callas (small towns) in the "Borderlands" between the "inner" or "mid" section of Roland's world and the "outer" regions. Many seem to reflect a similar culture and geography as the Southwestern American States settled by the Spanish and Mexicans of Spanish descent; and the northern (or "border" states) of Mexico. However, *these* Borderlands are greener than our world's desert states.

In the *Author's Note* to the fifth novel in the Cycle, *Wolves of the Calla* King acknowledges Akira Kurosawa—the Japanese director of *The Seven Samurai*, which was remade by John Sturges as the classic western, *The Magnificent Seven* (1960). The entire novel is a prolonged tribute to these two movies and has strong western overtones. He also credits the cinematic legacy of Leone, Sam Peckinpah, Howard Hawkes and John Sturgis (*sic*). King notes "the Calla did not come by the final part of its (slightly misspelled) name accidentally." This refers to the main setting of that book—Calla Bryn Sturgis, a small town that Roland and his "ka-tet" of fellow travelers he has trained as gunslingers decide to stand and defend against the depredations of raiding "wolves" (actually robots). The "Bryn" is inspired by Yul Brynner, a star of the American movie.

There is a livery in Calla Bryn Sturgis; a number of ranches in the vicinity, including Buckhead Ranch and the Rocking B Ranch; and Our Lady of Serenity place of worship is served by a Catholic priest from "our" world — Father (or Pere) Callahan, late of Jerusalem's Lot — the rural towns of Old Mexico were Catholic, of course. In other western imagery the Calla Badlands is a dry plain east of Calla Bryn Sturgis. And there's arroyo country near the town, with played out mines at the end of a dead-end canyon (those brought up on westerns can visualize the entire scene from this one sentence). There is even mention of a Calla Boot Hill! The Manni, a mystic sect who live in the Borderlands, may be inspired by the Mormon settlers of the 19th century as, among other things, the Manni are polygamists.

The setting for the fourth novel, *Wizard and Glass*, is Hambry in the distant Barony of Mejis. Another town near the desert it is known for horse breeding. It is also a seaside town and many buildings are adobe, so it might represent a Californian town from the Spanish/Mexican period. As well as Spanish family names such as Alvarez, Delgado, Ruiz and Torres there are many places straight out of a western — Hanging Rock, Eyebolt Canyon, various ranches, an undertaker, a cemetery, a Sheriff's office and jail, a livery, a bar/whorehouse, and even a town called Santa Fe in the Barony. Roland and his companions are threatened by a band of thugs called the Big Coffin Hunters, led by a man who had been exiled from the gunslinger autocracy. Tellingly, they are also known as "Regulators." It is surprising that in the *Afterword* to *Wizard and Glass* King goes so far as to describe the first four books as "cowboy romances," which is far from correct, as the only real romance of Roland's life is that with Susan Delgado, described in that fourth novel.

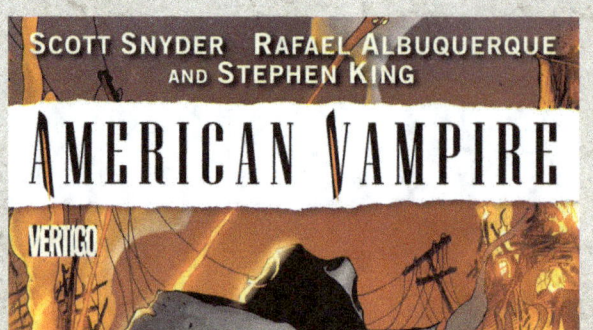

Those looking for an even more "western" feel for Dark Tower material than King's very cinematic description in the novels should access the Marvel Comics adaptations of the early events in the series (including some "new" material, not detailed in those novels). These were published from 2007 to 2013. Readers should note the original comic books contain a lot of background material about the Dark Tower Universe that are *not* included in the later hardcover collections. That background is described by King's former research assistant and writer of the comic series, Robin Furth.

The only pure western horror King has published is as part of *American Vampire*, a comic book series launched by Vertigo (an imprint of DC Comics) in May 2010. It also represents King's first original comic script. Each of the five issues in the first arc carried one story by King and one by series creator, Scott Snyder. After the first arc King had no further involvement. According to publicity material: "The series twists the well-trod vampire legend by allowing the creatures to evolve into a distinctly American creature and will follow the adventures of Skinner Sweet, a sociopathic outlaw in the Wild West who becomes the first American vampire. Unlike European vamps, Skinner is powered by the sun and, true to his native environment, has rattlesnake fangs. Each cycle, consisting of five individual comic issues, will take place in a different period of time in American history, tracing Skinner's descendants, with Skinner himself as a recurring character."

Snyder originally sold his idea for "a uniquely American take on vampires" to DC Comics then approached King for a blurb. King enjoyed the tale so much he replied that he'd be willing to contribute to future issues. Naturally enough, this excited Snyder and the editors at Vertigo, who agreed. King then wrote five stories relating to Skinner's origins in the American West. Again, according to publicity material: "King's arc will trace the origins of the first American vampire, Skinner Sweet, as he goes fang-to-fang with even nastier vamps, a group out to get rich by damming up a river to create a new town. 'It's really the vampire as American capitalist gone totally wild' (King said)."

King's story in Issue One is *Bad Blood*. Set in Sidewinder, Colorado in 1880, the tale is narrated by Will Bunting, who "only wrote one novel in my life — *Bad Blood*." Of course, Sidewinder is the imaginary town King created — it first appeared in *The Shining* as the town closest to the Overlook Hotel, and has since appeared in King's *Before the Play* (a prequel to *The Shining*), *Misery*, *Doctor Sleep* and *The Talisman* (co-authored by Peter Straub).

Bunting claims most of his "novel" (later revealed as *Bad Blood, or The Monster Outlaw — A Terrifying Tale of the Old West* by William Bunting) is actually true. His story opens with Skinner Sweet, "notorious murderer and bank-thief" in the custody of the Pinkerton Agency, operating on behalf of "Percy," a wealthy banker. As the train carrying Sweet and his captors proceeds from Sidewinder towards New Mexico Sweet's crew prepare to derail the train, intent on freeing their leader and killing all the passengers—"No Witnesses!"

Meanwhile, Sweet regales a Pinkerton agent with the tale of his gang's robbery of a bank in Bakersville, Colorado six months earlier. While his men were raping the women (and one man) a loan officer fired, beginning a shoot-out, in which a number of people including a three year old child were killed. The gang retreated to a nearby mine to hole-up.

Just before the train is derailed Sweet manages to unlock his handcuffs. Bunting watches the aftermath of the derailment: "What I saw next was surely colored by my imagination as well as by the dying hues of that terrible day's sunset … but what I saw is more real than any *dream* or *memory*." Sweet and his gang are confronted by "Old Man Percy" who surprises all by saying, "I think I've had enough of your shit, Mr. *Sweet*." The gang shoot Percy down but he immediately rises, bares lengthy fangs and *bites* Sweet in the neck. Sweet shoots Percy again and again before being shot dead himself. Sweet's gang flees and Percy and the survivors leave Sweet's body by the side of the railroad. Percy, now revealed as a vampire, is furious! Bunting closes this first tale, declaring, "I started writing that very night, and I think I knew two things even then: that what I wrote could only be published as fiction … and Skinner Sweet's story wasn't over but *just beginning*."

Percy has "very fair skin" and avoids direct sunlight as much as possible (he is seen carrying an unfurled umbrella) so, unlike the traditional vampire, he can go out in daylight (in fact he suffers mild sunburn). This begins the reader's understanding that these peculiar vampires are actually powered by the sun.

King's contribution to Issue 2 was *Deep Water*. It is 1925, Los Angeles as Will Bunting addresses a few people who've turned up to "celebrate" the reissue of *Bad Blood*, his "one-of-a-kind" dime novel based on the life and "death" of Skinner Sweet. The book is said to combine the western thrills of Zane Grey and the horror thrills of Bram Stoker! Bunting tells his audience that most of the tale is true, even

if he had to publish it as fiction. In Bunting's tale Percy and other vampires (who are originally from Europe) discuss Sweet's death—Percy is certain Sweet is dead but two other vampires remind him his blood had splashed on Sweet, so he might yet rise. Ignoring this potential threat Percy discusses his plan to dam the Baya River in Colorado and make a fortune irrigating cheap land the vampires had picked up in the New Mexico territory. In 1883 the Baya River dam is completed and Sidewinder flooded (of course, no such flooding occurred in *The Shining*/*Doctor Sleep* universe)—as a result water drains into the undead Sweet's grave on Boot Hill. Meanwhile, Bunting rides the West with the Pinkerton's Jim Book, and Felix Camillo, dispensing justice. Felix marries Benita Juarez, with Book as best man but four years later Benita dies in childbirth. Their daughter Abilena survives. By 1909, Lakeview, Colorado has replaced the flooded Sidewinder. Scavengers unwisely decide to dive on Sweet's grave—hoping to pick up artifacts of the famous outlaw they might sell. The first diver finds something entirely unexpected, a ravenous vampire of a new breed, one that does not burn in sunlight or drown in water. Newly fed, Sweet escapes his watery grave, heading into Lakeview, intent on taking revenge on Percy: "the time of the *American Vampire* has come."

King's tale In Issue 3 is *Blood Vengeance*. Lakeview, Colorado—1909. Sweet is back in town, confronted by the changes while he'd been underground— telephones, cinema, horseless carriages, and a Mexican mayor (Felix's father, Camillo), this last an affront to Sweet's racism.

The vampire rampages in Lakeview, killing all in sight, feeding and growing stronger by the hour. Meanwhile Percy's nest of vampires discover that Sweet has risen, and that he can easily walk in full sunlight! A posse is formed to catch Sweet; Chief Finch denies claims the creature is the famous outlaw, 30 years in his grave. Sweet kills Finch after extracting from him that Book and Camillo now live in Cruces, New Mexico. Having killed Mayor Camillo, Sweet telegraphs Felix that he wants Felix and Book to meet him at the Old Bakersvilles Mines, claiming to have Felix's father hostage—and signs the telegram Skinner Sweet. Bunting recalls being with Book when the telegram arrived. They, along with Felix and his daughter, ride out to meet the man "claiming" to be Skinner Sweet.

Photo Courtesy of Rocky Wood

Issue 4 carries King's *One Drop of Blood*: Two days after the events in *Blood Vengeance* Felix and the others arrive in devastated Lakeview, rife with tales that Skinner Sweet had destroyed the town—bullets couldn't stop him, and the creature had fangs! Bunting shares his suspicion that Sweet is a vampire, infected by Percy but he does not understand how any of these vampires can walk in full sunlight. When the group find Sweet at the mine outside town Felix Camillo enters but Sweet kills him. Felix's daughter Abilena picks this inauspicious moment to tell Jim Book she loves him. Another confrontation ensues; the mine collapses, apparently trapping Sweet. Bunting, Book and Abilena escape, although Book appears to have been infected by the Vampyric virus. The European vampires observe everything and mistakenly believe Sweet has been dealt with.

King's final contribution to *American Vampire* appears in Issue 5 as *If Thy Right Hand Offend Thee, Cut It Off*. Three years later in Cruces, New Mexico Sweet's legacy is alive and well in Book's blood and he is battling the infection. Abilena Camillo is still with Book and continues to express her love for him, despite their age difference. Some years later Percy sends men to dig Skinner Sweet out, but he kills them and decides to make for Percy's ranch, where Percy offers to let Sweet join the nest. But Sweet only has revenge in mind and drags Percy into sunlight, burning him to death. Elsewhere, Book asks Abilena to kill him, so he can escape his personal hell of vampirism. She agrees but only if he makes love to her as she is in her "fertile time." They have sex and later that night she kills him as agreed; a year later she leaves town with their daughter, Will Bunting tagging along. Back in 1925 Bunting concludes his tale by explaining his motives—to reveal to the world that "real monsters" are out on the roads and railways of America; and to celebrate Book's heroism. As he leaves the lecture hall he receives a note—from Skinner Sweet! Later, Abilena and her daughter Felicia observe Skinner as he walks down the street. Abilena promises her daughter they will deal with the man who'd destroyed her father, "Not today, but soon."

This is all classic King—creating a new species of vampire—not only solar powered, but uniquely American. Obviously, the western background is driven by the tale, rather than the other way around. As always, King delivers enough detail to ease the reader effortlessly into both the geographic setting and the era.

The *American Vampire* franchise continues today, with spin-off material. King's material is included in *American Vampire Vol. 1* (Vertigo, 2010).

It is obvious King has been influenced by the western genre, although this should not be overemphasized. After all even the Dark Tower Cycle is a blend of genres—fantasy, horror and science fiction among them. King has always read widely and immersed himself in popular culture, including movies, television and music. The vast majority of his canon is horror or mainstream, with fantasy and science fiction, crime and mystery also well represented. In fact, considering King's roots as a deeply American writer it would be notable if his canon was *not* influenced by the western.

* Rocky Wood is the two-time Bram Stoker Award® winning author of *Stephen King: Uncollected, Unpublished*, *Stephen King: The Non Fiction* and *Stephen King: A Literary Companion*, along with the graphic novels, *Horrors!* and *Witch Hunts: A Graphic History of the Burning Times*. He served as researcher on King's latest novel, *Doctor Sleep*.

Photo Courtesy of Rocky Wood

Fever Springs

By Norman Partridge

Mr. Beaumont bought the werewolf somewhere in Eastern Europe.

Actually, a foreign business agent purchased the monster for him. A man with a face like a pine knot. He arrived at Beaumont's bank on a Sunday afternoon. The bank was closed, which was just as well, because the agent had made the trip in a cast-iron prison wagon.

Not, of course, as an occupant. There was only one man locked in the wagon… or a thing that (at that particular moment) looked like a man. The agent had purchased the creature from a monastery where it had been locked away for years, howling in a solitary cell like a madman. At any rate, that was the agent's story. Beaumont believed the tale was little more than embroidery, designed to add an element of personal danger and (as a result) raise the agent's price.

In truth, Beaumont cared not at all where the creature came from. He cared about two things and two things only: 1) what the creature could do for him, and 2) the business at hand. And so Beaumont stared into the eyes of the man with the pine-knot face. Just as he had suspected, he did not like the particular gleam he saw there. In his experience, that gleam was a sign that a man had dreams. Beaumont himself had none at all. It was his belief that time spent dreaming was better spent planning. But the banker did not speak of that. Instead he spoke of other things.

"The full moon rises next Tuesday," Beaumont said. "I'll pay you after that."

"But Mr. Beaumont, I have other business to attend to. If you doubt the veracity of the goods—"

"I have no doubt about the goods. I have done my research. And I don't believe you'd have purchased a prison wagon to deliver a bucket of hokum to me."

"Still, I have pressing engagements," the agent said. "I can't linger here for a week."

"Then you won't wait for your money?"

"But, sir—my business…"

"Yes, sir. Your business." Beaumont opened a desk drawer and withdrew a small stack of letters. "At present it intersects with my own, and this is a matter I do not take lightly. You have an appointment with me today. Next month, you have another in Denver. And then another in San Francisco a month after that." Three times, Beaumont tapped a stout finger against the envelopes. "And it seems you're selling the same merchandise at each stop."

The man's pine-knot face seemed to split as his jaw dropped open. Only slightly. He searched for words with grim effort, not understanding that it was a pointless exercise. For now that Beaumont's accusation had been plainly spoken a feeling boiled up in the thick-set banker, a feeling that another man was of the opinion that Beaumont could be played for a fool. That was not a feeling that set well in Mr. Beaumont's gullet or belly, and especially not in his brain.

"You thought you'd sell the wolf to me. Then sell him again. Then sell him one more time after that. Was that your plan?"

"Sir, I—"

"Did you plan to kill me yourself, or was the wolf going to do it?"

"Mr. Beaumont. Please. If you'll only listen…"

But listening was a waste of time. This Beaumont understood all too well. He pulled a Colt revolver from his desk and put a bullet in the foreign agent's brain. The man's skull cracked like a walnut in a hot fire. A red flower, not unlike a carnation, seemed to bloom on what remained of the agent's forehead, and his puckered lips loosed his last breath with the same small effort they would employ in releasing a lie.

Soon the face and the lips were covered with blood. Then the dead man slid out of the chair. Beaumont returned his pistol to the drawer, along with the money he had intended to pay for the werewolf.

Next he rifled the agent's pockets and found the man's wallet.

The wallet was fat.

Beaumont smiled.

All in all, it was a good day's work.

* * *

The werewolf's name was Blasko. Of course, Beaumont didn't know that for a long time, as Blasko had been born mute. At first Blasko didn't even understand English. But listening to Mr. Beaumont and those in his employ, the little man learned quickly enough.

Mr. Beaumont was a banker. A most intelligent man. He had a way of making his needs clear. At first, he would simply present Blasko with a swatch of clothing, or sometimes an entire garment. Then he would draw a soft finger across his neck in a slow, slashing motion. Blasko would draw the scent and let it linger in his lungs. Later, as he learned the language and the particular way Mr. Beaumont employed it, the big man would whisper words to Blasko. Never many. Sometimes barely enough. But for Blasko, Mr. Beaumont's words were like snares. There was no escaping them or the actions they demanded. They were brutal, and simple, and (in their own way) as efficient as Blasko himself.

For Blasko was efficient.

Blasko would hunt… and Blasko would kill.

Sometimes he would kill those who had stolen things from Mr. Beaumont.

Sometimes he would kill those from whom Mr. Beaumont wished to steal.

It was all the same to Blasko. He was content. Life was far better in this country than the one where he was born. Holy men came few and far between here. The air was dry and clean. The land was open, often without trees. Sometimes there were valleys filled with cactus, many as tall as the tallest pines of his homeland, each one bearing thick spikes that might have crucified Jesus without so much as a single Roman nail. In fact, a single valley might hold enough cactus to crucify every man who had hunted or caged Blasko in his youth. And when the moon rose above the desert, its light washed the land like a great wave that carried the barbed cactus shadows into the night. In that wave Beaumont's enemies waited for Blasko like drowning men, pinned in the darkness, and though there was not much water here there was more than enough blood, especially when Blasko tore open his victims in the moonlight. That is what Blasko liked best. Claws and fangs and blood. Often, he slaked his thirst so deeply that he felt he would drown in a deep red sea.

Slip beneath the surface, into the pulsing blood.

Sink deeper and deeper as scarlet currents drove him down… and down… and down.

Until he found a bottom that was as black and empty as nothing at all.

* * *

And so it went that way for a few years. Beaumont's fortunes grew as his enemies dwindled. Blasko ate well, both as a wolf and as a man. His maw stretched wide when he devoured Beaumont's chosen victims. His belly was fuller than it ever had been in his miserable excuse for a life. And yet his own appetites grew as his world expanded.

Not enough to break the cinches of human (or inhuman) experience. Not that expansive. At first Blasko's only freedom came during the hunt. On the trail, beneath the moon, the land spreading before him like a thing that had no end. And then he'd find his prey in some small corner of it, and do what the banker demanded, and leave the land behind. He would return to the banker's estate, and he would bring Mr. Beaumont a scalp or a severed hand or sometimes a head, and Beaumont's lips would spread back and his teeth would gleam as if he were a predator himself, and then Beaumont would return Blasko to the cast-iron wagon. It was off its wheels now, its rusting axels cold on the floor of Beaumont's barn, its only door double-padlocked. And the locks would click closed, and the waiting would begin.

But each time the little mute returned from a hunt, he earned a greater measure of Mr. Beaumont's trust. This allowed a less cumbersome kind of confinement. Beaumont sold the cast-iron wagon and had a stable in the barn converted into a walled-off room. This room became Blasko's new home, and the full plates that arrived at the door three times a day seemed as effective as double-padlocks.

But there was more to fill than Blasko's belly, and Mr. Beaumont knew it. He had one of his clerks teach Blasko how to read, and then he opened his library to the wretch. And this was all it took. Soon Blasko passed his days among pages, seemingly solitary, but in truth inhabiting worlds and lives of which he'd never dared dream. And for him, this was a treasure greater than any he had ever imagined. Blasko was given to contemplation, but he could not contemplate leaving the library—and Mr. Beaumont—behind.

For life had put Blasko on another kind of chain, and the job had been done long ago. Indeed, where could the little mute go? Without a single word in his silent mouth, what life could this new land afford him? And what of the curse he carried? Blasko well-remembered its price in his homeland, where he had spent most of his years as a prisoner. No. The world was a mystery, and Mr. Beaumont was a certainty. Here Blasko was protected, and if there were chains, he found that he could ignore them.

Even so, he read. And as he read he began to imagine. Other Blaskos. Other worlds. And one night, as he read a book of poetry occupied by black birds of portent and dead lovers returning from unquiet graves, he heard thunder in the distance. Not far away. Perhaps in town.

In this dry land, storms were rare. Blasko longed to see a storm, for his homeland had been full of them. It was one of very few things he missed. He longed to revel in the feeling of rain on his face, just as he did the words on the page. And so he set his book aside and left his room.

Once outside, he discovered that the night was as dry as a desert grave. Still the thunder rolled. Or, at least, Blasko thought it was thunder until he caught the scent of dynamite on the air, followed by sharp, peppery bursts of gunfire.

The next morning Blasko was in the library, looking for more books by the man who wrote of ravens and dead women. He heard the servants talking… something had happened at Mr. Beaumont's bank. There had been a robbery. Gold had been stolen. And then the servants' words were cut off, as quickly as if Blasko had torn the windpipes from their throats.

This was an image he enjoyed, but he could not linger on it.

Mr. Beaumont had arrived. He came to Blasko with a black glove in his hand. Immediately, the smaller man thought of the raven… and portents. He took the glove in his own hand. It was light, thin—almost like skin itself. The black leather was smooth, worn only in unfamiliar places. The heel of the hand. Along the lifeline. The places that would naturally be filled by a pistol butt.

Yes. Blasko drew a breath and caught the sharp scent of gunpowder. He had a sense of the man who owned this glove. And then he drew the scent of the glove's owner through his nostrils, deeper this time, and it slipped down the back of his throat like a slice of meat that burned in his gullet.

Blasko smiled, pale lips drawing over his teeth. His fingers closed around the glove. He gripped it tightly, as if it contained bones he longed to crush.

Beaumont's lips drew near to Blasko's ear. "His name is Merrick Reece," the banker whispered. "Bring me his heart. And kill every bastard who rides with him."

* * *

Moonlight spilled across a dry wash on the edge of camp, but Blasko was unseen in the darkness. Pelt black, teeth long, he travelled the wash like a shadow, and he did his work with fang and claw, and he was gone long before the sun rose and spilled blood had faded to the color of rust on white sand.

* * *

"Jesus." Reece stared down at the dead Mexican, the corpse's naked ribs arcing above the empty red hollow of his belly. "Looks like the devil came to table and chewed our friend Mr. Gomez straight down to the sweetmeats."

"Apaches?" Colorado asked.

"Doubtful," Reece said. Softly, because the kid had gone pale. "Apaches raise some hell, but not this way."

"A wolf? Coyotes?" Rims—the dynamite man, thin as a confidence man's promise—grimaced as the words passed his thin lips. "Looks like whatever it was ate Gomez guts to black gravy and swallowed everything in between."

"Can't argue that," Reece said. "But if it was a wolf or a coyote, we would have heard something from the camp. Gomez was one mean *pistolero*. He would have got off a shot or at least had time to holler. So must be the thing that did this was quiet. Smart. Killing stroke came first, before Gomez even knew he was in deep water. Had to be a man did the job."

"Then who?" Rims asked.

"Not who," said Steinhart. "What."

The men stared at the big German, but the Heinie didn't say another word. So they stared at each other, gazes passing over the dead man's chest like prayers as empty as they were silent, for none of them were thinking of Bernardo Gomez now. Each man thought only of himself. Gomez lay there, a hollow where his guts belonged, gnawed down to shit-shaft and privates, torn flaps of skin dressing his bones like some bloodstained shroud. He barely looked human anymore. But he looked enough a man that each man among them wondered how he'd fit into Gomez's boots, wondered too how the quick-trigger Mexican had met his last moments.

The kid Colorado was the first to turn away.

"I can't stand here no longer," Rims said, following suit.

"We have a shovel?" the German asked.

Reece shook his head. "No shovel. No flowers. No time. We ride."

And they did. Over alkali flats, over earth as white and cracked as broken dinner plates. But there was no sound here apart from the wind and the occasional creak of saddle leather. The company made barely a whisper as they crossed the desert, the horses' hooves raising chalky dust so it seemed they were travelling a river of ghosts. Five miles of that, then ten. And then the men themselves were covered in dust, and they rode on as white and expressionless as the dead, each one a specter sloughing toward a solemn grave.

That night, around the campfire, Steinhart spoke again. He told the men a story. In fact, he told them a few. Speaking slowly, his thick tongue slapping his words, his accent harsh. These were stories from the place where he'd grown up. A place gone to hell and back in a dark German forest.

But that night, no one believed Steinhart's stories. Especially not Reece. Reece believed in two things: what he saw, and what he had in his pocket. Hell, wolves that walked like men? Once upon a time he'd heard a Navajo talk about demons like that, but Reece didn't believe in fairy tales. You bucked your horse through that gate, you might as well set your brand to all the rest of it, too.

Witches that lived in gingerbread houses. Pale ladies who drank blood. Men made of stone who'd do the dirty for those too weak or worn to manage the trick themselves.

Reece might be worn, but he wasn't weak. He turned his back to Steinhart and the campfire. But Steinhart kept talking, even so. Pinion sparked and crackled, and the smell on the air was like spiced meat. One by one, the men drifted away from the circle. The kid Colorado was the last one to go, and Steinhart was still talking when he left. But just like the others, the kid left the big German's words behind in the darkness.

That's the way it was that night. But a few nights later, when three more of the boys were dead, those who remained started to listen.

Even Merrick Reece.

* * *

Despite all those years locked up in a monastery, Blasko did not believe in God. He believed in the moon. It watched over him like a shining eye that never blinked. Bright, eternal, without judgment. The moon gave him strength when he was weary, and marked his path through darkness, and its silence was a twin to his own.

Wrapped within that silence, Blasko often thought of other places and other paths. Some he'd read about in books. But beneath the light of the moon, beneath a sky heavy with stars and full of black like an empty cauldron, words from books seemed somehow flat and artificial. They didn't mean what they'd meant to him when he'd turned those pages in Mr. Beaumont's barn. Out here in the darkness, those characters seemed like stick-men and women, their lives no more than lives imagined, or dreamed.

Yes. The whole wide world was here. Before him. Beneath the moon. And through it walked real men, not dreams. They pulsed with blood. And each of them carried a past, and each of them was bound for a future. But in truth their only future was a creature named Blasko, and as the moonlight washed over him he changed into a reaper that could cut them down just as easily as a writer could shear the puppet strings of a character in a book. His claws lengthening… his fangs sharpening. Skin alive as with a thousand scorpion stings, heart driving blood through his veins with the beat of the devil's own chorus.

And then Blasko moved. Through the night. Beneath the moon. Not the way a man would move. With the cunning and the speed of an unnatural predator. And as he slaughtered his victims he believed he could see the places they'd been and feel the things they'd done in a way no writer could describe. It was all his for the taking— each life, each moment, each experience swimming in their blood like a fat trout ready to be snatched from a very dark river.

And there it was, and just that fast—werewolf claws slashed a man's face. A splash of red on Blasko's wolfish tongue *and the slap of a scarlet water-wheel played counterpoint to the quiet rustle of shuffling cards on a Mississippi riverboat. Then laughter and the clink of champagne glasses, red chips falling where they may* and the werewolf's claws excavated belly, ripping in and up to find the pulse of a beating heart *as a frozen breath passed a young man's lips in the cold silence of Raton Pass, so high in the cold blue clouds that it seemed he could reach out and grab them like a fistful of heaven… so high he didn't dare whisper for fear his words would brush the ear of God.* And then another ruin of a man dropped to his knees, his last breath a whistle through a torn lung *as a whore's low whisper beckoned him from the card room, a tall black-haired beauty moving upstairs with fluid grace, and the man followed her laughter and the rustle of her skirts down a hallway to a door that opened on darkness but welcomed them both. He whistled low as they crossed the threshold and she laughed and took his hand and—*

Blasko wiped his bloody maw and howled at the beauty of it.

The moon's eye gleamed above, and the werewolf drank the cold light down like blood.

If all it held were dreams, then every one of them belonged to Blasko.

If all it held were imaginings, then their cold light would guide his way.

* * *

Others confined themselves to darkness on this night. Mr. Beaumont was one of them. He drew close to the fire. Even so, he was cold. He pulled cork from a brandy bottle and drank without benefit of a glass. Much too eager to dull his concerns, and for this task the brandy did not help in the least.

This brought Mr. Beaumont shame. His eagerness as much as his thirst. And so the banker stared into the flames as if challenging them, and he drew closer still to the fire, and (even so) he was cold.

Pinion and thick pine crackled, but there was no rhythm to the sound. This too disturbed Mr. Beaumont. The fire popped, and within it a pine knot sparked and bristled aflame, and Beaumont remembered the foreign business agent's ugly face along with the gleam in his eye that had sent the man direct to Charon's door—

Beaumont remembered the gunshot and the blood. And then he banished the memory. This was simple reverie, and a waste of time. He drew his watch from his pocket. It was silver. It was cold. He snapped open a top-piece etched with the image of his bank, and he held the glass close to his ear so he could listen to the simple music of the timepiece.

Tick tick tick. The sound was even. Measured. Sure and steady, like the universe itself.

Sure and steady. *Like Blasko*, Beaumont thought.

Or: *Like Blasko once was.* Days had passed since the wolf departed Beaumont's ranch, and the little mute had not returned. The banker had collected no trophy, no bandit's heart. And his watch ticked on and on. Even. Measured. Sure and steady. Waiting for a moment of reckoning that had not arrived.

Beaumont snapped the top-piece over the watch and returned it to his vest pocket. He lit a cigar, but it brought him no comfort. Soon he tossed the cigar into the fire. The cheroot went up in flames. The pine knot was gone now.

Nothing more than gray ash. The gnarled face Beaumont had seen or imagined—why, that was gone too. And in the darkness the fire cracked and spit and sparked as a thing alive… as Beaumont's own thoughts.

Beaumont listened. He could do little else.

Eventually, the fire burned down to nothing.

But the coals were banked.

And the ashes did not grow cold for a long, long time.

* * *

Reece threw his glove into the campfire. Damn thing. If only he hadn't lost the other one in Beaumont's bank when Rims blew the safe. If only the damn monster hadn't found it and caught his scent. If only—

If only. The way Reece saw it, those were two useless words. Still, it felt good to be shed of the glove. Reece stared into the fire, watched the fingers curl in on themselves as the leather crisped down to cinder. He didn't speak of the glove to the dynamite man or Steinhart.

All the others were dead. Only Reece and the German and Rims remained. The dynamite man hadn't spoken for two days. Hadn't eaten, either. Always sallow, now Rims looked like a dead undertaker, wrapped as he was in a black slicker's coat with big copper buttons. He moved only slightly more than a corpse would, and he looked ready for the dirt. Every day, they had to prod him into the saddle. Reece wondered just how many days the little ghost man had left. He had a feeling Rims would be the next to go.

It was different with the German. Steinhart was a whirl of activity. He'd been up before dawn, working with his big Bowie knife and a whetstone. Just as the coffee began to boil, he approached Reece and showed him the Bowie. It looked like there was some kind of brace on the end of the blade, jammed up against the weapon's hilt.

"That's a silver money clip," Steinhart explained. "Bought it in Denver. I sharpened it, and the Bowie's steel will guide it into the monster's belly. Silver will be the wolf's end. A wound carved by any other metal, and the demon will heal. But it has no hope against silver."

"Do tell." Reece blew loose a sigh. "You said that damn thing would only come around during the full moon, too. And the moon ain't been full the last three nights running. Still the wolf came. Every night."

The German jerked in his boots. "You call me a liar?" Then he shoved Reece, who was a damn sight smaller. "I tell you plain: That thing comes around tonight, he dies. And I will be the one who cuts his throat. After I cut yours, maybe."

The German was moving forward now, and fast. Across the fire, through the dull morning light. The Bowie streaked before him, its blade creasing the crisp air as it sliced a path toward Reece.

Reece didn't wait. He went for his pistol.

Before he had it drawn, two shots rang out.

One for the German. One for the dynamite man.

Both fell dead. Reece whirled. A stranger stood at the edge of the clearing in a patch of morning sunlight. Just a little man with a pasty face, dressed in black. But Reece understood who the man was, and instantly.

"You came in daylight," Reece said. "I'll be damned."

And then a big Colt bucked in the stranger's hand, and just that fast it bucked again. One shot missed Reece, and the other took the better part of his right ear. But that didn't slow Reece any. He put three slugs dead center in the werewolf's chest, and the pistol flew from the little man's fingers as he jerked backwards in his boots.

The stranger stared at Reece. Just for a moment, lips peeling back over a bloody grin. Then he bent down and grabbed his pistol. He snapped open the cylinder, fished fresh cartridges from his pocket and started to reload as he came forward, blood spilling down his shirt and dripping onto his boots.

Reece took time to snatch the Bowie from Steinhart's dead hand, but he didn't take another second beyond that. One blink and he was on his horse, slapping leather.

By the time the werewolf readied his pistol, Merrick Reece was long gone.

* * *

Reloading the pistol was only a bit of gamesmanship.

Blasko dropped the weapon, and his ass followed it into the dirt. He sat there, wheezing, watching the rider disappear into the distance. Quite suddenly, he couldn't move a muscle.

The sun poured down. A few minutes passed. And then Blasko's wounds began to heal. Slowly, of course. It would take an hour's time, maybe two. Blasko knew this well enough. But soon his wounds would crisp to scab, and then the scabs would flake to pink scars, and next his lungs would knit, and then—

And then Blasko would follow the rider.

That was his way.

But for now, Blasko sat, and bled, and wheezed. He thought of Reece's words, remembering the bandit's startled expression when he saw the pistol. And this memory made Blasko smile. Mr. Beaumont, too, had been surprised when Blasko wrote a note asking for a gun. He wanted the weapon simply because no man would expect it. A werewolf with a gun? Drawing down in the sunlight? It seemed preposterous. But, in truth, Blasko had killed many men just that way.

Blasko believed in surprise, just as he believed in secrets. He had many secrets. He guarded them, even from Mr. Beaumont. The moon was one of them. If he so desired, Blasko could transform himself into a wolf any time the moon shone. But just as the moon had phases, so did the wolf inside Blasko. When the moon was full and fat, the wolf was a hunter beyond compare. But Blasko's powers decreased markedly as the full moon waned, and this was another reason for the pistol.

Just as there were secrets Blasko guarded, there were many things people believed about werewolves which were not true. But what they said about silver was a simple, brutal fact. Blasko did not know why. He only knew that the metal's sharp scent lingered here in Reece's camp, and as he drew another whistling breath it seemed that the air itself was ripe with its horrible stench, and that

stench made him feel as if his guts were on the boil.

Blasko tried to ignore it.

He did not move as the sun rose higher, bathing him in its warmth.

But he moved soon enough.

And quickly.

* * *

Reece still had his Colt. He had Steinhart's Bowie, sheathed with its sharpened silver money clip, as well. What he didn't have was most of his left ear, but the blood had caked as he rode even if the pain hadn't tamped down an inch. He'd live with it. Hell, if he lived to tell this tale, he'd grow his hair long and that would be that.

After all, what was an ear? Just a little skin. The thing that mattered most now was the stake Reece and the boys had stolen from Beaumont's bank—a pair of saddlebags heavy with double eagles. Reece still had those. In truth, he hadn't so much as considered what he'd do with the money he stole from Beaumont's bank. Not until now. Reece never thought about such matters. For Reece, money was only a thing that filled his pocket and took him from one place to the next until he didn't have it, and then he set about the business of getting more.

But on this day, as he rode higher in the mountains with so many dead men behind him and a skinned ear that seemed alive with wildfire, Reece thought differently. This day, the money was for keeping. Maybe somewhere down the line he'd do something with it. If he lived to see tomorrow, and if he lived to see the day after that—

Reece had a plan for doing just that. It had begun with Steinhart's Bowie knife. The rest of it lay ahead, high above the timber, in a town called Fever Springs.

No springs there at all, of course. That was a laugh. These days Fever Springs was a desolate place, and dry. Abandoned. Home to leaning clapboards, and busted dreams, and rats. But once upon a time there had been more than a thousand people there, and something very special besides.

Until the mines played out.

Until the silver was gone.

Or most of it, anyway.

* * *

The houses leaned like sick men, casting shadows across the rutted street. A dead horse, gone to bone and tattered hide lay at the foot of a building with a faded sign: ASSAY OFFICE. And from the door of that office stepped the man named Reece. He carried a saddlebag over one shoulder, and his pistol was strapped down, and a Bowie knife hung from the other side of his gun-belt.

Blasko teetered in his boots. The sun was a brutal glimmer in the sky. He wretched and spit in the street. This place burned him… deep inside, everywhere, from guts to gizzard. The whole empty town, every inch of it stunk of silver. The earth, the air, everything. But Reece had come here. The man Blasko wanted. And so Blasko had followed, and—

"Looks like what they say about silver is true," Reece said, smiling. "Maybe you think I'm holding all the aces, leading you to a place like this. But me—I just figure I'm evening the odds."

Reece tossed the saddlebag into the dirt. One flap came open. Gold coins spilled into a rut of baked earth. Blasko stared down at them. That brutal glimmer of sunlight caught the metal. The coins gleamed, and the gleam caught Blasko's eye.

"You see, the stakes are high," Reece said. "I hope you'll forgive me. All this gold, and only two damn silver coins in the whole pot. I melted them down last night. Drilled a little hole in my bullets. Topped each of 'em off with a silver plug. We go at it with iron, I'll either kill you or maybe my pistol will explode in my hand. We'll just have to see."

Of course, Blasko kept his silence. That was his only choice, though Reece couldn't have understood that the man was mute. Even so, Blasko wouldn't have said a word. He was staring down at that gold. The brutal glimmer seemed to linger. And a fever burned in Blasko's brain. A fever apart from silver. A fever born of gold. Blasko thought of all the things he'd done in his life, and all the things he might have done. All he might still do. His life had amounted to little enough. He'd been a captive—with or without a glimpse of the world. But those lives he had tasted beneath the moon… those dead men he had devoured… now they were something different. And he saw bits of them in the sparks of light before him, and in that light… well, perhaps a different future.

A future that began with gold.

"So are we doing this now?" Reece wasn't smiling anymore. "You want to draw down and skin lightening? Or do we wait for night? You grow some claws and give me a chance at you with a knife?"

Blasko's guts boiled. He shook his head, wiped spit from his mouth. And finally his hand settled in the empty space above his holstered pistol, and his fingers twitched, and he nodded.

"Only one thing's for sure, then," Reece said, stepping into the middle of the street. "One of us will be eatin' dinner in hell."

Reece's smile was back. The bandit's hand drifted toward his side. Sweat seared Blasko's brow. He went for his pistol, and Reece did the same.

Neither one of them cleared leather, but two shots rang out.

Reece and Blasko fell dead in the street.

* * *

Mr. Beaumont stared down at Merrick Reece's corpse. Blood covered the thieving bastard's face, but his eyes were clear. For a moment, Beaumont considered carving the slug from Reece's skull, for it was a waste of good silver. Then he thought otherwise.

Beaumont scooped golden eagles into the saddlebags, tied them down, and stepped away. It was cold here, colder than the place he'd camped two nights ago when he'd first caught up with the werewolf and the bandit. He breathed deeply and tasted his own sour scent. Greasy. Unclean. He carried the stink of the campfire. Perhaps he'd cover the smell with another cigar. And perhaps, once he was shed of this empty place, he'd listen once more to the music of his pocket watch as darkness fell. That would calm him. Perhaps it was the only thing.

But Beaumont had no time for such musings now. Blasko lay before him, face down. Beaumont bent low and rolled the little mute over in the dirt. Blasko's dead eyes stared up at the banker, but they were not empty.

No. They gleamed. Even in death.

And, for Beaumont, that gleam was all too familiar.

In this manner, the banker's suspicions were confirmed. He rose and put Blasko's corpse behind him without a word. Beaumont did not like this kind of work. He walked down the street, his boots scraping over uneven earth. And then he slipped his rifle into its scabbard and mounted his horse, and he put Fever Springs behind him.

Beaumont rode south, descending the mountain. It was a cold night, but the cold no longer troubled him. He thought of Reece and Blasko as he rode. And then, as always, he put those names and the men who'd borne them behind him, and his thoughts returned to himself.

This, he understood, was the way of the world. Beaumont rode alone. Besides, there were other men out there. Lots of them. Other wolves, too.

Perhaps not so many of those. But others, surely.

Mr. Beaumont would find one.

For Mr. Beaumont's wallet was heavy.

Literature, Genre, Horror...and Mormons—What?

By Michael R. Collings

The whole debate over the relationship between "literature" and "genre fiction" is, in some senses, doomed from the start. Supporters of belletristic fiction see nothing whatsoever of worth in those groveling little tales based on plot and character, emphasizing as they do one element of, one perspective on, the "human experience," and often ignoring the darker parts, the suffering, the pain, the tragedy that make humanity (and one sort of literary expression of it) great.

Genre writers, on the other hand, frequently look with disdain on much of what is touted as "great literature," particularly by establishment critics and reviewers. They may harbor secret loves for Chaucer, Shakespeare, and Milton, of course; but when it comes to fictions that are relevant to *our* times, *our* conditions, *our* age, they find "establishment" stories and novels to be dull, boring, driven by style, symbolisms, or image and lacking in—you guessed it—plot and character.

The situation is particularly tense, I suspect, when it comes to horror as a genre. It is, in some ways, diametrically opposed to mainstream fiction. It often deals with the patently impossible…or at least the wildly improbable. It may easily reduce itself to clichéd images and figures: ancient castles, shadowy groves, sometimes ridiculously one-dimensional characters, and, perhaps worst of all, *monsters.*

Just as a number of first-class authors in the past rejected booksellers' attempts to place their books in the "science fiction" of "fantasy" shelves, arguing that they were merely using the *tropes* of those genres to write metaphors about essential humanity; so some of my friends and colleagues hesitate to come right out and say they write "horror." I frequently use the euphemistic "dark fantasy" when speaking to audiences that I know have little contact with horror beyond seeing previews for the latest buckets-of-blood slasher films. I especially use it when, in a church setting, people ask me what I write. It somehow seems too much of a disjuncture to say that I am the church organist—have been for fifty-five years—and that I write *horror.* The disjuncture becomes even more obvious when I admit that on occasion, when my hearing problems have made it impossible for me to get anything from the service, I have *written horror…in church.*

Most of the time, these various threads—writing, debates between genre fiction and literary fiction, the intersection of one's spiritual life and one's chosen form of literary expression—stay safely apart, often surfacing only in my own mind, where I deal with whatever issues arise and live with the fallout.

Recently, however, something happened that brought all of these issues, and more, to something approaching national attention.

When it was announced that the film adaptation of Orson Scott Card's multiple-award-winning YA/Adult science-fiction novel, *Ender's Game,* would be released in November, 2013, there were several immediate groundswells. One was unanimously positive. For nearly three decades the novel had helped form the imaginations of readers young and old, winning acclaim for its author. Regardless of the fact that it contained some intense scenes of real and imagined violence—not *horror,* precisely, but bordering on it—the story became one of the most highly anticipated films of the year.

One swell was distinctly negative. Based on versions of what Card was supposed to have written, sometimes years ago, about same-sex marriage, groups supporting it orchestrated grassroots boycotts of the film. According to their statements on the social media, many were distraught that the book should even continue to be published. One commenter said that she did not wish Card dead, but it would be nice if he were on a plane that was shot down on a desert island and all he had to read were the works of William S. Burroughs.

One swell was more ambivalent. The movie would be a SCI-FI extravaganza (and I use the term intentionally), full of special effects and topped off with a stellar list of actors…and the novel would get lost. Here people spoke of favorite scenes that would just *have* to be in the film or it would destroy the story. And with the term *sci-fi*, the issue of genre fiction entered the fray.

In mid-November, 2013, Mark Oppenheimer published an essay in *The New York Times* that brought all of these elements together and, for me at least, forced a moment of soul-searching. After identifying Orson Scott Card and Stephanie Meyer as members of the Church of Jesus Christ of Latter-day Saints (Mormons), Oppenheimer rapidly segued into a discussion of why so many members of that church in particular choose optimistic, "sunny" literary forms—more specifically, science fiction and fantasy—rather than opting to struggle with the grit and nastiness and tragedy of real life to seek literary greatness.

His argument rests heavily on his interpretation of comments made by Shannon Hale, an LDS young-adult writer. In particular, he relies on "Ms. Hale's theory…that literary fiction tends to exalt the tragic, or the gloomy, while Mormon culture prefers the sunny and optimistic." That Pollyanna-like perspective—resulting in what another source in the essay calls "faith-affirming and uncomplicated-type writing"—finds its natural expression in escapist genre fiction, "Because when you write sci-fi and so forth, things aren't as messy as with realistic fiction."

While there is much to quibble about in Oppenheimer's article, including his leaving out any significant investigation into the complex moral questions raised by *Ender's Game*, with its less-than-sunny conclusion, one major lapse lies in the fact that he completely ignores perhaps the darkest, arguably the most uncomfortable genre, one that (perhaps for him, inexplicably) thrives among authors along the Wasatch Front.

Horror.

Granted, horror is explicitly a form of genre literature, and, further granted, most readers of the *NYT* might hesitate to accord it "great literature" status under any circumstances. In a recent Facebook conversation, however, one participant commented that although

> [a]cademics dismiss horror writing…writing about terror and horror in human experience is one of the most serious things a writer can address. Fear, anxiety, and isolation are what drive us to our most cherished extremes. It is what forms the foundation for so much of our desperate achievement and scramble toward height and light. Even the crudest reach for significant themes is better than the most sophisticated sigh of emptiness, apathy, and despair. Let the blood spatter and the screams echo and revel in what is revealed as shadows flee. (—Samael Gyre writing as Gene Stewart)

While horror writers would certainly applaud these sentiments, critics, reviewers, and "establishment" types would more frequently side with the academics. In the hierarchy of literary writing (limiting it to the three genres in question) fantasy ranks low; science fiction ranks lower; and horror ranks lowest. Even its most eminent practitioner, Stephen King, appears to accept this estimation with his three grades of horror: *terror*, with its frisson of anticipation; *horror*, with its monsters creeping about in the darkness; and the *gross-out*, the physical representation of the gruesome and the gory—the visceral. And, he notes, if all else fails, he will go for the gross-out.

All this may be true, but the fact remains that a specific geographical area, a specific shared culture (or sub-culture), and in many cases, the same writers Oppenheimer wishes to associate with simplistic, highly optimistic, uncomplicated, less-than-sophisticated writing (if not his words, then the ones he chooses to quote) have written some intensely disquieting fiction.

He could, in fact, have looked no further than the first Mormon author he mentioned, Orson Scott Card. A multiple *New York Times* bestseller, winner of the Hugo and Nebula Awards back-to-back for a novel and its sequel (an unparalleled achievement), Card was in all likelihood the source of Oppenheimer's interest in LDS fiction, particularly because of the brouhaha over his authorship of one of the year's most anticipated movies, *Ender's Game.* That novel itself is sufficient evidence to refute many of Oppenheimer's claims: it is tough; it acknowledges both family togetherness and the tensions that rip families (and individuals) apart; it deals with complex issues revolving around the relationship between the individual and the community; it deals with aliens that are at once science-fictional and horrific in their non-humanness, and at the same time it urges readers to see beneath the surface and confront ugly, unpleasant realities about them…and about us.

But it is a walk in the park on a calm summer's day compared with some of Card's other works. "Eumenides in a Fourth-floor Lavatory," "Fat Farm," "Unaccompanied Sonata," "The Porcelain Salamander," and—for my money his finest, most disquieting, most horrific, and most sublime short story—"Kingsmeat" sufficiently indicate how deeply Card has penetrated into "our cherished extremes." In fact, a number of his early shorter works garnished not only praise but severe censure among LDS readers for their graphic depictions of horrors. And novels such as *A Planet Called Treason* (1979; extensively revised as *Treason,* 1988), *Lost Boys* (1992, expanded from an earlier short story), *Treasure Box* (1996), and *Homebody* (1998) show him fully capable of extending the tropes into full narratives.

Card is a far more complex, more sophisticated writer than the blurb in the *NYT* essay might suggest. His writings range from biography to historical fiction, from how-to-books to essays on contemporary LDS life, from scripts for religious tapes and films to full-scale theatrical productions. At one point, in fact, he told me that less than one-third of his total output could be considered sf/f. Yet in almost everything he writes, genre or not, there is an element of darkness, of awareness that life is more than a sunny outlook and an optimistic religion.

If Card were alone in his dedication to the darker elements of fiction, this essay would be superfluous. But he is not. For well over thirty years, writers throughout the Wasatch Front (south-eastern Idaho through northern Utah) have organized symposia, hosted conferences and cons, created workshops, encouraged writers groups that have produced a remarkable number of writers of fantasy and dark fantasy…and horror.

Just last night, a friend of mine, Dave Butler, posted a self-proclaimed screed on Facebook that included the following: "Big Storytelling (Broadway and Hollywood, and maybe to some extent Publishing) is in a serious rut. They rehash the same stories over and over. As an investment strategy, I get it—big dollars go into these things, so investors want to place bets on sure (or very likely) wins." He then lists, by name, authors whose works he sees as providing "more diversity of stories, more quirky stories, more local stories, more unique stories. I want stories that are awesome, not stories that are commercial." His list includes:

> Angie Lotfhouse's "syncretistic-Mormon science fiction";
> Steven Peck's "weird west lit fic";
> Bill Housley's "libertarian first contact stories,"
> Danyelle Leafty's fairy tales;
> Paul Genesse's "romantic epic fantasy";
> Michaelbrent Collings' "serial zombie survival epic";
> Tom Carr's independent films;
> Platte F. Clark's *Bad Unicorn* series;
> Eric Patten's Hunter Chronicles;
> Dan Wells' "I am not a serial killer" trilogy;
> Robison Wells' YA science fiction

To which could easily be added:

> Larry Correia, bestselling author of the Monster Hunter International series, the Grimnoir Chronicles, and others;
> Eric James Stone, Nebula Award winner and Hugo Nominee;
> Brandon Sanderson, Hugo and Whitney Award author of the Mistborn series and completer of Robert Jordan's *The Ring of Time;*
> Jeff Savage, one of the first to publish horror through an LDS publisher;
> Wilum Pugmire, an accomplished Lovecraftian;
> Jaleta Clegg, specializing in sf/f and silly horror—some of the best and silliest.

Two years ago, a remarkable anthology was published by Wm Morris and Theric Jepson, *Monsters & Mormons* (2011). Anyone unaware that the West has produced an enclave of Mormon horror writers might take a look at this 500-page tome containing stories, poems, graphic comics and illustrations… many emerging as if from the landscape itself. Some are humorous, others are straight-line extrapolations from present to future, but most at least touch upon darkness—even Jaleta

Clegg's, in which the "monster" is the infamous green Jell-O reputedly served at all LDS functions.

A year ago, a second remarkable anthology appeared, this time a group-project spearheaded by Nathan Shumate: *Space Eldritch* (2012). The concept: simple—Lovecraft in Space. The execution: far more complex, as stories by D.J. Butler, myself, Nathan Shumate, David J. West, Carter Reid and Brad Torgersen, Robert J Defendi, and Howard Taylor explored the infinite possibilities of other dimensions, of aliens and alien worlds, of space-and-time travel in multiple forms, all wrapped in the impenetrable darkness of H.P. Lovecraft's inimical, loathly universe.

And this year, a third anthology: *Space Eldritch II: The Haunted Stars* (2013). New to the volume are Michaelbrent Collings, Larry Correia (who provided the introduction to the parent volume), Stephen J. Peck, Steven Diamond, and Eric James Stone; the remaining stories are by five contributors from the first volume, myself included. Again, there are no limits—physical, spiritual, psychological—to the darkness of the imagined universes, to the terrors and horrors that, through fiction (and though fictive) help define what it is to be human.

Earlier this year, my son Michaelbrent Collings, began his most ambitious project. A multi-volume zombie-apocalypse-human-survival epic…set in southwestern Idaho. *The Colony:*

Genesis, The Colony: Renegades, and *The Colony: Descent* draw from the western landscape—from the anomalous mixture of city and wide-open spaces—to speculate on what might happen if, within a matter of minutes, the vast proportion of the human race transformed into zombies with powers of mutation and intercommunication, and others not yet disclosed. How would the remaining fraction survive, and what would be important enough to them to *want* to survive? As with his earlier horror novels—especially *Strangers* (2013), *Darkbound* (2013), and *The Haunted* (2012)—he has no fears of darkness, even darknesses where other horror writers might first hesitate.

And finally, a personal note. I have published two works that became Bram Stoker Award® Finalists for 2012: *Writing Darkness,* a collection of essays on the nature of horror, the nature of writing, and the intersections between them; and *A Verse to Horror: An Abecedary of Monsters and the Monstrous,* which deals alphabetically with monsters in folklore, literature, and film…with one limerick allowed per monster.

In addition, I have published eight novels: two sf (*Wordsmith* and *Singer of Lies*), four overtly horror (*The House Beyond the Hill, The Slab, Shadow Valley,* and *Static!*), and two mysteries (*Devil's Plague* and *Serpent's Tooth*). All eight are "genre fiction"; not one of them is, I think, cursed by sunny optimism. There is darkness in every story. And I have published over eight hundred books, chapbooks, chapters, essays and articles, and reviews, the vast majority dealing with horror. Two of my volumes of poetry are explicitly horror-oriented, particularly *In the Void: Poems of Science Fiction, Myth and Fantasy, and Horror.*

Now to the point behind all of the facts, figures, and blatant name-dropping.

What do all of these writers share?

For one, they share a love of and devotion to genre fiction, specifically sf, fantasy, *and* horror. Not all write in each genre; certainly not all are quite comfortable being called "horror writers." But in the search for truth—even the truths underlying the universe and all of creation—they find the ideal outlet in an "escapist" form of fiction that allows them to rise above the grittiness of day-to-day tedium and enter far more into the realms of darkness—again, physical, emotional, spiritual, psychological—where we scramble toward "height and light." nd none would deny the implicit greatness of the scrambling.

For another, they all have deep roots in a single geographic location: they are Westerners. Almost all either live or have lived in Utah, Arizona, or Idaho. Many come from families who settled those regions and, as the saying goes, "made the desert blossom as the rose." My great-grandfather was carried across the plains in his mother's arms while his father and the remaining children pushed a handcart. They settled southern Utah—that landscape, with its painted cliffs and neat valley farms, is as much my homeplace as any of the cities I've lived in. Simply by being part, to whatever degree, of the land, I share its history, its struggles, and its successes. So,

in their own ways, do most of these writers.

For yet another, they mostly share a single religious heritage. Not all are Mormons, but most of those who are not have chosen to live within LDS environments, which gives them glimpses into the intensity of family and community. Those who are Mormon understand a point that Orson Scott Card articulated a number of years ago. In "On Sycamore Hill," he talks about the genesis of two stories in *The Folk of the Fringe,* a collection set in the landscape of a post-apocalyptic Utah. One evening, when the rest of the workshop group had left for dinner, he remained behind, at first thinking that he wanted to work on his stories. Gradually, however, he realized that, as a Mormon, he was not truly one of the group:

> …this wasn't my community. These guys were Americans, not Mormons; those of us who grew up in Mormon society and remain intensely involved are only nominally members of the American community. We can fake it, but we're always speaking a foreign language….

From this comes a fourth, crucial point. Most of the writers listed above, whether Mormon or not, whether directly from the West or not, can understand the sense of being *isolated*…by vistas and landscapes, by religious beliefs and commitments, by shared historical heritages that set them apart…and by their choice to work within a genre that emphasizes, that embraces, that makes essential *isolation*. Horror by its nature begins in aloneness—whether in an old, creaking house, or in an ancient forest redolent with secrets and fear, or in the farthest reaches of space. And out of that aloneness, it struggles to create some kind of community, to establish ties with fellow humans, or, when that is impossible, with fellow aliens.

To return to the beginning of this essay: the most important points about Orson Scott Card and *Ender's Game* that Oppenheimer misses are *not* that Card writes genre fiction or that he is a member of a religion that has a peculiar and peculiarly optimistic outlook, as important as those might be.

What he misses is that Card and all of these other writers—*genre* writers, *western* writers, *Mormon* writers, progeny of pioneers of varying sorts—all of them have *chosen* horror in one way or another as a unique, for them ideal way of, as has already been said, scrambling "toward height and light."

And the struggle can be sublime.

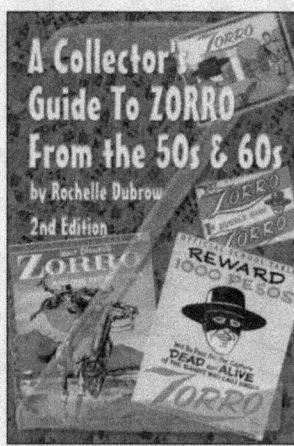

WHAT THE HELL EVER HAPPENED TO...?

An interview with Mark Clements

By Robert Morrish

The horror genre is, of course, by its very nature a *dark* place. But even in that context, the 1990s were a very, very dark time for the genre. The boom period of the 1980s resulted in a glut of horror novels published, many of them of poor quality, and not surprisingly sales figures nosedived. In reaction, many publishers abandoned their horror lines and many horror writers found themselves abruptly jettisoned. Mark Clements was one of the victims of those cutbacks.

Clements had published his first novel, *6:02*, as a paperback original through Popular Library in 1988 before moving to hardcover publisher Donald I. Fine for his next three books—*The Children of the End, Lorelei,* and *The Land of Nod.* After that, though, the aforementioned bust in the horror market, combined with Penguin Books' swallowing up of Donald I. Fine, led to an involuntary halt to Clements' writing career, although he has subsequently served as ghost-writer for several books.

Clements grew up in Indiana and graduated from Indiana University, but has lived in the San Diego area since 1981. As is the case with many authors, he's held a wide variety of "day jobs" in order to pay the bills while pursuing a career as a novelist, including pizza maker, farm hand, factory janitor, frame maker, bookstore clerk, proofreader in an accounting firm, tech support, tech writer, ghost writer, artist, editor, and teacher.

Clements teaches and runs read-and-critique workshops at three conferences: the Southern California Writers Conference, the La Jolla Writers Conference and the San Diego Writers Conference. He's also attending National University, working on a master's degree in creative writing with the goal of teaching at the college level.

Although his fiction-writing career has gotten sidetracked, Clements has by no means abandoned the dream, as he explains: "When I decided to start writing seriously I made myself this pledge: 'I am going to become a very successful published writer.' To me, 'successful' meant being able to support myself and my family by writing the things I like to write. Fortunately I was smart enough to recognize how much of a role luck plays in this industry, so I didn't include a time limit in the pledge. Good thing, because I'm still only halfway to where I swore to be. And I'm never giving up."

DD: Your first book, *6:02*, was published by Popular Library. How did you place your book with them? Did you have an agent for that first book, or did you connect with the publisher through their slush pile?

MC: Ah, the good old days of what's now called "conventional" publishing. Back then a handful of publishers, even big ones, still accepted unsolicited submissions. So what I did was send out two manuscripts at a time—one directly to a publisher and one to an agent. As it happened, I landed an agent first, Jane Jordan Browne, and she got two offers on *6:02*. One was from Warner Books, of which Popular Library was an imprint, and the other was from Pocket

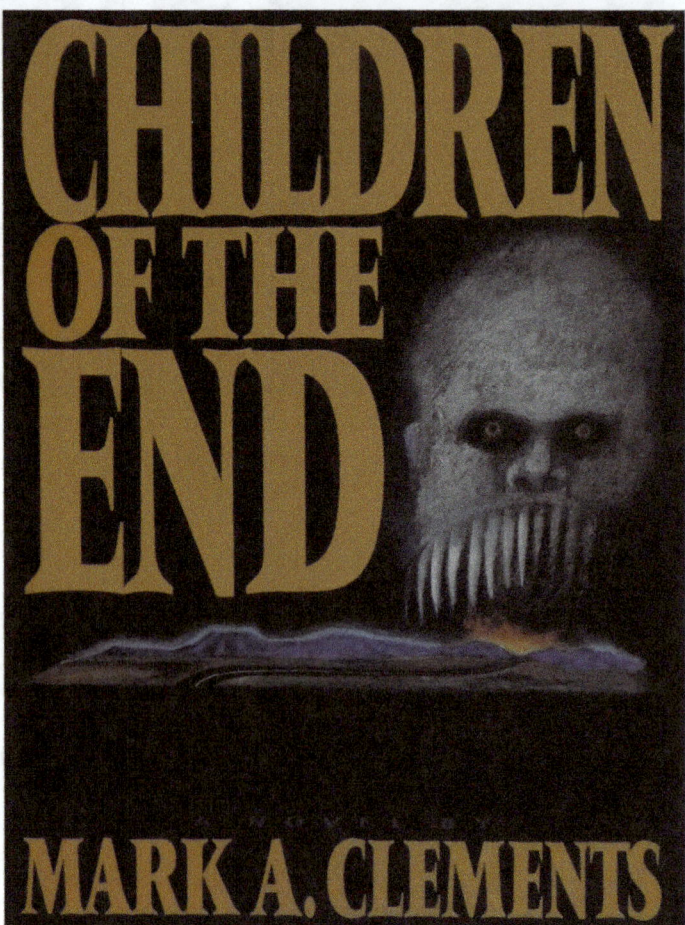

CHILDREN OF THE END

A NOVEL BY **MARK A. CLEMENTS**

Books. We went with Warner, which turned out to be a mistake due to plain old bad luck. My editor was wonderful until the crucial moment of the novel's release, when she left on maternity leave and nobody else picked up the ball. I had TV appearances and signings set up—all from my own efforts—and virtually no books to sell. A trickle here, a trickle there. Still, when I submitted my next novel to Warner as stipulated by contract, the same editor was hot for it. Then the book went to the editorial committee for consideration, and the reaction was, "Hey, his last one didn't sell, so forget it." And my editor didn't defend me—because she couldn't. She was out on maternity leave again.

DD: Your next three books were published in hardcover by Donald I. Fine, Inc, with paperback editions by Leisure. How did the move to those publishers come about?

MC: Fine was known at the time as "The Last of the Mid-Sized Publishers." He was famous for finding and promoting then-unknown writers like Ken Follett, Leonard Elmore and John Lecroart. Not so famous for finding me, alas. But at least he was willing to roll the dice on books he liked, regardless of what the markets were like at the time.
DD: Which of your titles sold the most copies?

MC: I suspect it was the last one, *The Land of Nod*, but I honestly can't be sure because Donald Fine died shortly after the hardcover was released and DIF was absorbed by

Penguin. I got orphaned, as they say—no editor at Penguin, no support system—and that was that. They didn't care about a novel they hadn't published themselves, and were very lackadaisical about providing figures. Plus, by the time they got around to doing so, the success of the novel was already a moot point, so why worry about it? Back then, especially, once a book left your hands there was very little you could do about its sales.

DD: On your website, you mention that *The Land of Nod* is your personal favorite among the books you've published. Do you think that's a case of appreciating your most recent work the most, or is there more to it than that?

MC: Hopefully I'll always like my most recent book the best, but yeah, in this case there's more to it than that. *Children of the End* was a way of recapturing a bit of the magical past—good and bad. It let me pit my own light and dark sides against one another, and compare adulthood with childhood. For the latter reason the novel has been compared to Stephen King's *It*, and understandably so. But it's no kind of copy.

DD: You also mention that you have a soft spot for *Children of the End.* Why is that?

MC: Two reasons. First, monsters. I just love them. Second, I had some serious points to make about human behavior, and the creatures in *Children* let me do so via a rewarding mixture of bloodshed and black humor. It's probably too over-the-top for some people, but so be it. I love my Loners.

DD: I'm guessing that the end of your relationship with Donald Fine came about due to lower sales than the publisher was looking for, combined with the fact that the mid-1990s were not the best time to be peddling fiction with supernatural elements. Is that the case?

MC: You know, there were a lot of factors involved. Like I said, Don Fine died, which made him harder than usual to work with—and he was a notoriously difficult to work with. But as far as Penguin was concerned, uninspiring sales figures certainly had the same effect that they'd had at Warner, exacerbated by the fact that I was working in a genre that was, as you say, not doing particularly well at the time.

DD: Did you continue trying to sell novels during the next few years? Do you have unpublished "trunk" novels from that period, or from earlier in your career? If so, tell us about them.

MC: I wrote two unpublished novels before selling *6:02*, and another between *Lorelei* and *The Land of Nod*. The first manuscript might have been salvageable, but all existing copies were lost in a fire and I've never had the heart to try it again. The second novel was a monster story whose creatures happened to end up in F. Paul Wilson's *The Tomb*. I mean, literally the only difference between his Rakoshi and my aliens was the color of the critters' eyes; Wilson and I even described them using the same metaphors. Of course there was no theft involved; it was just weird serendipity. I even wrote to Wilson and told him about it, adding that I'm a big fan of *The Tomb* so it didn't bother me that much. Also, I'm cribbing some of the settings and situations from that novel to use in the one I'm working on now, so it wasn't a complete waste.

As for the later unpublished novel, it was simply stillborn. I finished it and it had some cool moments, but never a pulse. Then there was another novel I began right after *The Land of Nod*, but never finished. I could tell it was never going to come to life. Then, of course, there's the book I'm working on now. It's been slow going for a variety of reasons, some associated with the book itself and others having to do with marriage, children, money…all the things I'd never expected to get in my way!

DD: On your website, you list your five current favorite authors as being Martin Cruz Smith, Mitchell Smith, Andrew Klavan, Mo Hayder, and Thomas Harris, all of whom are crime or thriller writers. Given that, it seems surprising that you haven't tried writing a straight crime or thriller novel. Or have you?

MC: All my current favorite authors have blurred the genre line into horror at least once. I guess the only thing you can say for sure is that none of them write *supernatural* horror novels. But while Martin Cruz Smith is best known for his Arkady Renko mysteries, one of his early works was a gem about vampire bats and the plague called *Nightwing*. Mo Hayder's absolutely hardcore all the time; her novels *all* challenge the distinction between crime novels and horror; *Karma* by Mitchell Smith does the same, as do several of Klavan's novels. As for Harris, well, he created Hannibal Lecter; what more need I say? It's true that I read less supernatural fiction than I used to, mostly because I don't find much of it convincing. But when I do get convinced, I love it as much as I ever did. I just finished *Dr. Sleep* and to me it's the best King novel in many a year.

DD: When did you start ghostwriting? Was it strictly an economic decision to venture into that line of work, or was there more to it than that?

MC: Oh, it was economic. My first child was on his way and I'd been laid off from my job, but I thought, hey, I'm a

writer, and I'd rather write someone else's book than work in a factory. Of course the big advantage of ghostwriting is that the other guy takes all the risks, right? You just get paid and move on, right? Piece of cake. That's what I thought.

DD: How many books did you ghostwrite? What types of books were they? Memoirs, other non-fiction, fiction? Are you able to list any of the actual titles, or are you contractually prevented from doing so?

MC: I ghostwrote between six and eight books, depending on where you draw the line between "editing" and "ghostwriting." I guess I shouldn't mention titles, but the books included thrillers, memoirs, a tome on New Age healing and a military techno-thriller. That one was memorable because I actually wrote it for a woman who was herself writing for an ongoing series produced by a stable of writers working under the same pseudonym. My client considered these books her meat and potatoes, but wanted to concentrate on something else, so she hired me to handle one project for her. In other words, I ghostwrote a book for someone who was ghostwriting books for a ghost.

DD: When and why did you stop ghostwriting?

MC: I stopped for two reasons. First, the client I mentioned above told me, "You can tell which of my books you wrote because it's good." What she meant was that I treated the nonexistent author's novel the way I treat all my own writing: painstakingly. Writing is the one area of my life where I'm a perfectionist, and since I'm also slow at it—a re-re-re-writer—I'm a poor ghostwriter. Non-writers don't understand. They think we can just crank stuff out like fresh linguine. Well, some of us can, but not me. As a result I tended to end up with frustrated, unhappy clients while earning the equivalent of about a buck-fifty an hour. Not a great combination.

Then there was the matter of my own work. The last thing my writing career needed was to come to a dead stop, but there it was: year after year after year went by, and I was producing nothing in my own name with which to follow up on *Children of the End*. So a couple of years ago I gave up ghostwriting entirely.

DD: Given your relative proximity to Los Angeles, have you dabbled at all in screenwriting?

MC: Yep. For eleven years I worked for a company that produced screenwriting software, and an independent filmmaker here in San Diego bought our program so she could write a TV pilot called *Dreamweavers* she was developing. But she didn't have the time to actually learn the program, so she hired me to turn her notes into a script. Since the notes were *very* sketchy, I ended up not only transcribing them but fleshing them out and basically co-writing the script. She and her husband, a cinematographer for Stu Segall Studios (which at the time made shows for cable TV), hired a cast that included Robert Carradine and Frank Gorshen, and shot a twelve-minute trailer entitled *Dream Weavers.* Although the trailer and concept were both cool, the series unfortunately never got off the ground. It would have been great.

Also, all my novels have been optioned at one time or another. *Children of the End* got to the script stage a couple of times, and one of those made it to the final cut at a production company before joining the smoking pile of wreckage below.

DD: In a 2012 interview with DearEditor.com, you answer a question by saying (partially) that:

"My current novel features an organism that is alive but does not become conscious or self-aware until a third of the way through the story."

What more can you tell us about that novel? Is it still in progress or are you shopping it at this point? Have you started (or completed) any other new novels in recent years?

MC: The book you mention is the one I've been working on for eight or nine years now. It's a very complicated, difficult piece, a sort of bio-horror story, and I chose a rather idiosyncratic approach to it by including the point of view of an organism that doesn't actually *have* a point of view for a long time. But that's sort of the point. I wanted to challenge myself, really put myself to the test. Hopefully the result will be a novel that's terrifying, thought-provoking, and memorable, all at the same time. Anyway, at least it will be a novel of some sort after all these years.

The intended title was, alas, *The White Queen*. Of course, now there's a popular TV series with the same name, which sucks because it was perfect for my novel, which is about an organism that arises in opposition to the "Red Queen" of Darwinian natural selection. So far no alternative has leaped to mind, so I'll continue to use *The White Queen* until I get nearer the end. As for the date of completion, my goal is to have the novel done (finally) and out on the submission trail before the end of 2014. I plan to go the conventional route at first—agent, publisher—because I'd just as soon have someone else handle the publishing and marketing end of things. But we'll see—one advantage of writing today is that there are actually alternatives, if need be. I've made all my old titles available as ebooks, so I have some understanding of how that works, and if I don't feel there's enough interest in the conventional publishing world for my new book, I'm willing to go that route. We'll see….

✿ ✿ ✿

Photo Courtesy of Mark Clements

PHANTOM HILL

By Hank Schwaeble

The demon had been there, right at the spot where his boot met the ground. He could feel it in the pulsing of his wound, smell its wake in the dead air. That scent meant he hadn't missed it by much. Two hours, he reckoned. Maybe less.

He tied off the horse and patted its neck. It needed water, but it was spooked. He glanced over to the saloon. His horse was too nervous to drink. He was too nervous not to.

Sand and dirt caked his hands and face and neck, sweat turning it into pasty smears. He untied his bandana and wiped away what he could. Puffs of desert and prairie plumed off his longcoat. He pulled the goatskin from his saddle bag, slipped his arm through the sling and took his hat off to tug it over his head. He left his Henry rifle in its sheath.

How many, he wondered. Town this size, couldn't be more than three. He drew his Remington and checked the cylinder, reholstered it, checked the replacement cylinder in his pocket. He'd assume three. But he'd been wrong before.

The saloon was quiet. His spurs clinked on the wooden platform, the way they disrupted the stillness another reminder he wasn't far behind. He stood in front of the swinging doors and tilted his head, cracking the cartilage in his neck.

First contact was always difficult. The demon's presence hung in the atmosphere like a funk, inhaled and absorbed by the townsfolk. There was always a mood. Eyes lurking with suspicion, conversations laden with distrust. He knew what to expect.

A young girl in a frilly dress and a bonnet scampered onto the platform near a far edge and stopped. He shaded his face to see her, blocking out the late afternoon sun. She stared for a few beats then ran off around the corner.

Please, he thought. *No kids. Not again.*

He clenched his eyes shut, took in a long breath, then pushed through the doors.

The place was almost empty, but the air was still heavy with stale body odor and acrid breath. And dust. He had to stop himself from sneezing. Two men—former soldiers wearing the threadbare remnants of cavalry uniforms—were sitting at a card table. Another man sat alone in the corner huddled over a glass of beer. A woman in a red and black dress, her puffy skirt ballooning in layers, sat on a stool next to the door, eyes fixed and **chary**. The saloon keeper was sweeping out the floor in front of the bar.

The man sweeping straightened up, hands on the broomstick, elbows hanging.

"No whiskey," he said. "Stage is late with supplies."

Of course it is. "Beer's good."

The man lingered an extra beat, face sagging, then leaned the broom against the bar and circled around to pour a glass.

"Two bits."

Pricey, but he paid it. It was at least as warm as the room. Pulpy, too.

He lowered the glass and wiped his mouth on the back of his sleeve. "I have a question."

"Hotel is down the street, can't miss it. Four rooms. Three vacancies. There's a house of soiled doves four buildings past it. You can buy tokens here, if you like."

"Not that kind of question."

The man propped his arms on the bar, looked over to the two at the card table for support. "I'm not obliged to take questions from strangers."

"Name's Pierce." He placed a five dollar gold piece on the bar. "Now you know me."

"What is it you want to know, Pierce?"

"How many men in these parts have taken a squaw for a wife?"

"What the hell kind of question is that? How would I know?"

Pierce glanced over the man's shoulder at the mirrored wallspace, watching the men at the card table. They were interested, but didn't look like they wanted trouble.

"This town ain't that big. You'd know. Talking about white men. Indian wives."

"The hell, you say! Mister, I think you'd best leave."

Pierce took another sip of his beer, finger of his free hand still on the gold piece, then he thrust his arm out and grabbed a scruff of shirt. He yanked the barkeep over the counter and pulled the man's face near his lapel. His beer hand set down his glass and pulled back his coat just enough to reveal the coin-metal badge. A silver circle around a star. *Texas Ranger*.

"Answer the damn question."

"Heck, Mister. You didn't say you was a lawman. I can only think of two."

That was definitely welcome news. Fewer usually meant quicker, and quicker meant an easier time picking up the trail.

"Either of them Comanche?"

The barkeep blinked.

"The squaws. Either of them Comanche?"

"Slocum's. Tom Slocum. He's got a place just south, over the hill. Trail follows a creek right to it."

Pierce let him go. The man slid back over the bar. He straightened his shirt out and swallowed. Pierce took another sip of beer, saw the man eye the gold piece. Tipping his head back, he drained the glass, then scooped up the coin and dropped it into the pocket of his vest. Lawmen didn't pay for answers.

"One more question. I passed a church as I rode in. It looked like it was starting to go to seed. You got a preacher in this town?"

Over his shoulder, Pierce could hear the two men at

the card table snicker.

The man pointed to the corner. He didn't smile, but whatever frustration he felt over being roughhoused and losing five dollars seemed more than countered by the satisfaction of making that gesture.

"*Reverend* Swain," he said. "And you're in luck. He's still conscious."

More snickering. *Great*, Pierce thought. *Just great.*

The men at the table stiffened and made coughing noises, pretending to be analyzing their cards as Pierce turned and marched past them.

Pierce stopped next to Swain's table and stood there. The man was dressed in a tattered black suit. A black string tie drooped from his stained collar. His shirt had once been white. Beneath his flat-brimmed hat, graying hair poked out in various directions like quills. He didn't look up.

"You really a preacher? Devout servant of God and all that?"

"Who wants to know?"

"Someone who isn't, but could really use one."

"The Reverend Jedediah Swain, First Methodist Episcopal Church of Phantom Hill, at your service." He raised his glass and took a long swig, but still didn't look up.

Pierce pulled out the chair across from him and sat.

"I need a true man of faith, Reverend."

"Buy me another beer, Lad, and I'll be as true and as faithful as you want me to be."

"You're not going to make this easy, are you?"

"Son, I have no idea who you are or what you're talking about, but the ways of God are never easy."

"Maybe not, but some are definitely easier than others."

"Just another glass and I'll hear your troubles. Your burdens will be lifted. Through God, all things are possible..." His voice trailed off and he waved his hand, as though swatting the rest of the thought away.

Pierce studied the man for a long moment. Then he pushed himself away from the table and stood. He would have to use a child. God. Damn. It.

"Sorry to bother you, Pastor."

Swain grabbed him by the wrist as he started to walk away. His grip was surprisingly firm.

"Wait. I apologize. Please, sit."

Pierce sat.

"I assumed... It's been a while since anyone has sincerely sought my spiritual guidance."

"And why is that, Reverend?"

He swept his arm in a long arc, indicating the rest of the saloon behind him, and beyond. "You'd have to ask them."

"I'm asking you."

"You don't want to concern yourself with my misfortunes."

"Indulge me, Reverend. I want to know."

The man tipped his glass and looked down. "I suffered a lapse in judgment. You might say it set off a chain of events. My price to pay. Some things are not easily forgotten. Or forgiven."

Pierce watched the man peer into what was left of his beer.

"You sure it's not just a matter of you worshiping a different kind of spirit? Like the kind that comes in a bottle?"

" '*Not that which goeth into the mouth defileth a man.*' Are you determined to humiliate me, son? Is such easy sport your purpose after all?"

"No. I need a man pure of heart. Right with God. Not one that can merely quote scripture."

"It's not my place to judge my own heart. As for being right with God, how is one to ever know? I've confessed my sins without pride or excuse, asked for His forgiveness daily. And I'm sure He has forgiven me, for the Bible tells us He shall. Forgetting, however..." The reverend shrugged, swallowing the last of his beer. "*That* is another matter entirely."

Only one culprit tended to make a man act this way, Pierce knew. A story formed in his head, swirling thoughts coming together, debris in a dust devil. A Sunday sharper, preaching virtue and attacking vice from his pulpit to a flock of rough men and painted women, determined to clean up this frontier Sodom. A young wife plucked from some far away town, obediently playing her role, respecting her husband but not loving him. The pastor in all his pious glory reaching out to ladies of the evening, ministering to them, visiting their house of ill repute. One of them deciding to toy with him one slow, languorous night, maybe luring him to a private area, maybe casually slipping out a tit while he's trying to pray with her, maybe reaching right down and grabbing his loins, a look of delicious sin in her eyes. A woman so different than his innocent, boring mate, a woman representing the promise of pleasures long denied him. A guilt-ridden preacher taking to the bottle afterwards, finally confessing his transgression in a drunken, maudlin stupor. His young wife feeling both betrayed and relieved, running off with some carpet-bagger or soldier first chance she got. The man she left behind now the source of hushed whispers and stinging barbs, a minister with no respect, fallen, cuckolded, hardly ever sober for more than a few hours. Sticking around for lack of anywhere else to go. Waiting for a sign he was forgiven. Waiting for another spiritual assignment from his Boss. Waiting on the stage to bring whiskey.

Or something like that. The details weren't important.

"Tell me, son... why do you want to know about who or what I am? What troubles you so that you worry about the pureness of my heart?"

"The lack of pureness in mine."

"I don't understand."

"Come with me, Reverend." Pierce stood. "We've got the Lord's work to do."

The fire popped and snapped, flames clawing the air. The pungent pine smoke singed his nostrils. Hell is greedy.

"Don't you think it's about time you told me what we're doing here?"

Pierce prodded the fire with a stick. Sparks whirled into the air and died out. *Greedy*, he thought, *but patient.*

"We're waiting for the moon to be up."

The preacher lifted his hat and scratched his pate. "Even if that made any sense, that's not what I meant. You tell me to grab my Bible and horse, show me a badge when I object, then you make me ride with you until we see Tom Slocum's place. Every crack of a twig and your hand slaps the handle of your revolver—the presence of which, I might add, makes it rather difficult for me to resist your edicts. But I must insist you at least tell me, why are we here?"

They were crouched around the fire, obscured from view by a large weeping willow. A rocky creek gurgled nearby, filling the air with a damp, earthy smell that the smoke couldn't quite mask.

"I have a question for you first. Why is this place called Phantom Hill?"

"Why, it's named after the Fort. Mile and a half north of town. Town's just a camp, actually. A place that sprang up in the Fort's shadow."

"In that case, why is the Fort named Phantom Hill?"

Reverend Swain sighed, scratched his stubble. "I'm told it's because when you ride in from a distance, it looks like you're approaching a steep hill. But then it levels out as you get closer, flattening out into a plain. Disappearing. Like a phantom."

Pierce nodded, peering into the fire.

"There's another story some say," Swain continued. "Something about an Indian being spotted by a sentry when the cavalry first made camp. Shots were fired, but none of the soldiers dispatched to investigate could find any sign of Indians, anywhere. So everyone started saying the man had fired on a ghost."

The fire burned hot now. Pierce traced the horizon, found the moon peeking through the trees. He unslung his leather goatskin. Then he reached into his pocket and removed a small pouch, closed off with a drawstring.

Reverend Swain shifted his weight from one side to the other. "Now, about why we're here?"

"Tell me, Reverend. You ever heard the Comanche's version of creation? Their tribal myth?"

"Maybe. I'm not sure. Why?"

"The Comanche believe the Great Spirit created them from dust, just like it says in Genesis. They also claim something else was made, that from all the bits of darkness in the Earth that God brought together, a demon was formed, an evil, shape-shifting devil. To protect the people, the Great Spirit cast that demon into a bottomless pit. But its presence can still be felt in the fangs and stingers of various creatures, sources of pain and death meant to torment us in revenge."

"That is not so different than what the Bible teaches. Eden had its own serpent, and there has been enmity between such creatures and man ever since."

Pierce stared at the fire, flames digging their way out from below. "No, not so different."

"What's going on, son?"

"Let me tell you another story, Reverend. A story about a young officer assigned to assist the Confederate Indian Agent. The Union had withdrawn at the start of the war, and left a string of broken treaties in its wake. The Confederacy couldn't spare enough men to ward off Comanche attacks. So this man helped negotiate treaties, keep them from declaring war. He was hardly a statesman, and had never negotiated for anything more than a plowhorse, but he'd grown up on the edge of the *Comancheria*, spoke a few phrases of their language. That was enough for him to be volunteered."

Swain lowered himself from a crouch onto the ground, sitting. He rubbed his knee and listened.

Pierce kept his gaze on the fire, watching his story play out in the glow of the orange and white embers.

"Then one day this man was introduced to a Comanche shaman. A tribal elder named Dark Horse. It was his role as respected advisor to the council to determine the worth of the officer's words, the value of his promises. The soldier was not allowed to negotiate in his presence. His daughter acted as translator and intermediary. She was very young. In English, her name meant Morning Flower.

"Now, this soldier had lost his wife a few years earlier, watched her die from consumption. He was a lonely man, far from home. He spent long hours with Morning Flower to explain why the Confederacy was more trustworthy than the Union, why our words meant something. Hours talking with her, watching her eyes watch him as he spoke. Understanding eyes, inquisitive eyes. Breathing in her raw scent, both pure and wild at the same time, and he fell in love."

The reverend cast a glance over his shoulder in the direction of the cabin, but did not speak.

"Dark Horse forbade it, of course. He cut off the negotiations as soon as he realized what was happening, withdrew all support. But Morning Flower let this man talk her into leaving with him. Abandoning her tribe, her family. Her people."

Pierce loosened the string around the pouch and gently shook his palm, feeling the shifting of its contents.

"I wish I could tell you this had a happy ending, Reverend. But I can't. You see, the war was almost lost, and this man decided one more soldier couldn't make a difference, anyway. So he set off with Morning Flower with the idea of deserting, and happened to cross paths with a detachment of Magruder's Texas cavalry. He tried to talk his way out of it, but they weren't buying it. Maybe they saw the way he looked at Morning Flower, the way she looked at him. Maybe they just didn't like anyone who rode with an Indian. They took him into custody. She broke free of the blue-bellies holding her and threw herself at him, screaming his name, wanting one last embrace. And they shot her."

Nobody spoke for several seconds. The fire and the creek continued their rhythms.

"That's quite a story, son."

"It gets better."

The fire had sucked all the moisture out of the branches and was now in full glow. Pierce stood and sprinkled some dust over it from the small pouch. The flames flared high, and he quickly leaned over the fire as they receded and inhaled as deeply as his lungs would allow. The smoke scalded his nasal passages and throat, made his chest burn from within. He opened the end of the goatskin he'd been carrying and, coughing, breathed into it, inflating it like a bladder, its liquid contents weighting the bottom. He pinned a thumb over the opening and shook it. The large sack sloshed loudly. He coughed his lungs clear.

After giving it some time to absorb, he let the excess air out then closed the top off. "I'm going to need you to take a swig of this, Reverend."

Swain looked at the goatskin, scratched his head again. "Why don't we head back to town. Continue this discussion over a proper libation?"

"Please, Reverend." Pierce held the canteen sack out for Swain to take. His other hand pushed aside his coat and rested on the butt of his revolver.

The man said nothing for almost a minute. The fire crackled patiently. "Is it some sort of poison? Did you bring me out here to kill me for reasons I cannot fathom?"

"It's not the kind of poison you think. I promise the stuff in this canteen won't kill you."

The preacher took the floppy canteen and looked at it. Then he looked at Pierce, who dipped his head.

"Do it."

"Bleh!" Swain coughed and spat, wiping his mouth. "What in blue Hades is that?"

"Boiled sassafras root, with juniper and honey, mostly. What's offending your tongue is silver nitrate. And some special powder ground from things you don't want to know about, I assure you. Keep drinking."

"Why?"

"I haven't finished the story."

Swain started to say something, but it came out as little more than a cough. His eyes slid from Pierce's to the holstered gun Pierce was tickling.

"Blahk!" he said, spitting. "That's awful!"

Pierce nodded. "So is what happened next. Magruder's troops were on their way to the coast, ran into some trouble near the Louisiana border. That soldier went from being a prisoner of the Confederacy to a prisoner of the Union. Ironically, he thought himself lucky, since the Yankees didn't seem too concerned about whether he was a deserter. He was shipped by wagon somewhere, then by train somewhere else, then all of a sudden they told him the war had ended, and he was set free. Paroled, they called it. Made him sign some document promising not to fight anymore."

"But that's not the end of the story, is it?"

"That's enough." Pierce reached over and took the goatskin. He slung its cord over his head and sleeved an arm through. "Too much will make you puke."

"You're not really a Texas Ranger, are you?"

"No."

"This, us being here, it has to do with the Indians, doesn't it? The shaman."

"A bottomless pit just isn't deep enough for some things, Reverend."

The preacher peered into the darkness beyond the fire before settling his gaze on Pierce. "Are you saying this shaman conjured up some sort of evil spirit?"

"Down at that cabin, Reverend, you're going to see some things. I'm going to need you to remain calm. You're the only one that can defeat it."

"Defeat it? Me? You're not making a bit of sense."

Standing almost over the fire, Pierce opened his vest and began to unbutton his shirt.

"Son, I'm afraid you're a bit... touched. I have a little place near town. How about we go back there, get a good night's sleep. We can talk about this at length, come back tomorrow if—"

The preacher drew back, his body recoiling at the sight.

"My God..."

"Take a good look. This is one bite."

Swain rubbed his eyes. "I've never..."

"I'm a cursed man, Reverend. This gnarled flesh of mine is its way of never letting me forget it. Not even for a moment."

"What could possibly inflict such a wound?"

Pierce started to button his shirt. "I can't describe it. It's vague and shadowy, sometimes people see it as a figure in a black hat and a blood red serape. Others have seen it as a tall, thin man in tails and a bowler cap with a cane. I don't bother to even ask anymore. I just let the wound tell me how close I am."

"But—"

"Listen to me. You have to keep your wits about you. I can't have you running away in the middle of things. This devil I'm chasing, this is what he does. On the day of a full moon, he finds traitors to the tribe and infects them. When I arrive, it is too late, always too late. But if we don't stop them, stop what he's set in motion, they will wipe out everyone around. And I do mean everyone. It's up to you. It all comes down to you."

"Me? I don't understand."

"I need someone pure of heart, which I am not. This, you see, is my curse. The shaman knew my heart, inside and out. Only I can track it, he made sure of that, but track it is all I can do. Others must do the killing."

"I think you're greatly overestimating my heart, son. And let's drop this talk of killing, okay?"

"Just meditate on your Good Book there, Reverend, and get yourself as pure as possible. That concoction you drank is working its way into your blood. It's a special blend. Powerful medicine. Once it's done, we'll be ready."

"Is that supposed to protect me, that awful stuff I drank? Do you really not see the lunacy of all this?"

Pierce didn't respond. He looked up at the moon, allowed a few moments to pass, then started to kick dirt onto the fire.

"It's time. Say a prayer, Reverend. A good one. Cleanse your soul. Then we head down there."

***

The cabin was made of sturdy wood planks over a rubblework foundation. Flat sod roof, but even in the moonlight, Pierce could tell it was well constructed. Built by a man who intended it to last.

Pierce dismounted quietly and hitched his horse. He spoke in a hushed tone.

"How many children Slocum have?"

"One boy, I think." The reverend's horse reared and he gave it a sharp tug on the reins until it settled. "Now, listen. I'm only doing this because you're obviously troubled and need help. I've heard of war doing strange things to men, contaminating their minds. Of course, I'd be lying if I didn't admit the fact you have a gun and look like someone not afraid to use it doesn't continue to weigh in the decision. But you have to promise me that we knock and politely ask him how he's doing, okay? Tell him there's been talk of Indian trouble in the area and we just wanted to check on him. Once we see that everything's okay, we're heading back. You and me. Promise?"

"Whatever you say, Reverend."

"I'm serious. You have to promise."

Pierce patted his horse's neck. "You have my word."

Swain hitched his horse next to Pierce's and swung off the saddle.

"Doesn't it strike you as strange there isn't any light coming through the windows, Reverend? Not a single candle?"

"Maybe they settle in early."

Pierce walked up to the door, his spurs pinging with each step. He looked back at the preacher, one hand on his revolver, then gave the door a solid rap with his knuckles. Once more. Then again.

"Heavy sleepers, wouldn't you say?"

Swain didn't respond. Pierce tested the door, could feel it was braced. He drew his Remington, took a step back. The reverend started to object, but Pierce lunged forward, stomping the door with his heel. It cracked and splintered some, but held. He kicked it two more times, then finished it off with his shoulder.

The air that greeted them seemed to hiss as it escaped. A gamy odor scrambled aggressively up Pierce's nose, harsh and fetid, excrement and rotten eggs. Pierce was used to it. Swain covered his mouth and turned away.

Pierce let him gag for a few seconds, then took him by the arm and led him inside.

"I need you to be strong now, Reverend. I can't kill it. Only you can."

The interior was littered in shades of darkness. A slice of moonlight cut across the floor, illuminating a severed limb. A very small severed limb.

Pierce eased to his left, groping the wall for a lantern. He bumped a table, patted it until something rattled against his hand.

"Keep blocking the door."

The match sizzled, an explosion of light, before shrinking down to a small flame. Pierce set down his revolver and wasted no time lighting the lantern. He grabbed his gun, turned and held up the lantern in one fluid motion.

"Good God in Heaven..."

A wash of yellow light flickered across the floor, chasing shadows to the corners. Pierce let the reverend take in the scene. The headless body of a man, almost certainly Tom Slocum, was in the middle of the floor, intestines coiled next to him like noodles. The body of a young boy, torn at the limbs, lay inches away. A heap of body parts sat nearby, including a man's head, like the aftermath of a giant child at play, pulling the wings off things it considered flies.

"You with me, Reverend?"

The man said nothing, standing fixed to the spot. Pierce thumped him on the ribs.

"Keep your wits, Preacher."

Swain's voice was wavering and weak. "What on Earth could wreak such carnage?"

Pierce stepped forward and lifted the lantern, allowing its light to flow into the corners of the room.

A figure stood against the back wall, its bottom half visible in the glow of the lantern. Legs bare from the knees, feet coated in dark blood. The rest of its shape a darkness within the shadow, interrupted only by the red glow of two eyes, an outline of long straight hair descending around them.

"It's... it's a woman," Swain said. "It's his wife! She

survived!"

"No, Reverend. It's not. And she didn't."

As if to make the point, the figure lurched forward into the light, baring an impossible number of teeth, its head and shoulders in a feral lean. The blood vessels in its eyes had burst, making them swell red, bulging over the edges of the lids. It let out a long hissing, growl. The taut peel of its lips stretched over jagged rows of tightly packed fangs, slicing at angles like miniature daggers.

"*Sweet Christ Almighty...*"

The thing paused to sniff the air. Its skin was a pale green, almost blue. The bones of its fingers protruded through gnawed tips like ivory claws. It raised one of those hands and dug the bone-claws into the flesh around its mouth, ripping its lips away with a violent jerk. Freed from the constraint, its lower jaw dropped and its teeth jutted farther out. It seemed to enjoy the new range of motion.

It looked at the reverend and reached a long arm up, stretching its body, extending its legs, pointing its feet, until it was able to dig those claws into the wood of the ceiling and as soon as it did its body sprang up, defying gravity, pressed against the wood. It bent its head down, an insectile motion, still sniffing, its neck stretching beyond anything that should have been physically possible.

"*Now*, Reverend! *Go*! You're a man of God! Face it down!"

"I have no weapon!"

"Your faith is your weapon! Go!"

Pierce pushed the man forward. The preacher stumbled, barely keeping himself from tripping into the pile of eviscerate. He slowly raised his head to look at the creature. It was almost directly overhead. A thick rope of saliva stretched from the tattered flesh beneath its gums, reaching for the floor.

"Please, Reverend. Show me you have faith. You have to have faith!"

The man glanced down at the Bible in his hand as if seeing it for the first time. He straightened up, holding it aloft. When he spoke, his voice bellowed with a newfound authority. Pierce sensed a glimpse of what this man had been like on the pulpit, how his sermons had sounded during those times of devout piousness.

"*You have no power here, demon! The Lord Jesus Christ is the protector of my soul! I do not fear you!*"

Pierce felt the breath leave him in relief. The man had faith, after all. He hung his head, then raised his revolver, ready to fire.

The creature twisted its head one way, then back. The preacher met its gaze and did not blink.

Then the creature launched itself onto him from the ceiling, its jaws stretching wide and clamping down on his chest. The reverend gasped once, cried out in pain at first. Then the cries turned to screams and the pain to terror.

Pierce fired once, hitting Swain in the head. The creature feeding on him didn't flinch.

"Sorry, Reverend."

Powerful jaws crunched through the chest plate and quickly got to the heart. The thing ripped the heart out with its teeth, head snapping back in triumph. Blood gushed from dangling tubes with each bite. Within a second or two, the heart was gone.

Pierce didn't wait. He backed out of the cabin and yanked on his horse's lead. He mounted it with a running start and spurred it to a sprint.

The thing would be dead in moments, if not already. The reverend's blood would do it. It always did. The concoction was fatal to whatever the hell it was. He'd worried for the pastor's soul, right up until the last moment. But that, too, worked out. It had to be a pure heart. And it was. He was just thankful he didn't have to use a child this time.

The horse slowed to a trot after almost a mile. He picked up the creek again and let it drink. The stage would be arriving in town soon, and he was sure there were people on it looking for him. But that, of course, was part of the curse. Stages would always be delayed. Sheriffs would always be distracted. Posses would always get lost. Whatever it took to keep him going. He would always be one step ahead. And one step behind.

He thought of the dead boy on the floor of the cabin. At least it was only one. And it wasn't his doing, he reminded himself. The consolation rang hollow, as usual. He bent over and held his breath, waiting for the feeling to pass. The familiar sting seared through his scalp, the burn of shame somersaulting in his gut. But what choice did he have? Dark Horse was long gone, years dead. But the curse lived on. If he were to give in, by his own gun or otherwise, how could he be sure that would end it? How could he risk such a thing?

He raised his head to the sky, looked at the stars shimmering above. He wondered again, as he always did, how one man could know another man's heart so well. To know what he was capable of, to make him face it, that was the cruelest curse of all.

He would ride all night, then start up again after a few hours rest. It would take some roaming to pick up the trail, some guesswork, but he always managed. Another town. Another name. He rubbed his face. One of these times it would be different. Yes. One of these times, he'd catch up with it. Maybe the very next time. The very next town. Each time he came a bit closer, didn't he? Yes, he would find it soon.

The horse finished drinking, and he set off on it heading east. The moon was high, lighting the way.

❦❦❦

LEAH JUNG PRESENTS

THE DARK SIDE OF BEAUTIES:
CHELSIE ARYN

Interviewed by
Joel B. Kirkpatrick

Photography by Dan Doyle

Photography by Dan Doyle

The angel-faced Chelsie Aryn once stated "people know me as the quiet, simple country girl." However, if you browse through her impressive portfolio of modeling work, you would see that she is capable of demonstrating an intensity in her vampire-like eyes that is the startling opposite of wholesome. She can blame it on acting all she wants, but I am on to her charade. A little bit of research reveals she may not be as quiet and well-mannered as she implies.

This Atlanta, Georgia transplant, born in Upstate New York, admits to a leisurely love affair with thunderstorms, the murder-mystery television program *Criminal Minds*, and Harley-Davidson motorcycles. She has a subtle tattoo that represents the saying "curiosity often leads to trouble." Chelsie Aryn is an unassuming seductress with a sweet giggle and an affinity for mischievous adventures; I *had* to put her in *Dark Discoveries*.

As for this beauty's professional career, consistent for over four years now, she has gained massive popularity after working with dozens of photographers all over the country. Her more notable credits include a campaign with cosmetic giants *e.l.f* and a first-place title in an extremely competitive event that *Playboy* produces, spotlighting non-nude models, called "Playboy's Miss Social." Hopefully this feature will inspire our cover model to embrace her dark side and slip a few Peter Straub works among her collection of Sarah Dessen novels.

Photography by Dan Doyle

JBK: Chelsie, I saw photos of you where you were calm, cool, and collected with a giant snake wrapped around your neck. That was a real snake, yes? If that photo shoot was, say, the set of a reptilian horror flick instead, would you have been comfortable enough to act terrified while laying inside a coffin filled with snakes? Have you ever acted in film before?

CA: Yes, that was a python. Her name is Adrianna. We actually had a lot in common being we are both the same age and both Virgos. Believe it or not, she was more of a camera diva than myself, and she had just given birth the month before to 38 babies. I happen to like snakes so I enjoyed the shoot. Now, if they were untamed and poisonous snakes in a coffin with me I wouldn't be acting;

it would be real fear. I am not a fan of video cameras, and as much as everyone wants me to try acting, I just have no interest. I have done a commercial and a few music videos in my past, but that is the extent of my acting career.

JBK: You began modeling just out of high school. How did that come about? Were you 'discovered', or did you work hard to get into the business?

CA: When I turned 16 my parents said I needed to get a summer job or take my modeling seriously. So I figured modeling would be better than scooping ice cream and would leave me with more free time. I researched modeling websites online. I found one that allowed you to have a free modeling profile. It required you to post a few pictures and wait to become approved. I added a few pictures my mom took of me and got approved. Then the emails began to show up. Photographers were asking to work with me and I ended up with very little free time that summer.

JBK: Were you nervous at all, or did it seem perfectly natural and normal to you?

CA: I was a little nervous on the way to my first shoot. It was with a photographer from out of state. The shoot was set up to be 3 hours long. I went with my mom. We arrived 30 minutes early to the studio location. We went right to work and it ended 7 hours later. The only reason it ended then was because we ran out of things to shoot. We had used every prop and outfit he had and it was 11 pm. I found it to be fun and I was a ball of energy with the flashes popping. He was impressed and I made money having fun.

JBK: The unique tattoo on your left hip—the goldfish. Tell us about it. Was it your first, or was that the one below your ankle? Do you have any new tattoos?

CA: Oh this is going to start some controversy. My first tattoo is my flirty fishy on my hip. I was 15 when I got her at a home tattoo party. (NY legal age for a tattoo is 18.) I had originally wanted the Playboy Bunny logo but my mom said that my Playboy obsession was just a phase and I would outgrow it (ha-ha) and if I wanted a tattoo to choose something with more meaning. So while looking at tattoo flash I came across this image of a flirty, fancy goldfish blowing a kiss and it reminded me of a story my Grandma Miller told us. The pond we went swimming in as kids used to be known as "Mud hole pond," and it was where she and my Grandpa used to go to make out. Each bubble around my fishy is for a family member of my immediate family.

The tattoo of the three stars on my foot I had done when I was 16. The blue star is for my brother, yellow for my sister and pink for myself. When I was 18 I had some swirls added to that tattoo. Then when I turned 20 I got the one behind my ear.

JBK: *"Curiosity Often Leads to Trouble"* — that tattoo behind your ear is a flirty, shy little thing. What inspired it, and what inspired that location?

CA: The tattoo is of a little birdie (designed by my sister) whispering in my ear "Curiosity Often Leads to Trouble." The location is because I enjoy neck kisses and we all know that leads to trouble!

JBK: You once said you had wanted to be a Playboy model since your early teens, and to travel to exotic locations for photo shoots. Where have you travelled now? And where is your favorite location?

CA: I am a firm believer that everything happens for a reason and this will all make perfect sense to your question, I promise. Everyone remembers their first copy of *Playboy*. Mine was March 2009. Jennifer Pershing was the centerfold model. When I won the "Playboy Miss Social Miss March title" I was shooting a calendar at the most exotic place I have ever traveled to, Villa Castellamonte in the Dominican Republic. As a Playboy Miss Social winner you get a trip to the the Playboy Mansion, the second most exotic place I have ever been, and Miss March 2009 Jennifer Pershing was my tour guide. That was pretty exciting for me. But my favorite place will always be my hometown. In my heart I will always be a small town country girl and this is where I am the most relaxed and confidant.

JBK: What locations are you still dying to go see while being photographed?

Photography by Dan Doyle

CA: I wouldn't mind going to Alaska or Hawaii. I am not a huge fan of the beach and sand or snow but everyone says they are beautiful locations and something you must add to your bucket list.

JBK: Are your photo shoots fairly private events, or are you sometimes surrounded by crowds when working? Have you ever had any trouble with fans or the public during a shoot?

CA: I have to say it depends on the photographer. I am comfortable with crowds as long as we are not causing a distraction. I think only once did I attract a vulgar man who stopped to watch a shoot happen on the street. He wanted me to take my top off, said the picture would look better that way, and he refused to go away.

The worst thing that ever happened was once while shooting on the side of the road in an overgrown lot in a simple sundress. We were doing a beauty headshot with an old barn in the background. A man came down the road in his car with his head stuck way out of the window and yelled, "You just made my day." As he took the corner he smashed into a mail box, debris went flying all over, and he just barely missed hitting a telephone pole. Then he kept right on going. The photographer and I looked at one another dumbfounded and my mom said, "I don't think he thinks you made his day anymore!"

JBK: You've become a fairly good photographer with your cell phone, and Instagram has a bazillion images as proof. Who is catching the most "real" Chelsie Aryn? You, or professional photographers?

CA: I think I am the same goofball in my selfies that shows up to a professional shoot. I do however think my Instagram is more verbally uncensored than any of my other sites.

JBK: The Internet has the ability to create almost instant stardom sometimes, and you are certainly comfortable with your Internet exposure and fans. Yet, most celebrities shun such public lives, and try to keep fans at a bit of a distance. Have you ever been cautioned that it could be

images of you, which we were delighted to find on your Facebook page. Were those images for an ad campaign? How did you get the opportunity to work with Oddo?

CA: I have been lucky enough to work with Javier Oddo twice. Both photo shoots took place at his location in NYC. The first shoot was arranged for us through a NYC modeling agency. The images were for the agency as well as our portfolios.

JBK: Who did the amazing make up for those images? Do you ever do your own makeup?

CA: I think you are referring to the the first photo shoot I did with Javier Oddo and the MUA was Ingrid Okola Dubberke and the Hair by Betsy Reyes Hair. I always try to post credits online to everyone involved. If no MUA or Hair Stylist is named then it means I did my own. I always try to credit everyone next to the photo when I post them. Not only do I feel it is professional etiquette but I feel like they have the hard job. All I have to do is show up. I am the blank canvas; they are the artist.

JBK: Your mom gets credit as Assistant at that photo shoot in 2012. What was she doing, besides having a huge amount of fun?

dangerous to be so "visible?"

CA: I keep some things private. There is a lot that I don't post. I really only post about work-related issues and events. I stay away from religion, politics, family and relationships. I will post about my family and boyfriend once and a while but not very often. I do try to not cross any personal lines with people on social media sites. I will not send "special photos," skype, text, make phone calls or go out with people I don't know in real life. I do however think that your "friends, fans, followers" on social media sites are like cyber neighbors and I am a small town girl where we greet our neighbors with a wave, have small chit-chat, everyone gets along, and you look forward to seeing them daily in passing.

JBK: Javier Oddo has taken some stunning, painted

CA: My momma has been on pretty much every shoot with me since I started modeling, including Playboy. She does everything from being my stylist to my chauffeur. For that shoot or any shoot she is like the photographer's third eye. She catches things like tags sticking out, stray hairs, hot spots, she holds reflectors, adjusts clothing, etc. She has been hired by several of the photographers I have worked with to come help out on other shoots (other than mine) because she is a good assistant. Many of my other model friends seek her out for help also. She has been everyone's mom for as long as I can remember, but she is *my* momma.

JBK: Your mom was your first photographer, wasn't she?

CA: Yes, my mom has always loved photography. When I was born I became her favorite subject. She would dress me up, do my hair, add props—this all started when I was just a week old. We just never knew we were doing all the same things that happen on a professional photo shoot.

How much of modeling is "just work" and how much is "living the fantasy?"

CA: There is a fine line between the "just work" and "living the fantasy" statement. It's a creative output for everyone involved. I call it playing dress up for adults. You get to look and dress unlike your daily self, pretend to be someone else for a bit. All while trying to look natural, comfortable, and make a living at the same time.

JBK: Lots of aspiring young women may imagine that modeling is just sitting in front of some camera being pretty. It takes much more work than that, doesn't it. What would you like to tell those hopeful young women, that you might wish you had known yourself, early on?

CA: I get a lot of messages from people who want advice. I do tell them it's not as glamorous as one would think it to be. Your hair and skin get pretty abused, and you have to maintain a very healthy lifestyle to keep everything looking fresh and healthy. This is not a 9-5 job. This is a 24/7 job and shoots are just a part of it, and they never finish on time. It's hard to make plans with your friends because jobs pop up last minute and after a shoot you will find yourself not only physically sore but mentally exhausted. Most of all, expect to be in a relationship with your career. It can be difficult to find a mate who is confident enough with his/herself to accept what you do and fully understand this line of work.

JBK: How many photographers have worked with you now? Can they even be counted? Do you have any favorites, or would that be a professional discourtesy to say?

CA: I used to keep a list but gave up on that. I do have my favorites but that would be a long list. I have what I call my "modeling family." I love each of them for different reasons based on their talents. I will say every new shoot gives me new favorite images and memories to take with it.

JBK: Your pics from the Big Paw photo shoot in Albany, April 2012 are just hilarious. It certainly looks like you were freezing your ass off up there. Where is the most difficult shoot you've had to do? Why was it such hard work?

CA: Oh, you got that right! That would have to be the most challenging shoot I have ever done, thanks to Mother Nature and her *PMS*ing on us that day with 32 degree below-zero wind chills as I am wearing a bra, booty shorts,

and standing on a cliff with a kite strapped to my back like a cape. The wind hitting my bare skin stung like razor blades. I was purple. Everyone on the team suffered with me (in their hats, coats, boots, mittens and scarves, of course) but we got it done. Then the sun came out as we drove home!

JBK: You once worked in a motorcycle shop, until your modeling career made that "normal" job impractical. If you were not modeling, would you still be doing that or would you follow your other dreams into the fashion world?

CA: My job for the motorcycle shop was a bit staged. They wanted their spokesmodel to be familiar with how the company ran, the parts of the bikes, and their customers. They were also being considered to do a reality show and wanted me to be a part of that. It didn't end up happening. When I was in high school my plan was to go to college and get a degree in Early Childhood Development. My teachers at the time said that I should follow my dreams and go for the modeling, that college buildings have stood their ground for hundreds of years but my eighteen-year-old body won't last that long. Every time I post something online stating that I am traveling to some fun place for a shoot, I get a message from some of them saying, "Bet you're glad you're not stuck in a classroom now!" They're right.

JBK: Do you get time to make any of your own outfits? Are you "fashion crazy" or do jeans and a sweatshirt suit you just as well?

CA: I don't know how to machine sew but I do like to cut up jeans and tops. Distress them, dye clothing, and add personal little embellishments to things to make it an original, one-of-a-kind "Chelsified" item. If I am going out I do get a bit fashion crazy but everyday life I am in jeans/

Photography by Kimberly Cook

legging and something oversized, comfy, with no make-up and messy hair.

JBK: That cycle shop job really turned you on to bikes. What was your first bike? Who taught you to ride? What do you ride now?

CA: I was always into motorcycles. I don't know why. My parents don't ride. Just the sound of the rumble always turned me on. I still don't have my own bike but if I did it would be a Harley Nightster, flat black with no chrome. I took a motorcycle safety course for my bike certification. I highly recommend it to anyone looking to become a rider.

JBK: Are you a collector? If you could purchase any classic bike in the world right now, what would you pick?

CA: Can't really say I collect any one thing as much as I have a lot of stuff. If I could purchase any classic bike right now I would be looking at an old Indian Motorcycle with a Goulding Rocket sidecar. Now that would be fun to travel in.

JBK: If you could hop on your bike and "just go," where would that be?

CA: I would want to zig-zag from Bike Weeks, from Daytona to Sturgis, hitting all the sights, like the Four Corners, Route 66, the Rocky Mountains, Yellow Stone Park, and hit the side roads through small towns in every state.

JBK: Living in Atlanta may have cured you of your love affair with thunderstorms by now. Have you been shaken out of bed by terrifying storms yet? Do you miss the snows of upper New York at all?

CA: I have not experienced an earth rattling thunderstorm yet here in Georgia. I have gotten a taste of the cold fall rains and we have had light snow here twice this winter season so far. NO, I am not missing the cold north-east winters back home.

JBK: Where is your favorite place to just chill?

CA: Home Sweet Home. Home here in Georgia or New York as long as I am surrounded by the people who love me and my pets, I am content.

JBK: You once said your motto is "I am a what-you-see-is-what-you-get kinda girl." What exactly does that mean?

CA: It simply means everything about me is real. My attitude, hair, nails and so on. Everything about me is real expect maybe eyelashes for public events and photo shoots. I gave up getting fake nails, using hair extensions, and indoor tanning in my personal life. I have never had any plastic surgery. Even though lots of people swear my boobs are fake. Not to say that if a shoot requires me to use any of the above items, I would of course use them. It's part of the job, like any prop on a set.

JBK: *Dark Discoveries* is about modern horror, dark fantasy, and dark sci-fi, so we must ask: Are you afraid of the dark? And do you believe in ghosts, aliens, and the dark forces?

CA: Oh, hell yes. I am a big baby when it comes to scary things like abandoned houses, dark woods, when the power goes out, and all the things that go bump in the night. I totally believe in ghosts, that aliens are out there, and in the dark forces of evil. I personally have not been affected by any of these, except that my sister and I swear we had a ghost/spirit in our house as kids, but she was not evil in any way. My sister is a huge fan of scary movies and she would make me watch them with her. Then it would take weeks before I could sleep in the dark again!

❦ ❦ ❦

Photography by Kimberly Cook

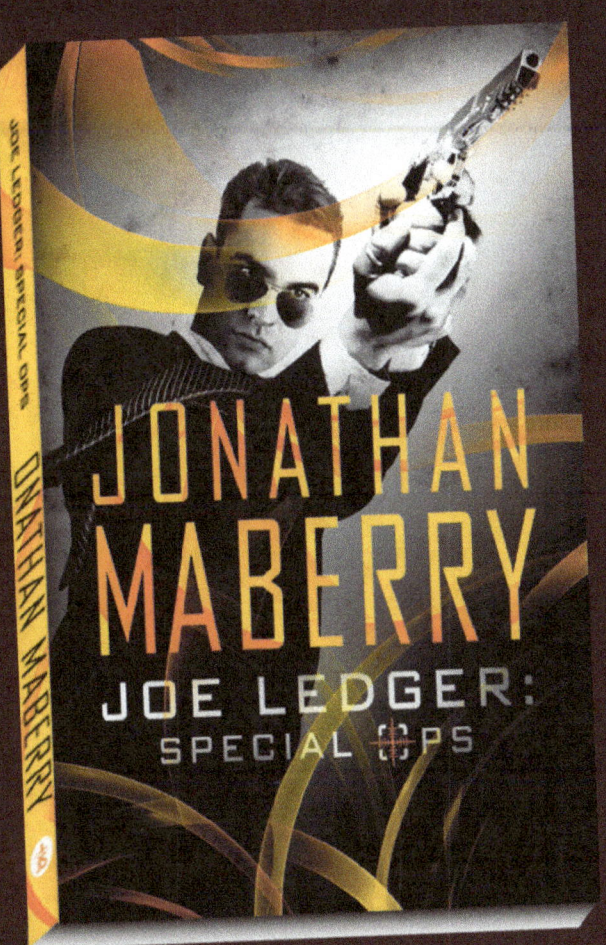

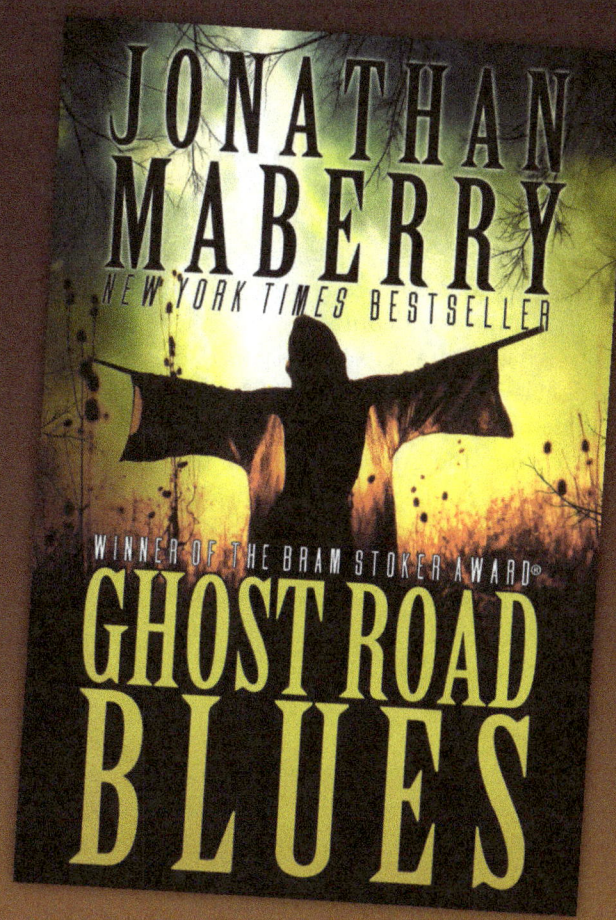

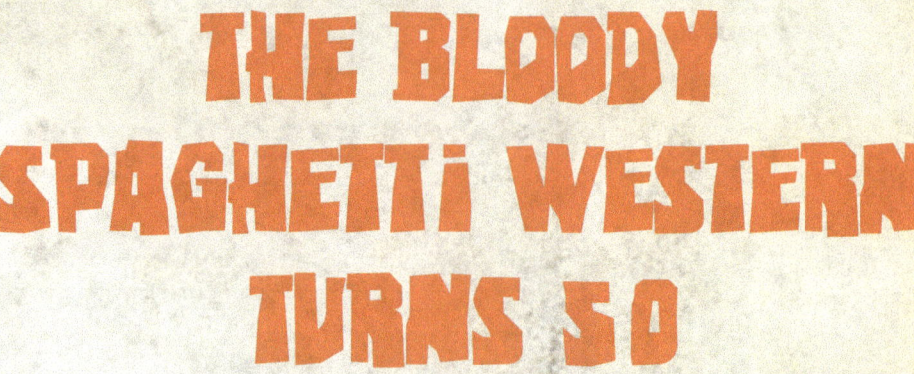

THE BLOODY SPAGHETTI WESTERN TURNS 50

By James R. Beach

In preparation for this horror western special, it occurred to me that it is the 50th anniversary of the Italian western—Sergio Leone's classic hit film A *Fistful of Dollars* from 1964. So, in light of this fact, I think a revisit to one of the most popular genres of the big boot is in order. Since this is a horror magazine, I thought I would focus on the breaking of the violence barrier that (along with Herschell Gordon Lewis and his pioneering low-budget gore films starting in 1964 in America) helped open the door to horror films to do the same.

Although not the first Italian western certainly (Giorgio Ferroni, who later directed the Gothic classic *Mill of the Stone Women* (1960) and *Night of the Devils* (1972) fired that first shot in 1942 with *Il Fanciulla del West*), more than any other *Fistful of Dollars* defined what became known as "The Spaghetti Western." Loosely based (or influenced at the very least in many people's minds) on Akira Kurosawa's *Yojimbo* and starring Clint Eastwood, it signaled a new direction for westerns—one of more overt violence and sex—something missing quite conspicuously from American westerns prior (Sam Peckinpah's *The Wild Bunch* did not break the violence barriers in the US until five years later in 1969). Gone were the bloodless deaths of the villains. Now they died realistically and in full bloody color. The heroes too. Leone's hugely popular "Dollar Trilogy" included two follow-ups—also starring Eastwood—*For A Few Dollars More* (1965) and *The Good, The Bad and the Ugly* (1966). And those three movies spawned hundreds of westerns to follow.

The anti-hero debuted in the spaghetti westerns. Often you had a hard time telling which character was the good guy, and which one was the bad guy. A prime example is Franco Nero's cruel, but charming character Django, from the film of the same name in 1966. Dragging along a coffin behind him, Django comes to a mostly dead town in the grips of the racist Captain and a Mexican horde. Director Sergio Corbucci lays on the violence and bloodshed—the famous ear-cutting scene inspiring Quentin Tarantino (although initially censored and cut from a number of non-Italian prints), the ballet of violence with the coffin reveal at the fort scene and the finale—obviously influencing both him and likely John Woo, as well.

Django's motivations may be revenge but he uses his wits and pits both the racist Captain's men and the Mexican bandits against each other for his own purposes. The film itself is brilliant and the grim and gritty feel, also the gallows humor of it, help to add to the tension. Corbucci's Old West is definitely a crueler one than Leone's. And its high violence quotient helped turn around the censorship laws against depicting violence and gore. Corbucci continued this violent trend in his subsequent films, *Navajo Joe* (1966) starring a young Burt Reynolds (as a rare Native American

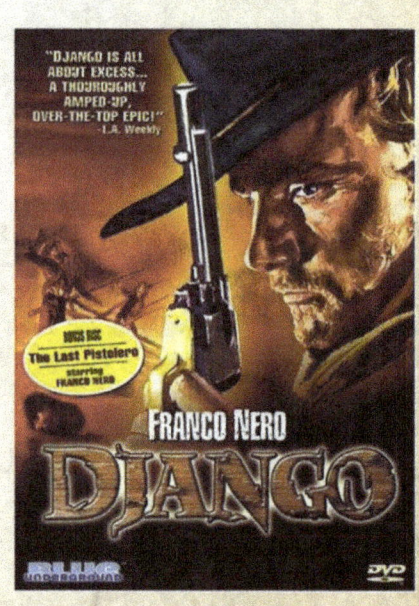

"DJANGO IS ALL ABOUT EXCESS... A THOROUGHLY AMPED-UP, OVER-THE-TOP EPIC!"
—L.A. Weekly

BONUS DISC
The Last Pistolero
starring FRANCO NERO

FRANCO NERO

DJANGO

BLUE UNDERGROUND

DVD

revenge hero), *The Hellbenders* (1967) with Joseph Cotton, and *The Great Silence* (1968) with Jean-Louis Trintignant and Klaus Kinski—amongst others. As Quentin Tarrantino said recently: "In a particularly violent Rory Calhoun western, maybe eight people are killed. In a Corbucci western, 38 people could get slaughtered in one scene." *Django* remains a seminal classic in the western fields and my personal favorite (I'm even showing it as part of my Retro Film Series in all of its uncut and restored glory!).

Franco Nero returned opposite George Hilton (*The Strange Vice of Mrs. Wardh, Case of the Scorpion's Tail, The Killer Must Kill Again*) later that same year (1966) in Lucio Fulci's first western, *Massacre Time*. Sold as a *Django* sequel in other countries, it is not related but tells instead of a gold rush prospector named Tom who is called back to help his family. The town he left is now ruled by a rich plantation owner and his cruel son Junior. Tom is out for revenge with the reluctant help of Hilton's Jeff—the town drunk and local laughingstock. Although less violent than Fulci's later gore efforts he became known for, *Massacre Time* still lays on the bloodshed with a gory close up of a murdered family, a particularly brutal whipping of Nero and the operatic and ultra-violent shootout finale (another obvious influence on Tarantino and Woo). Fulci later revisited the West in the early 1970s with the Jack London- inspired *White Fang* (1973), also starring Franco Nero, and *Challenge to White Fang* (1974). But it was with *Four of the Apocalypse* in 1975 that he truly revisited the cruel and violent West from *Massacre Time* and stepped it up even more with a gory skinning, a brutal rape of Lynne Frederick's Bunny, and even a bit of cannibalism.

Well-regarded giallo and adventure/fantasy director Sergio Martino also took a stab at westerns first with *Arizona Colt Returns* in 1969 and later with *Manaja: Man With a Blade* in 1977. *Arizona Colt Returns* is the weaker of the two, a sequel to Michele Lupo's superior *Arizona Colt* with Giuliano Gemma in the title role. Anthony Steffen (*The Night Evelyn Came Out of The Grave*) is not as good of an actor as Gemma, but is okay and plays a grittier and slightly more psycho Colt. The very beautiful Rosalba Neri (*Devil's Wedding Night, Amuck!, Lady Frankenstein*) also co-stars which automatically gives it an extra star (in my book at least). It smacks as an effort by a new director

handed a sequel and trying to make something decent out of it. *Manaja*, by comparison is leaps and bounds better. Maurizio Merli (of *Violent Naples*) plays Blade, a fur-coated stranger who likes to toss axes at people. It has its share of violence to compete with Corbucci and Fulci with a couple axes to the head, chopped-off limbs, some bullets between the eyes and to the heads, and John Steiner burying Blade up to his neck in the sand and pinning his eyes open so the sun burns them out.

Jack of all trades Antonio Margheriti did a few westerns. His best, *And God Said to Cain* (1969), stars Klaus Kinski and incorporates elements of his gothic horrors into the Old West tale. A man, Gary Hamilton (Kinski), is framed

for a crime he didn't commit. He of course comes looking for the man who sent him up the river after he is released from jail. Margheriti uses slamming windows, flapping curtains, tolling bells and even the cries of birds when Hamilton's name is pronounced to help add to the creepy feel. He also dispatches his enemy's men in violent and gruesome ways in tunnels underneath an old Native American burial ground. Margheriti directed four other westerns: *Dynamite Joe* (1967), *Vengeance (Joko invoca Dio … e muori* [original title]) (1968), *Whiskey and Ghosts* (1974) and *Take a Hard Ride* (1975).

Sergio Garrone directed some good westerns such as *No Room to Die* (1969) (aka: *A Hanging for Django, A Noose for Django*) also starring Anthony Steffen, *Django the Bastard* (1969) also starring Steffen, and *Vendetta at Dawn* (1971) with George Eastman (a Joe D'Amato regular later on). None feature Django (just by name only in some countries), but all three are violent with *Vendetta* often being compared to Wes Craven's *Last House on the Left* in terms of cruelty and exploitation factor.

Giulio Petroni directed six westerns total—including one of the better Italian westerns, *Death Rides a Horse* in 1967 (one of my favorites as well). Much like Petroni's other films, it starts off strong and sets a dark tone for the rest of the film. A gang brutally kills and rapes a family in front of a boy who survives. Later when he is grown, he vows revenge on the gang. It stars John Phillip Law as the revenge-minded young man, Pasta pistol regular Lee Van Cleef (from Leone's *Dollar* trilogy) as the reluctant side man also out for revenge against the gang and giallo regular Luigi Pistilli as the vicious leader of the bad guys. This is a great character study of two contrasting men and how they slowly change along the way.

Other notable horror and giallo directors also got their start on the violent westerns before moving behind the camera. Dario Argento, who later became Italy's biggest horror director, started out as a co-screenwriter on Sergio Leone's epic *Once Upon A Time in the West* (1968). Argento also co-wrote the story and screenplay for *Five Man Army* a year later, starring Peter Graves and Bud Spencer (*Trinity* series). Another director known for cruelty and the high level of violence in his cannibal, horror and crime films, Ruggero Deodato, got his start as an assistant cameraman on Django. Interestingly enough, Enzo Barboni, who also served as a cinematographer on the seminal film, later went the other direction and helmed the comedy western series *Trinity*.

Notorious director Joe D'Amato (Aristide Massaccesi) (*Blue Omega/Buried Alive, Emanuelle and the Last Cannibals, Porno Holocaust, Erotic Nights of the Living Dead, Anthophagus*) got his start as a cinematographer and worked on a few westerns like *Dead Men Don't Make Shadows* (1970), *Django and Sartana!* (1970) and *A Barrel Full of Dollars* (aka: *A Coffin Full of Dollars*) (1971) before moving on to filming gialli and later directing his own erotic horror and exploitation films.

Last but certainly not least, although not a spaghetti western, a Spanish production directed by Joaquin Lewis Romero Marchent, *Cut-Throats Nine* (1972) is one of the most violent westerns ever made. Bordering on a slasher flick level of gore and violence, it tells of a group of vicious murderers who get the upper hand on their transporting officer, rape his daughter and then burn him alive and turn against each other. With hacked-off limbs, bodies being burned to a crisp and a few disembowelings, *Cut-Throats Nine* feels a lot like a horror movie and definitely rides the exploitation wave of the seventies. Marchent also made a number of other very good westerns between the period of 1955-1972 (including his first, *El Coyote*, which was one of the first westerns produced in Europe), but *Cut-Throats* remains his most violent picture. Honorable non-spaghetti mentions also go to US westerns such as: Sam Peckinpah's seminal and barrier breaking *The Wild Bunch* (1969), *A Man Called Horse* (1970), and French director Robert Hossein's *Cemetery Without Crosses* (1969) is also excellent and stars the lovely Michelle Mercier (Dario Argento has been credited as a co-screenwriter in some prints, but Hossein denies his involvement).

Recommended Spaghetti Westerns:

A Fistful of Dollars (1964) – Directed by Sergio Leone

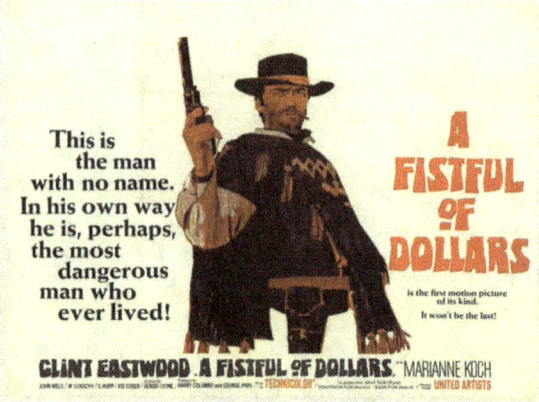

Minnesota Clay (1964) – Directed by Sergio Corbucci
A Few Dollars More (1965) – Directed by Sergio Leone
A Pistol for Ringo (1965) – Directed by Duccio Tessari
The Good, The Bad and The Ugly (1966) – Directed by Sergio Leone
Django (1966) – Directed by Sergio Corbucci
Massacre Time (1966) – Directed by Lucio Fulci
Navajo Joe (1966) – Directed by Sergio Corbucci
Arizona Colt (1967) – Directed by Michele Lupo
The Hellbenders (1967) – Directed by Segio Corbucci
Death Rides a Horse (1967) – Directed by Guilio Petroni
Once Upon A Time in the West (1968) – Directed by Sergio Leone
The Great Silence (1968) – Directed by Sergio Corbucci
Five Man Army (1969) – Directed by Don Taylor & Italo Zingarelli
Django the Bastard (1969) – Directed by Sergio Garrone
And God Said To Cain (1969) – Directed by Antonio Margheriti
No Room to Die (1969) – Directed by Sergio Garrone
Vendetta at Dawn (1971) – Directed by Sergio Garrone
Four of the Apocalypse (1975) – Directed by Lucio Fulci
Manaja: Man With a Blade (1977) – Directed by Sergio Martino

Recommended Reference Books:

Spaghetti Westerns – By Howard Hughes. 2010; Kamera Books.
Spaghetti Westerns: The Good, the Bad and the Violent – By Thomas Weisser. 2005; McFarland.
Violent Italy – By Daniel Dellamorte and Tobias Petterson. 2002; Tamara Press.

❦❦❦

Joe Bob Briggs:
King of the Drive-Ins

By Steve Holetz

Joe Bob Briggs on Panel
Photo Courtesy of Anthony Kay

Back in high school during the eighties, my friend and future co-host Gord and I had this ritual. Before going to our summer job, we would visit the bakery around the corner for doughnuts and coffee, then return to his parents' kitchen to read the morning newspaper. Invariably, the highlights of our habit would be the comics and the weekly film review by Joe Bob Briggs. At the time, we knew nothing of Mr. John Bloom or his career as a journalist for the Dallas Times Herald. But we found ourselves captivated by Joe's crazy tales of Cherry Dilday, Rhett Beavers and many other colorful Texas denizens, the numerical lists dedicated to everything from barbecue to his own rules for livin', and the brilliant reviews of Drive-In masterpieces replete with beasts, breasts, and blood by the gallon.

Joe Bob's reviews gave us an illicit window into films we weren't yet old enough to rent, and a steady stream of hilarious lines worth repeating to anyone who would listen. A few years later, we would devour the book versions of *Joe Bob Goes to the Drive-In*, where we caught up on all the reviews we'd missed, and thrilled to his work on *Joe Bob's Drive-In Theater* and *Monstervision*, where we finally got to see these gruesome and garish works of genius hosted by the man himself, as God intended.

Joe Bob Briggs left an indelible, Godzilla-sized footprint on the impressionable psyches of two kids who would one day grow up to run their own comedy horror film festival, and as such, it was an absolute thrill to have the opportunity to interview him for The BoneBat Show during Seattle's 2013 Crypticon Horror Convention.

STEVE HOLETZ: It used to be that kids went to the woods and partied. Slashers and serial killers were there to teach them a lesson. But in 2013's *Evil Dead* remake, the kids are going to the cabin to detox their friend! Are you dismayed by the lack of aardvarking and tomfoolery in today's horror films?

JOE BOB BRIGGS: You know, there wasn't a single nekkid breast in that remake.

SH: That's what I'm saying!

JBB: Yeah, absolutely! You know, the main thing that was screwed up about that movie is it wasn't that scary. They had all those millions of dollars to create all those horror set pieces, and it just didn't really scare the crap out of you like the original one did. I mean, it's not like the original one had that much plot to begin with. "The zombies must rise." That's the whole plot of the original movie.
But…well first of all, how do you do a remake of *Evil Dead*, and leave out Ash? Hello? There was one character that everybody cared about in the original, right? Ash! They go to extraordinary lengths not to put Ash in the remake, so right there they show you what you're working with.

SH: Do you think that was because Bruce Campbell was essentially irreplaceable? How do you replace somebody who is that iconic?

JBB: You can replace anybody after 30 years, c'mon. I know they are probably saying, "We might do *Evil Dead 4*." Sorry Bruce, everybody gets old, we're not gonna do that. And if you *do* do it, we're not gonna watch it, probably. No, I love Bruce, but I don't think holding out for *Evil Dead 4* is a reason not to put Ash in the remake.
I saw that movie the year it came out, at one of the first screenings of it. They showed it at the Cannes Film Festival, and

I think the only two critics that were in the room were me and Rex Reed. And Rex liked it as much as I did. The great thing about it was that it was so elemental. And people don't understand today that as of 1982, there had only been like 5 zombie films in history! It was like *White Zombie*, and one in the forties that some French guy did, and maybe three others. *Night of the Living Dead*, you know? But there was no such thing really as a "zombie film."

SH: It wasn't a genre yet.

JBB: And Sam Raimi says "I wanted to establish the real zombie rules." Well, what zombie rules, Sam? Just make 'em up! But the great thing about that film, that George Romero did not do, is that there was only one way to kill the zombies. Arms, legs, head, everything had to go!

SH: Complete dismemberment!

JBB: Complete dismemberment. Which is really what made that film so appealing when it first came out. Even though Sam Raimi was, like, stealing equipment from Michigan State or wherever, and doing the animation in his attic, or whatever he did to make those zombies disintegrate and everything, it was like ten times scarier than all this digital stuff they did in the remake in 2013. So, as you can tell, I'm not a big fan of that movie.

SH: Have you ever seen a movie that did actually scare you? Is *Evil Dead* that film? You are pretty much a connoisseur of the gristle and gore.

JBB: It's true, there's not much that scares me, but I'll tell you. This'll be a surprising answer because there aren't even many people that like this film, but there was a film called *Wolfen*, in I think the late seventies or early eighties (1981-SH), about the wolves roaming around the Bronx, and it was actually the first film that used the steadicam. The steadicam had just been invented, and they used the steadicam to show the wolf's-eye view of these rabid wolves that would roam across the barren landscape of the worst part of the South Bronx in the late seventies and early eighties.

SH: Where you'd find wolves, their natural habitat.

JBB: They're all trying to kill Albert Finney. That movie scared the living crap out of me. I don't know why, if it was something about the steadicam, and getting dizzy from the steadicam, and the red wolf eyes and everything. If you watch it today on DVD, you probably won't be scared, but in the theater that was extremely scary.

SH: Nice. All right, it's been dark times here in Seattle, Joe Bob. In 2010, the Puget Park Drive-In closed after 42 years. They just announced the Valley 6 Drive-In is closing after 45 years. What does this mean for the youth of today? Where are they gonna go to grope each other and drink lukewarm beer?

JBB: All that means is it's too damn cold and too damn rainy in the Pacific Northwest. That doesn't mean anything about the future of the Drive-In. (Laughs) I admire somebody who held out for 45 years in this kind of weather. I mean, Drive-Ins are kinda made for warm weather. It's not too surprising that you can't make a go of it. Drive-Ins have nine strikes against them to begin with. You've got to have all this land, but you've got to have all this land that's close to people, which means it's gonna be expensive land, and then you can only show the film once a day! Whereas an indoor theater can show it, what, nine times? They can start at 10:30 in the morning and show the film nine times! You've got one shot, people want to see it right at sundown, and to make a go of it, it takes deranged people, who own these Drive-Ins and run them for years and give them to their grandchildren and everything. So the fact that they stayed open all that time is admirable. I'm sure in the seventies they were showing porn just to stay open. Remember, it would cause wrecks on the highway when people would drive by and see the giant porn on the outdoor screen? That was because Drive-Ins had to figure out some way to survive in the seventies, and that was the only way.

No, it's sad. But there have actually been new Drive-Ins built, and old Drive-Ins revived over the past three or four years, and mostly it's not the grandchildren of the original founders of the Drive-In, it's new people who just love the Drive-In. There's a huge one in Texas, there's a new one in Florida. But they do seem to be in warm weather places.

SH: That's great to hear. I did manage to get my kids to the Drive-In a couple of times, to experience that, so hopefully one day they will live somewhere warm, and be able to take their kids, and it will continue on.

Speaking of the perils of living in Seattle, in 1992, in an aside on Iraqi beer steins, you said: "Bread and wine. Wine and Bread. That's all these guys like to talk about. It's like they spend all their time in Seattle or something." Have you been able to get a decent meal since you've been here?

JBB: Well, I've been mostly in the hotel since I've been here. I've been to Seattle several times, I have this really vivid memory of being in Seattle to do a book reading, this would be way back, at least two decades ago, at a really cool bookstore downtown, and being here on the same day as Hunter S. Thompson. Hunter's last book was just sort of this deranged series of snippets of essays that didn't make any sense, that he just kinda jumbled together and published. I can't remember the name of the book, but anyway, he was reading the same day that I was reading, and my reading was a lot more coherent than his reading.

I remember that very vividly, and I remember, you know when you come into town to promote a book, they always schedule you to do radio interviews? I'm sorry if I'm going to offend somebody by saying this, but they would always send me over to this public radio station at the University of Washington. Everyone would be nice to me when I got there, and then when I would go on the air, I don't want to say they were ultra-liberal, but they would read stuff out of my columns and say: "Now, did you write this? What did you mean by that?" In many cases I wouldn't be able to remember what it was that I had written or why I had written it because it would be from years ago, and I'd be thinking, "What are you people doing? How did I offend you? What brings you to assault me?" I would have these sort of hostile interviews at the University of Washington, and I would be totally unprepared for them. So I remember that, and I've told comedians this, I've said: "Now when you go to Seattle, don't make a coffee joke, they've heard all of those, and if you make a coffee joke, they're not going to like it anyway, because they are proud of their coffee!" I've made that mistake nearly every time I went on TV in Seattle. Then it's like, "Oh, I shouldn't have made that coffee joke." I went for the simplest thing you can do. So don't do that. They don't like that here.

SH: Now Joe Bob, you are, if nothing else, a practical man, and nothing is more simple and practical than the metric system. Do you see a day where you start rating movies by liters of blood instead of gallons?

JBB: No, I'm too damn old to do that. (Laughs) It's like, I can't even drive in Europe, much less figure out liters of blood. So, no.

SH: All right, wrapping this up here, how about three great Drive-In flicks no one has seen?

JBB: Three that no one has seen? I'm not that great on titles, but you know, the eighties was the golden age of direct to video, most of it crapola. I talk to a lot of young people who really romanticize the eighties and say, "Boy, I wish I lived in the eighties." I'm like, "Why?" "Well, because I love all the movies that came out." And I say, "97% of 'em was crap! What are you talking about?" But, in the eighties, because you could make a movie for $60,000—I mean, today you can make a movie for $2,000 dollars—but (then) you could make a movie for $60,000 on film, and a lot of people like Fred Olen Ray did do that. So there were extremely wildly inventive plots in no-name movies—movies that you would probably only watch one time. I'm thinking of *Nightmare Sisters*, which

is the only movie that had Linnea Quigley, Michelle Bauer, and Brinke Stevens, the three acknowledged scream queens of the eighties.

Then if you go back, there is a film that I did a commentary for. If you find the DVD, it has my commentary track on it, so you'll see why it's a brilliant movie. *Warlock Moon,* from the early seventies, is a really, really strange movie that virtually no one has ever seen.

And then *Hell's Angels '69,* which starred the actual Hell's Angels. Now, there were a lot of movies about them, but in *Hell's Angels '69* they tried to use the actual Hell's Angels as actors.

SH: And not in a *Live at Altamont* sort of way.

JBB: No, No, No. They are actually doing actor roles, and they had a major plot problem, because they are filming the Hell's Angels, and the Hell's Angels are acting like Hell's Angels, they're not acting like nice guys at all. They are supposed to be the heroes of the movie, and they're supposed to pull off this heist in Las Vegas, but they're just so disgusting that you can't ever identify with these guys, who are first of all really bad actors, and secondly they are like really beating people up. If you ever see that movie, it's one of those strange "Only in America" kind of things that could happen between about 1968 and 1975, when all the rules were changing with movies. So basically, anyone who walked into a film executive's office with some new idea, they would say, "Yeah, go shoot the sonuvabitch. Try it, we don't know what works!" And so you had this great period in film history where you could make anything, and one of those movies was *Hell's Angels '69.* They were saying, "Forget that *Easy Rider* crap. We're the real motorcycle guys!"

SH: Now shit is getting real!

JBB: Yeah! With mixed results. (Laughs)

SH: All right, man. Once again, the last question we always ask all of our guests on *The BoneBat Show*: Joe Bob, what pisses you off?

JBB: *A Chorus Line.* 1985, starring Michael Douglas. THAT really pissed me off.

SH: (Laughs) Thank you so much for joining us. It was an absolute pleasure.

JBB: All right, glad to do it.

~~~

* **Steve Holetz** is producer and co-host of *The BoneBat Show,* a comedy, music, and pop-culture podcast that has been rocking the virtual airwaves since 2007. He is also director of Seattle's BoneBat *"Comedy of Horrors" Film Fest*, recently named "One of the Top 5 Coolest Comedy Film Festivals on the Planet" and the world's ONLY dedicated Comedy/Horror event. When not interviewing independent creators for *The BoneBat Show*, manically screening films for the festival, or sharing his favorite movies, comics and video games with his family, Steve can be found spinning independent metal, rock and punk music on the *Bonehand Heavy Half Hour*. All of Steve's projects can be found at www.bonehand. com.

☗☗☗

Steve Holetz on panel with Joe Bob Briggs
Photo Courtesy of Anthony Kay

Steve Holetz on panel with Joe Bob Briggs
Photo Courtesy of Anthony Kay

Steve Holetz on panel with Joe Bob Briggs
Photo Courtesy of Anthony Kay

Gaming in the Weird West: A Run through the Deadlands

By Richard Dansky

Oddly enough, western-themed video games, and horror-themed westerns in particular, are rare on the ground. In recent memory only *Red Dead Redemption's* zombie-themed DLC has really been a breakout hit. Game developers seem to prefer post-apocalyptic as their wasteland of choice; it offers all of the desolation and openness of the classic western, with the added bonus of higher technology, a wider range of potential enemies, and bigger guns.

Tabletop RPGs, however, have provided an enduring example of the horror western in the form of Deadlands. Described as "Spaghetti...with meat" and symbolized by iconic artwork by Brom, it was an instant hit. Nearly two decades on, *Deadlands* remains vital on the RPG scene, an audacious setting where six guns meet magic, and the walking dead go toe-to-toe with Pinkertons and Texas Rangers. Taking full advantage of the fact that once the game's in the player's hands, all tabletop RPG assets are free, creator Shane Lacy Hensley and the writers and designers at Pinnacle Entertainment Group created an ambitious world of monsters and spirits, riverboat gamblers and desert desperadoes, all moving through a steampunk-inflected, half-familiar landscape.

According to Hensley, the game that became *Deadlands* was originally inspired by another Brom painting, one showing an undead Confederate soldier (later used as the cover art for the *Wraith: the Oblivion* sourcebook *Necropolis: Atlanta*). Fourteen hours of pondering the image on the drive home from GenCon eventually led to a homebrew game set at the Battle of Gettysburg, which eventually morphed into *Deadlands* and the need to create Pinnacle to produce it.

The original version of the game identified it as being set in 1876, though subsequent editions have moved the clock as far forward as 1882. Given access to Earth through a spell cast by Native American shamans to drive the white settlers of North America back into the sea, inhuman spirits called Reckoners have set about reshaping the world to their liking. Needing a certain ambient level of fear to materialize on Earth, the Reckoners use their powers to distort the landscape, create monsters and—starting with the Battle of Gettysburg—raise the dead. By the time the game opens, monsters and Harrowed roam the West while the Texas Rangers try to keep a lid on things to keep the population from panicking. Magic—done by haggling with spirits called manitou—is real. California has largely fallen into the ocean, leaving in its place a Great Maze of rock. The Great Maze is also the source for Ghost Rock, a mysterious stone that powers the jury-rigged tech of the setting. It was a marriage of westerns, horror and steampunk unlike anything that had been seen before.

What really set *Deadlands* apart, though, was its marriage of subject matter to mechanics. The game brought playing cards and poker chips into its resolution mechanics, conjuring up western imagery with every round. Writer and designer Matt Forbeck, who was brought onto the project early by Hensley, said the use was absolutely intentional:

> We decided to braid the game's theme to its mechanics as tightly as we could manage. Poker cards and chips figure large in the American West, so we tried to find places they'd work in the game. Old miniatures games sometimes used playing cards to help keep track of things like order of movement, so it was a short move for us to use them to generate and keep track of combat initiative in our game.

Graphic designer and line-editor Hal Mangold agreed, saying, "*Deadlands* was a case where the balance was also right between meta-story, and the gaming environment. That's a really hard balance to make...and *Deadlands* did it."

But the first book nearly didn't make it to its official GenCon release—according to Forbeck, the delivery of the initial shipment of *Deadlands* in 1996 got cut so close that in order to have the books on the table when the show hall opened on Thursday, Forbeck had to lead a contingent of Pinnacle staff out to the parking lot where the truck was waiting in line. Convincing the driver to open the back, Forbeck and his crew unloaded the fifty-pound shipping boxes and ferried them by hand to the booth so when the doors opened, they'd be ready.

Deadlands went on to go through multiple editions, not to mention rules sets. In 2006, *Deadlands: Reloaded* was released, using the Savage Worlds rules systems. The game's also spun off non-RPG products, like the *Doomtown* collectible card game, a wargame called *The Great Rail Wars*, and board games like *FRAG Deadlands* and *The Battle for Slaughter Gulch*. Several of these won Origins Awards, demonstrating that the iconic nature of the game could easily be translated into other contexts.

A great deal of this was due to the art style; Mangold thought that "one reason *Deadlands* really did well was the artistic presentation. It was a good melding of style with subject matter." In addition to Brom, Ron Spencer also made an essential contribution by designing the game's logo and the look of iconic monsters like The Hangin' Judge. Other artists like Loston Wallace, Paul Daly and Alan Nunis also made significant contributions to the look of the game, as did cover artist Paolo Parente. But it was Brom's work, particularly the Gunslinger, that really struck a chord. It was, as Mangold recalled, "sort of the Platonic Ideal *Deadlands* image that all others were compared against," one that starkly and elegantly summed up the game's aesthetic at a glance.

With success came multiple additional settings, set at various points in the timeline of the *Deadlands* world. Drawing on classic genres like noir (*Deadlands: Noir*, set in 1930s New Orleans), post-apocalyptic (*Hell on Earth*) and science fiction (*Lost Colony*), they offered players the chance to transplant core elements of the game into new situations. And it wasn't just its own timeline that Deadlands explored. In an innovative series of "Dime Novel" adventures, the game crossed over with *Call of Cthulhu* (published by Chaosium) and *Werewolf: The Wild West* (from White Wolf), respectively. Crossing company lines was a big step, but also indicative of the respect the game and its creators had within the industry

No matter how far from home the games strayed, the heart of *Deadlands* remained in the haunted wastelands of the Reckoner-infested west. Forbeck's feeling was that the blend of the familiar—you don't have to explain a stagecoach—and the eerie was what made the setting so compelling. "Traditional westerns are so close to reality that they can feel dull ... [but] westerns have a lot of elements that lend themselves to blending with horror. The isolation of the plains, the knowledge that you're usually on your own... That's some of the fun with it, of course."

For freelancer and history buff Christopher McGlothlin, it was the combination of the supernatural with the American Civil War that made the game so appealing—that and the broad creative freedom Hensley gave his authors and artists to "play with his cool zombie toys." As for Hensley, he has a different view, that *Deadlands* "resonates so strongly with players because we all wrestle with our mortality. Fighting against the inevitable end—even in something as ultimately trivial as a roleplaying game—gives us at least a simulated view of spitting in the Reaper's face."

As of 2014, *Deadlands*: *Reloaded* is still very much alive (or Harrowed) and kicking, with both the classic setting and *Deadlands Noir* releasing new material and an ever-rabid fandom clamoring for more around the globe. Says Hensley, "the roleplaying game just keeps going and going. Everywhere I go—from Poland to Russia to Australia to Ireland and our own fifty United States—people tell us how much they love roleplaying in the weird west." And with various transmedia projects in the pipeline—both comics and novels are on the way—new audiences will be meeting the likes of Reverend Grimme and Dr. Hellstromme

The iconic visage of The Gunslinger, ever so slightly reminiscent of a certain Man With No Name, still peers out over the Reckoner-tainted deserts, and fans new and old wander the weird west ready for anything the dusty trails can throw at them. It's a remarkably enduring game, creating a western horror experience that was simultaneously engrossing and seamlessly accessible. For anyone who's ever wanted to step inside a Joe R. Lansdale novel, there's no better way than to find a Posse of fellow *Deadlands* players, saddle up with a Marshal to gamemaster, and ride.

And when you do, as Hensley says: "Keep your powder dry and your finger twitchy."

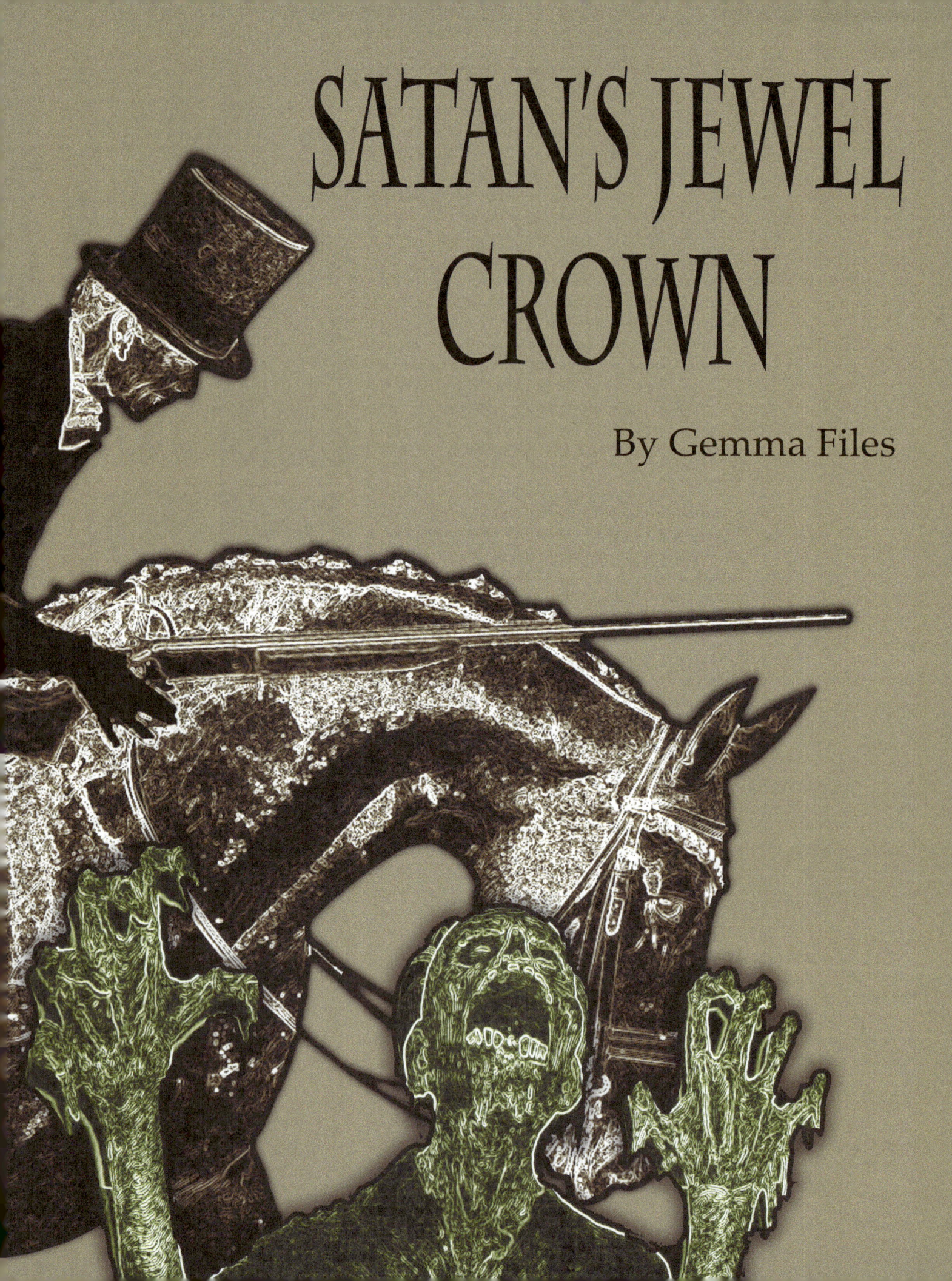

SATAN'S JEWEL CROWN

By Gemma Files

I walked into Satan's Jewel Crown, having no horse, then stopped a while at the town pump to order myself before going any further, taking time to splash my face and beat the dust from my brother's old coat. As I did, a little girl playing by the saloon door looked up when my shadow fell across her, gawping—maybe at my height, which has always been noticeable, or the bandage 'round my throat, which I suspected might have commenced to bleed through once more, during the last and hardest phase of my travels.

I had a rifle across my back and a knife in my belt plus another, smaller knife in my boot, all donations; my pack was full of dead things' heads, well-wrapped, which I'd heard some towns were now paying good money for, then turning in themselves later on for government bounty. I hoped to at least be able to swap these for a few nights' room and board, and perhaps (if I was lucky) a fresh pair of boots, since the ones I was wearing were both down at the heel and slightly too tight, as my blisters could testify.

So I smiled down at the girl, hoping to make a better impression. But: "Are you a lady?" was all she asked, at which my heart lurched, thudding traitor against my ribs, where I'd wrapped myself to bind those poor things I'd once called breasts down far enough to imply their lack. Yet I trusted in my voice—that awful rasp, made worse by thirst and rough weather—to give that very idea the lie.

"I look like a lady to you?" I inquired of her, therefore, in return. And on hearing me, she shook her head, falling properly silent...though to be frank, she still did not seem *entirely* convinced.

Such an odd little thing, all eyes, in a solemn, peaky face. We stood there admiring each other a moment, while I studied on what to say next. Luckily, it was at this very point that her mother came out, dressed in low-cut muslin, hair gold-glinting in the last of the sun. Saying, as she did—

"My daughter's touched, sir—has been ever since the War, the night her father died. It's these times, y'see; they weigh particular hard on small things, and the soft."

I nodded at that, honestly enough—I'd certainly found them so, after all—then smiled again, to which she gave me just the slightest sketch of a smile back, both faint and weary: something worth cultivating, even in that state, polishing up and finding its full shine, so you could admire it at closer quarters. And I knew I was lost.

"Have t'keep my eye on her from now on, I s'pose," I told the woman—Anthea, her name was, and is. The girl's was Esmee, called Meem, for reasons I never thought to ask. She I let go, at her own request. Yet Anthea, my lovely wife, I hold to still.

And thus it began, the tale I'm calling on you to pen. Take it down at my direction, leaving nothing out, but I warn you, do not think to elaborate, either—for though my handwriting may be disreputable, I can cipher with the best of them.

"I have a secret wound," I told Anthea, on our wedding night, several months from that same day. "From the War—don't like to speak of how it happened, as I'm sure you can understand. So let me do for *you*, my darling, please. Tell me what *you* like, and let me do my best to supply it."

"You're the only man I've ever known who talks like that," she said. "Sometimes..."

"Sometimes?"

"...you talk like you're not one at all. A man, I mean. But only sometimes," she hastened to add, for she did not wish to offend me. And hid her face in my shoulder, embarrassed.

"Perish the thought," I said.

It was a good choice, in hindsight, though I mostly do not count myself philosophical. For what is life but a series of secret wounds, as well as what those wounds leave behind? Our scars hold us together, more than anything else. Wouldn't you agree?

Well. It's a thought, only; an opinion, whatever that's worth. Even in my current position as mayor, not to mention this cursed place's sole surviving citizen, I surely can't legislate you share it.

***

Now, we all know that the bodies of the dead had commenced to rise long before I ever got into the "business" of killing such creatures again. Some people date this turn of events back to the War Between States, or even to slightly before it, claiming it a sign of God's impending judgement on America for harbouring hexation. For those slightly more well-read, however, it's easy enough to prove how the first *true* incidences had far more to do with the influence of two heathen Mex demons who called themselves gods allied with a passle of duelling hexes than to anything the Good Book ever predicted.

To begin with, in the wake of the Mexico City earthquake, there was a springing up of what would come to be called Red Weed all across Arizona and New Mexico—pernicious stuff, well-known to infest livestock, causing them to move about long after they'd been drained of all true life. And it's true that the first dead things I killed, back on my family's farm-land, were definitely Weed-infested, staggering here and there with little scarlet flowers a-bloom from all their orifices—they'd twist their vines as I approached, snapping and creaking, juicy with anticipation of seeding my flesh and mulching my remains. These I took down from a distance when I could, popping their knees, then stamped on their heads and jointed them as they lay twitching, stacking the remains up afterwards to burn.

But then came the Hex War, in which those old Mex demon-gods met their downfall, along with plenty of others. By its end, mages who'd never before been able to meddle formed compacts and founded whole cities, the Pinkerton Agency gave way to the Thiels, and a crack opened halfway down to hell itself, some said, releasing all manner of bad things into this world: horse-sized spiders, bone-dust monsters, dogs with human hands. Was only after that when the dead we know today began to make 'emselves evident, either clawing up out of graves or fresh-turned, with no trace of Weed to be seen. They spread their sickness through biting and ate all in their path, which was why the government fixed so high a bounty on evidence of their destruction.

Thus the era we now live in was formed, so far as I can reckon: a place of black miracles where towns feed their Weed-banks blood in exchange for fertile soil, where hexes can finally be diagnosed through arcanistry and expressed at their own request, either emigrating to Hexicas to live with their own folk or joining up with the Thiels to fight the unnatural with yet more unnaturalness, after. And we poor unmagicals are mainly left to flounder, finding our own way through darkness, with corpses nipping at our heels.

I had left Caxton, back Georgia way, as a too-tall, ugly woman with no prospects, monetary or otherwise. But by the time I crossed the border into Tennessee, circumstances had conspired in such a way that I now passed for a towering, raw-boned man, my general lack of beauty suddenly rendered "noble" and "distinctive" by a mere change from skirts to trousers. Which is how I eventually came to stride these streets like Lincoln reborn, though by necessity rendered beardless.

It was nothing to me to alter my sex in such a manner, since I have been treated as a work-horse all my life, which may well be why I've grown to look it. I was not raised gently, nor am I gentle by nature, and thus it ever seemed to me I was probably not made for gentle things, long before later experiences managed to prove that thesis well beyond a shadow of a doubt.

My family claimed to have been of some stature at one point, long before the War (though that conflagration might be, and often was, credited with marking the utter end of their fortune's downwards turn), and as is often the case, they had long pinned all hopes of social resurrection on my brother, sole heir to what tiny fortune we retained. Unfortunately for them, as is equally often the case, Phillip turned out to be both completely uninterested in and woefully inadequate to the task at hand; instead of delivering on his supposed promise, he instead chose to use the Hex War's final spasms as an excuse to betray them by taking whatever he believed himself entitled to and running off, never to return...one of those things, as it ensued, being me.

I suppose I could have fought him on this point, but given I had no great interest in helping to redeem my family's name either, it was easier by far to leave with him than to do so alone. We did not long stay in company, at any rate, only reaching so far as it took Phillip to find a low groggery, some fools to try and cheat at cards, and enough drink to get him in the mood to do so.

I fell asleep in the corner and woke to find myself alone, aside from the man I'd previously seen pouring drinks, the night before. His friends were outside, hooting and hollering. When I asked him as to Phillip's whereabouts, he all but rubbed his hands together at the prospect of shocking me with a revelation that proved no great surprise at all, before commencing in on whatever else he might've had in mind.

"Left you to us in trade, that brother of yours," he said. And: "Oh really?" was all I replied, reaching for the slim-ground paring knife I'd secreted in my sleeve.

Though thus disappointed in his intentions, he nevertheless approached me without any sort of fear, perhaps assuming me as stupid as I was ugly, or that I had some sort of investment in thinking myself a frail flower in need of rescue. Whilst I, on the other hand, simply waited for him to draw close enough, then drove my blade deep into his eye.

He had a belt with a gun on one hip, and I buckled it 'round me, though I knew it unlikely to do me much good; indeed, there was barely enough time to do so before his friends kicked the door open and saw me all over bloody, their leader at my feet. They made threats and I listened, then laughed. "Little pleasure to be had from a corpse," I told them, palming the knife's hilt once more, "but you're welcome enough to it, I suppose."

A second later, I'd already drawn its still-sticky edge 'cross that place where my adam's apple should have been, quick as a wink, and lay there watching them dissolve into darkness even as they stood looking down on me, cursing. Yet I woke later, alone, surrounded by fresh carnage. The place was silent, bloodier still than I'd left it. By the marks left behind, I took it that a herd of dead things had passed through, coming and going, leaving ruin in their wake. That they had left me untouched was indeed an oddity, but my throat hurt far too much for me to ponder on it long. Like them, therefore, I rose again, albeit in a very different manner.

The rest of the man's clothes fit me as well, to a point. I covered up my wound, cut my hair. And so I became myself, at last, leaving the creature once called Myrtella in the dust behind me; I was "Mister Phillips" from thence on, with no real need of a first name, seeing how I'd already reclaimed my brother's and thrown away my father's.

Looking back, I now see that much of what I've accomplished since has been in the service of turning myself *into* him, only better—becoming in truth the man he only professed to be, between the big talk and the sister-selling. One way or the other, I know beyond a shadow of a doubt how in my own odd way, I've done more for others than he ever would have looked to, and ten times more effectively. This whole town stands testament to that, as I believe you'd agree...

...if nothing else.

I well-knew I should've left Satan's Jewel Crown right after I turned in my haul and got my coin, but the plain fact is, I just didn't *want* to. Instead, I felt a new and aching need to stay 'round Anthea for as long as I could, to follow this hook she'd set in my heart, and see where it might lead. It posed a puzzle, since to be near other folks was usually never much more than trouble, or so I'd always found: they soon enough started to want to know me, to ask after where I'd come from, where I'd been. What-all I might—or might not have—done.

Anthea's boss, Mister Colquitt, who ran the saloon she worked in, thought paying her was tantamount to owning her. She'd been able to cry him off thus far by citing her widowhood, but when he saw her look to me, that all fell by the wayside. He was high up in the town council and commenced to whisper in ears, making them wonder what it was I was after, 'sides from what *he* already wanted.

"You're looking to marry my mama, ain't you, Mister Phillips?" Meem asked me. "Why?"

"To look after her, 'course. Don't you want that?"

"I guess. She does need looking after."

"You too, I bet."

"...maybe."

That very same night, the first of the dead came in, and while others ran and screamed, I stood and fought. I'd already been noticed, but that got me some credit. Was enough so that three nights on—once we'd dug the trenches I suggested, and filled 'em with pitch against new incursions—I slipped into saloon-keeper Colquitt's room with a particular head I kept deep in my pack, too rotted up to sell but still straining to bite, whenever I set my hand on it. In the morning, he came staggering down with his eyes rolled back and his teeth all a-snap, so I drew Anthea out of his way and let him get far enough outside that nobody near could see, before pocking him through the forehead.

The verdict came in he'd died in the night of wounds he'd kept hid, then risen back up. And I was good and in after that, clung fast, dug deep as a tick...so close to the town's beating heart I could not only feel its pulse but taste its blood as well, sipping it down like finest victory wine.

Meem saw me bury the head, later on; made certain I saw her see me, too. But she never said anything, so I gathered it must've suited her I stay, as well as the rest. Strange little girl.

I'd been one of those myself, once.

"*Are* you a man?" she asked me, whilst Anthea was elsewhere.

"I am now," I said.

"You *were* a girl, though. Like me."

I paused, thought hard about it for a moment. Then allowed: "They did call me so at home, for all I don't think they treated me much different than they would've a boy, so long as he wasn't their favourite. But I never really thought about it, one way or t'other—not 'till I needed folks to assume I was somebody your mother could love, and feel comfortable doing it. Which would *you* prefer I be, honey?"

"Well, I already have a mama."

"You could call me Papa, then. If it suits you."

And I guess it did, because *she* did, from then on. Right up until the day she died.

That night, I looked in on Anthea watching Meem sleep, and thought: *I want to stay here, to do what I can to keep you both safe. I want to be the man you think I am. Want to kill anything that threatens us, same as I'd kill anyone who'd even try to prevent me from doing so.*

And—I will. Oh yes.

You best be very damn sure, I will.

***

By that winter, I'd been less elected mayor than acclaimed so, for the dead things kept on coming, and I was the best they had at knowing how to protect ourselves. Wouldn't've thought the earth held so many, but that it always seems to be the most unwelcome creatures which seem limitless— they flocked in from miles around, when they weren't propagating by the usual methods. As each day was increasingly given over to clean-up and every evening to funeral pyres, we were also struck with corpse-fever, which thinned our numbers somewhat, while consolidating my own base of power—for it was the nay-sayers who tended to drop hardest, and those who acknowledged me as best choice for role of war-time leader to recover.

But in and between these misfortunes, we did see the first instances of something no one else had, thus far: an apparent cure for infection, as mysterious as it soon proved (thankfully) complete. There were those who lived, for once, after having been caught in the dead's jaws—fell silent a few hours, suffering bad, yet got back up the very next morning, apparently unscathed. And amongst these was Anthea, who'd already put two bullets from her little gambler's derringer through the thing that had hold of her before I could rush over and shear its head off, even though it'd already buried its teeth so far in her shoulder that they stayed there, lodged fast, when I finally pulled it off.

I spent the whole night crying over her, with Meem's solemn little hand on my bent head, stroking away at my shorn hair. At last, worn out, I fell asleep beside the bed—then woke to find her down in the kitchen, making flapjacks.

Beautiful Anthea, her long curls gold in the morning sun. Smiling. Talking. Better.

"You all right?" I asked her, to which she answered, brightly: "Oh, 'course. Shouldn't I be? Did something happen?"

I studied her a moment, unsure what-all to say, given

her wrap had just slipped far enough to let me see how those two raw holes in her flesh were still visible—not bleeding, not anymore, but not exactly healing, either. Much like that wound at my throat.

She noticed, started a bit, and covered them up again. Gave me the same smile I'd sold my soul for, sweet enough to stop my breath.

And: "No," I said, "nothing like that, darlin.' Just had a bad dream, is all."

"Oh? Well, you're awake now—so sit down and eat these, Mister Mayor, 'fore they get cold. Give they sell my cooking 'cross the street, it's not everybody gets their own private sample."

"But Papa," Meem said, once Anthea'd gone back upstairs to freshen herself, in anticipation of opening up the saloon. "She *isn't* really better, not at all. She just isn't done, yet."

I swallowed. "What do you mean, honey?"

"That she's still here," she told me, sadly, "though she shouldn't be. 'Cause you love her so much, you just won't let her go."

And did I notice, looking back, how all those who survived their brushes with the dead were people I had use for, while those I disliked failed outright and rose back up, necessitating a second destruction? No more than I ever traced the endless wave of plague-bearing Weedless dead we now fought back almost daily, not to the Hex War at all, but to one very particular instance of the chaos following in its wake.

My neck remained tetchy, never entirely sealed over. Sometimes it wept blood. Anthea would soothe it with compresses, brew me sweet tea, then bandage it anew. I used whiskey to treat it too, increasingly—medicated myself from the inside, so to speak. No one thought any ill of me for that, since I ran myself so ragged in service of this town, and its folks.

My town, now. *My* folks.

"Papa," Meem said, a little further on that winter, "you really should let Mister Corcoran move on, at least."

"Oh, but I couldn't do without old Corcoran, honey. He's my right hand."

"Well, then Missus Yee—let *her* leave, while you still can. Her girls, too."

"Now, but where would they go *to*, exactly, with all the dead things out there sharpening their teeth for 'em? Think, Meem. I have a responsibility to Missus Yee, just like t'everyone else."

"But Papa..."

"You don't want me to lose my job, now, do you? Where would your mother and I live, then? Or you, either?"

I was only teasing her, gently, or at least I thought I'd been. But she looked down right then, and by God, I almost thought she was about to cry. I'd've done about anything in this world, at that same moment, to take my clumsy mockery back.

"Just don't bring *me* back, please," she told me, at last, soft enough I had to cock my head to catch it. "When it comes to me, at last, I mean. I know why you kept Mama, but I see how it is, for her...for *all* of them...and all things considered, I'd really rather not."

"You have my word," I swore, though I still didn't really know—wouldn't allow myself to see, more like—what it was, exactly, I was swearing to. And I've kept that promise, as it happens...thus far.

Can't say what may happen in the future, for loneliness is a curse. Yet so long's I have Anthea, I believe my sweet Meem can continue to sleep easy, unlike the rest of this town's citizenry. Her presence, though sorely missed, is no longer required.

I do owe her that much, given all she did for me.

***

Right about here, meanwhile, is where *you* came in, with your shiny Thiel Agency badge and your cunning arcanistric instrumentation: Agent Lucas K. Law, at my service, or so you claimed. I remember you standing in my office, sipping the whiskey I'd poured you, while down in the street below, I could see my people going to and fro, doing their jobs; by the saloon door sat Meem, as ever, playing with her doll in the dust, which set me to thinking about that first day, and all that'd followed after. Listening with only half an ear as you told me why you'd come—that Doc Asbury's measurements reckoned Satan's Jewel Crown as close as made no never-mind to "the very epicenter" of this latest outbreak of (possibly) hexation-created unnaturalness. How it was part of your rubric to investigate, and that you hoped I'd give you every sort of aid in your quest to discover exactly why the dead seemed to find this area—the place, even—so damnably attractive.

"People do say Satan's Jewel Crown's prospered under your rule, Mister Phillips."

"I'm only a mayor, sir. We don't elect any kings, 'round here."

"Of course not. Still, to brave such continual incursions from these, eh, graveyard emissaries and survive—no, more than just that, surely. To *thrive*..."

"We've been fortunate, that's true, though we've suffered our share of losses: corpse-fever, brawls, the regular range of insults, as well as gettin' bit. But as to that, we do seem to have an amazing survival rate, even amongst those took down in battle."

"Excuse me?"

"Oh, a good third of our folks've shook it off, thus far, even once the poison's took hold. My own wife, for example—"

You blinked. "I'd...like to meet that good lady, if so."

"Well, sure. She's just over that-a-way, if you care to cross the street."

As we walked out together, you casting your eyes

'round in obvious curiosity, something began to mount in me that I barely recognized, so long had it been since I'd last felt it—anxiety, doubt. *Fear*, not only on my own behalf, but on behalf of all.

My town, my people, my family—I, me, mine. All I'd built up and kept safe even in the besieging face of death, and so much worse.

"Those fortifications look military-grade," you said. "You have soldiering experience, I'd wager."

"No, sir," I replied, pulse starting to stutter. "Learned it all from books, or veterans' tales. My brother—"

"No? But you *must*'ve fought the risen before, somewhere—back along the original line of infection, perhaps."

I nodded. "In Georgia, when the Weed first came up, we got our share of infestation: live animals, dead bodies. We soon learned how to deal with 'em."

"But nothing like this new strain, exactly."

"No, t'be sure. Wasn't 'till just before I crossed the border that I first saw ones like these-all, and then only their tracks—before the bounty laws came down, and I started in to hunting."

You paused in your step, a spark of sudden interest lighting your eyes. "Really. You know, Mister Phillips, our investigations while back-tracking the herd's migration eventually uncovered tales of a certain long-burnt-out watering-hole—so close between states, apparently, it almost didn't matter exactly which side it lay, while the place still existed—that might've witnessed this country's very first mass conjunction of plague-bearing dead. We examined its ruins a month ago, and found evidence of great hexational discharge still resonating; its foundations gave off an Asbury Scale reading of 68.5 even after several months' inactivity, seemingly collected 'round a bloodstain on what was left of the bar-room's floor..."

"I did pass through that area," I admitted, feeling my throat contract, "and it's a hard road to travel, full to the brim with all manner of untrustworthies, or was. Don't ever recall hearing much about any hexes, though."

"Well, they do exist almost everywhere, inherently—everywhere *I*'ve been, anyhow, since joining up. By the by, if I may ask you about that wound you bear, under your neckerchief...is that from your recent toils, or did you sustain it earlier?"

My hand went to the offending bandage. "Some time ago, thank you kindly. I hardly notice it now, given all my other distractions."

"Really? It looks quite painful."

"Oh, once, yes—but these days, it's nothing I can't deal with. Just can't seem to get it to seal up, not completely."

"I'd think that would make things...very difficult."

"I'm not sure I take your meaning."

"No? Let me rephrase, then: that does not, in fact, seem like a wound it would be possible for a man *to* survive, no more than it's usually possible to survive a revenant's attack where the bite breaks skin, everyplace else but here. Would that be your wife I glimpse there through those doors, the lovely woman tending bar?"

I bristled. "It would."

"Well, well! She, too, looks in remarkably good health, given what you say she's been through."

"You think I'm lyin' 'bout her getting better, is that it? Just like Mister Corcoran did, over there, or Missus Yee and her girls, down at the wash-house? What possible reason would I have to misrepresent our triumphs, small's they might be, when the losses we've had remain so much greater?"

"None at all."

"Then why're you quizzing me on all these whys and hows, exactly? I'm no arcanologist, not like your bosses, or yourself."

"Well, this *is* your town, isn't it? Who else should I think to ask?"

We stood there glaring a moment, eyes locked, like we were about to draw down; you reached into your fancy waistcoat, and I fairly twitched. But instead of a shooter, you brought out one of old Doc Asbury's famous hexation-measuring Manifolds, the latest model; it could drain spellwork too, as I recalled, though I think you somewhat forgot about that part, once things'd gone fully to perdition. At any rate, you held it outstretched my way like a dowsing rod, attempting to explain how the spinning of its various dials revealed there was far more to me than I'd hitherto suspected.

"You see, sir," you said, "I believe that *you* are *causa generis* of this infestation—unintentionally and all unaware, I can only guess. As most new-turned hexes are, concerning the damage they do."

"A hex. *Me*."

"Can't see any other explanation, really. There are those who've shown similar powers, already, upon expression...what the witch-hunters of old once called necromancy, whether demonstrated by bringing the dead back to life, or keeping those already on the cusp from, uh—going any further. That said, of course, I frankly can't think there's been a case before recorded in which one man did both at once, spreading revivification in his wake like typhus...or re-ordered an entire town to his personal liking, either, using a threat *he himself* was author of to keep its populace under his rule..."

God, the pure shock of it. Though it *did* fit, I had to admit, if only to myself: if I couldn't recall having had anything like magical powers previous to that truncated attempt to cut my own throat, things certainly had gone to my benefit ever since, albeit in odd and awful ways. Even the idea that I should have made my change in the manner a man usually does, rather than a woman—for I'd received my monthly gift years ago, and never made much of it, aside from an excuse to change trousers more frequently—that, too, seemed right, when placed in context. As right as any of it could be.

The way you regarded me, though, when you thought I wasn't looking; it was like you thought I'd done it deliberately. And the rage rose, kindling me from head to toe, pumping me full of poison and fire admixed—up, and up, and up. My fingers itched, longing to form fists.

Yet at that very instant, I heard my sweet little Meem yell out, from behind: "Papa, don't! Papa, they're coming—they're almost here—you just *got* to stop them, Papa, *please*—"

We turned as one, then, you and I, Agent Law. Just in time to see a fresh passle of rotten, reaching dead come charging down the street as though summoned, all sunken eyes and moaning, open mouths.

How'd they get past my barriers? I remember wondering as I whipped out my knife, fast enough it must've looked like I was fixing to juggle it. *My sentries? The catch-pits? Christ's sake, how damn deep we got to* dig *those trenches, anyways, 'fore they finally start to do the trick?*

Then I saw the whole range of their faces, just as the first wave broke against us—those intact and fresh as well as grave-kissed, same ones I'd called out greetings to that morning, on my daybreak stroll from one end of Satan's Jewel Crown to the other.

And I knew, finally. At last, that was when I *knew*.

You should let them all go, Papa—let them leave, let them move on. While you still can.

Before...

...the crush was on us, and everything turned to carnage, with you and me back-to-back against the horde. I saw you put down six, a round for each, before you were forced to throw your gun away and grab whatever came to hand, instead—first a good, solid length of log, snatched off the nearest pyre pile, followed by the Cavalry saber old Mister Hudgens no longer seemed to know how to use. I found myself trying to thrust aside those I recognized while taking down those I didn't, but that went by the wayside soon enough, once the berserker-fit was on me. And at some point I stood gasping, glancing down, only to realize that the figure crouched beside me was Anthea—Anthea, her long hair blood-dabbled, hugging Meem to her like some awful Madonna and munching away on the side of her neck all the while, like it was the world's best slice of watermelon.

I groaned out loud, then, and punched my wife full in her beautiful face—knocked her sidelong, slapping her down further, so I could wrest what was left of the only child I'd ever be likely to call my own from her still-grasping arms. Saw you from the corner of my eye, Agent, watching me do it, even as Missus Yee's eldest took a chunk out of your nicely-dressed calf. But I didn't have time to note what happened next, let alone to care.

Oh, but I held Meem tight, tight. Gripped her like she was salvation. And then—

"You all *stop*, goddamnit!" I cried, cradling that poor girl close. "All of you, just...*stop*."

Which, without further ado—they did.

***

So...here we are.

Even after that wonderfully useful explanation of yours, I've no doubt you were startled when I roused you up once more and burnt the fever from your veins, sealing that ragged wound with a touch (just like my own throat, at last; like Anthea's pale shoulder, under her muslin gown). And saying, as I did, in true Galileean style: *Awake, O sleeper—Lazarus, I command you, roll away the stone. Come out. Come back.*

I am not done with you, Agent...no, not yet.

Maybe not ever.

Here you are again, though, after all that—made almost good as new, barring some ill-usage. And it's thus I'll send you back to your masters, to Doc Asbury himself, who I reckon may well wish to study you for years: a living dead man, walking and talking, to demonstrate the untapped depth of my powers. But one way or the other, I'll trust you to warn them to leave me alone, from now on—not because Satan's Jewel Crown is far too small a place for them to trouble with, so much, but because if they do not, far worse things may...hell, *will*...happen.

Think about it this way, Agent Law, and inform others accordingly. When *I* die, whether by natural means or otherwise, I expect the town will go with me—fall silent forever, like a stopped clock. That's what I hope. But there's always the alternative: a general exodus in the wake of my passing, these people I've sacrificed so much for streaming out across the land like locusts, rotten and hungry, to spread their awful sickness everywhere they turn...

And why should this be my legacy, anyhow? Well, we know that all hexes' power centers around what they know best, the thing most familiar to 'em: Chess Pargeter with his guns, Reverend Rook his Bible. The Chinee and Indian hexes have their traditions. I once heard of a woman burnt back in Caxton who'd used embroidery, sewing her desires onto the world around her. So is there something in me that's equally hungry and cold and rotten, at my core? Or is it just that when it came upon me, when I cut my own throat and first made sacrifice to myself, I had already given myself up for dead?

Little enough pleasure to be had in a corpse. Yet I will take what I can, and call myself thankful for it.

You see, I know what I am, now, for which I really do thank you—my true nature, what I've *been* capable of, thus far. Yet I don't think I know the extent of what I might still achieve, if I'm given reason enough to push things further. Which is why it's better for all concerned that I not be—you, most especially.

If (when) I die, *you* die, too—finally, fully. It's a foregone conclusion.

Better to leave me alone, again, from now on: here on my throne, king of all I survey, danced attendance on by dead wife's body and my dead daughter's ghost. A lost, uncertain thing no more, though forever damned to wear what my town's named after; if the shoe fits, as they say. And after this, all who meet me—thanks to you—will surely know it does.

(Meem knew already, it occurs to me. Perhaps because she was as I am, or might have been; another hex, potentially—a friend, a companion, far more than her mother is, or can be. But still I let her lie, as she asked me to.)

Mister Phillips, Myrtella; it's all the same. I'm both, and neither. I'm what I am, only—nothing ever seen before, and nothing to be trifled with. And this much is certain, either way…

…even if I don't want anything more than what I already have, I will *never* settle for anything less.

☙ ☙ ☙

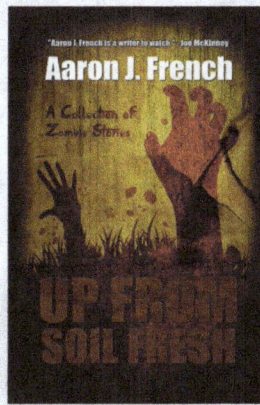

THINGS THAT BITE

Legends and Folklore of Supernatural Predators

By Jonathan Maberry and David F. Kramer
Bram Stoker Award-winning authors of THE CRYPTOPEDIA

CRYPTIDS AND THE SCIENCE OF CRYPTOZOOLOGY
Part One of Three

(1)

SOMETHING IS OUT THERE

Truth is stranger than fiction.

Seriously.

There are some pretty weird things out there, and we're not talking about vampires and werewolves or creatures from myth. No, our own physical world has its fair share of very strange things. You've heard of some of them: Bigfoot, El Chupacabra, the Loch Ness Monster, the Jersey Devil; but there are many dozens of these unknown animals.

Are they real? Good question. Opinions vary wildly.

If they do exist…what are they?

Well, some of these animals may be UMA's (Unidentified Mysterious Animals) that, due to lack of physical evidence, spoor or DNA, resist scientific classification in the known biology. This is why there's always a race to attempt to classify any new animal that is seen, captured, killed, or washed up on the beach.

A second classification includes all of the Legendary Creatures such as the Cyclops, Pegasus, Harpies and similar monsters from myth.

Still others are relicts, surviving examples of species believed to be extinct or so close to extinction that living examples are rarely found. This category ranges from the common horseshoe crab (which is actually more closely related to a spider or tick than a crab) is a surviving example of a family limulidae, and are descended from eurypterids (sea scorpions). They evolved during the Paleozoic Era (540-248 million years ago) and all of their close relatives have long since become extinct while they remain virtually unchanged. Another more exotic example is the Coelacanth, a large fish believed to have become completely extinct over sixty million years ago; and yet one was netted in December of 1938 by Hendrik Goosen, the captain of the South African trawler Nerine. Since then living populations of them have been sighting (and caught) in the waters around Indonesia and South Africa.

But there is a fourth group of unknown animals, the cryptids, for whom we do not have a clear understanding of whether they exist or not. Like UMAs, cryptids (which means 'unknown' or 'hidden' animal) rarely leave physical evidence and any continued belief in their existence is based on eyewitness reports of varying credibility. There's even a science to locate and classify them: cryptozoology, a term coined in by Bernard Heuvelmans (1916-2001) for his 1955 book, On the Track of Unknown Animals. Heuvelmans was one of many scientists, explorers, hunters and others who felt a compulsion to know the truth about the things people have reported seeing in forests, in lakes, on mountains and in their own backyards.

Cryptozoology refers to the scientific search for unknown and non-supernatural animals believed or purported to exist but which have not yet been included in the official fossil record of known creatures. Generally cryptozoologists search for the more sensational megafauna cases, such as Bigfoot, rather than new species of beetles or flies. As a result, their work is often dismissed by more conventional biologists. Mainstream scientists dismiss cryptozoology with the same thoughtless disdain with which they pooh-pooh parapsychology and the hunt for UFOs. And just between us, blind disbelief is not supposed to be a part of the empirical process. Maybe those folks don't want to believe, or are just so stubborn that they need a carcass or measurable data before they can accept even the possibility of reality. Good thing Columbus didn't share that view -- or Archimedes, Galileo, or other more open-minded thinkers.

Despite the criticism, the cryptozoologists persist, however, and in recent years their work has been received some validation and support from the general public and from the media. Documentaries on the hunt for cryptids have become a staple of cable TV, ranging from the Sci-Fi Channel to the Discovery and National Geographic networks.

A recent cryptid sensation was the 'Montauk Monster', a bizarre-looking animal that washed up on Montauk Island. However scientists now widely agree that it is a dead and partially decayed raccoon. People who want to believe in cryptids patently reject this explanation. And that's kind of how it goes. So many people want to believe.

The search for unknown megafauna (lit 'large animal', the term in biology used to describe any animal weighing more than 40 kg) has also received some credibility sabotage from within. It turns out Roger Patterson and Robert Gimlin actually fudged the legendary Bigfoot film footage in 1967; and Christian Spurling's world-shaking 1934 photo of the Loch Ness monster was similarly faked. That kind of sensationalism (or, if you're in a tolerant mood you could call it 'prankishness') does real harm to progress of serious research. Even so, there are plenty of scientists and researchers out there in the field using sound scientific methods to prove--and in many cases disprove—the existence of cryptids.

Consider how few of the world's many animals were known to science even a century ago, and how many new species are discovered every year. It puts a lot of egg on the faces of those who mock cryptozoology out of hand. Consider that two hundred years ago the first explorers to claim to have encountered a web-footed, egg laying aquatic mammal with a duck bill and a poisonous sting were not believed. And yet the duck-billed platypus exists. As does the Giant Squid, Mountain Gorilla, and the Okapi--each of which were considered myths for years. In May of 2005 a new species of long-tailed tree monkey (Highland Mangabey) was discovered in Tanzania, East Africa. The following February a section of previously unexplored Indonesian forest was penetrated to reveal entirely new species of butterflies, frogs, giant rhododendron, and a type of honeyeater bird that was previously unknown to science. In March 2006 National Geographic News broke the story of a new shark species (dubbed Mustelus hacat) discovered in Mexico's Gulf of California; and in June of that year a team from Hebrew University in Jerusalem excavated a cave and discovered six previously unrecorded species of animal: four seawater

and freshwater crustaceans and four terrestrial species of invertebrates. And the real jackpot was the discovery by an international team of scientists of hundreds of rare and previously unknown and ultra rare plants and animals in the mountain rainforests of New Guinea. The scientists discovered new species of birds, four new species of butterflies, egg-laying spiny anteaters, tree kangaroos, twenty new species of frogs, a number of plants including giant flowers.

We may have mapped the human genome but we're nowhere our inventory of what walks, crawls, slithers, hops, swims, flies or grows in this big old world of ours.

Given the frequent discovery of new species it's a marvel that people can still be so closed minded about the possibility of other new species.

One of the frequently used arguments against the possible existence of a creature such as Bigfoot is that there has been no physical evidence recovered. Granted that we don't have a forensic workup on the big hairy guy, but consider how much evidence we have on the Neanderthal. For a species that existed for hundreds of thousands of years there are remarkably few skeletal remains, and no complete skeletons.

Given all of this, why is it so difficult to accept the possibility of even stranger creatures out there? Who knows what ancient species that somehow dodged the evolutionary bullet or which unknown animals are just waiting to be discovered?

In this section we'll meet several kinds of cryptids, divided into two groups: those on land (including flying cryptids) and those found in lakes and oceans.

(2)

CRYPTIDS AROUND THE WORLD

Here are some of the stranger cryptids from around the globe and throughout history.

Achiyalatopa: The Zuñi Indians of Western Nevada have legends of a gigantic bird-monster with feathers made from sharpened spikes of flint. Though immensely powerful and massive (its body weight is necessary to counterbalance the stone-knives that make up its quills), the Achiyalatopa is not an evil predator. Quite the reverse, in fact, as the Achiyalatopa taught many secret and holy skills to the Zuñi. Even today, archeologists frequently find Zuñi altars that bear carvings of this ancient creature.

Ahool: This giant, batlike cryptid from the rainforests of Java gets its name from its distinctive cry, "Ahh-hOOOoool!" Eyewitness reports claim that the Ahool has a simian head, a strong body covered in gray fur, clawed hands, and a ten-foot wingspan. Based on pure description it's like that the Ahool is actually the more common wood-owl of that region. Uncertain lighting in the sun-dappled (or moonlit) forest can play a lot of tricks on even the most skeptical observer.

Almas: The Almas are another of the world's many as yet unclassified species of hominids. For five hundred years they have been spotted in the wastelands of Siberia, the Caucasus and Pamir Mountains of central Asia, and the Altai Mountains of southern Mongolia. Unlike either the shorter hominids such as Ebu Gogo or towering wildmen like the Yeti, the Almas are approximately the same height and general build as regular humans, though with longer arms and, like their cousins of both statures, covered with coarse reddish-gray hair. They are not aggressive and generally disregard humans, and when approached will melt away into the forests or snowy wastes. For additional research on this elusive creature we recommend Still Living?: Yeti, Sasquatch and the Neanderthal Enigma by Myra Shackley (W. W. Norton, 1983),

Alom-bag-winno-sis: Among the Abanaki Indians of New England there is a legend of a water monster that delights in upsetting boats and drowning people. The Alom-bag-winno-sis glides along beneath the water, sometimes in the form of a sea snake, sometimes in the form of a dwarfish human, and then surges up beneath the canoe of a fisherman or river traveler and overturns the canoe. The Alom-bag-winno-sis often chooses spots where the water is already turbulent, hoping that the rapids and the surprise dunking will be enough to cause pain, injury or drowning.

Altamaha-ha: Though the South Atlantic does not have quite as many monsters as the South Pacific, there are still quite a few cryptids plying those waters, including the Altamaha-ha who is seen most often around the scattered islands of South Georgia and the South Sandwich Islands. These islands are territories of the United Kingdom but the waters are ruled by a 30-foot long sea monster that has a serrated ridge running along its back, rows of powerful dorsal fins, and a tapered mouth like that of an alligator packed with rows of conical teeth. Despite this fierce armament, the Altamaha-ha appears to either be placid in nature or timid and tends to shy away from contact with humans.

Aniukha: Deep in the icy wastes and frozen forests of Siberia there is a legend of a small but deadly predator called the Aniukha. Perhaps the most rare and least documented of Europe's many cryptids, the Aniukha nonetheless appears in occasional folktales, especially among exiled Jews sent to Siberia during and after the era of Josef Stalin (1879 - 1953).

This creature has been variously described as being as small as a praying mantis or as large as a squirrel. It runs on all fours like a woodland mammal, but can also stand erect and leap great distances, much like a cat. The Aniukha has a pale body covered in scales with patches of sparse gray or dark brown fur. Its face is like that of an emaciated cat, with huge dark eyes, ears that rise to tufted points, and a short snout filled with very long hollow teeth.

Aremata-Popoa and Aremata-Rorua: Polynesian cultures depended on water traffic. Boats of all kinds would ply the waters between the thousands of islands in the South Pacific, engaging in trade, exploration, and occasionally a bit of warfare. For the most part the seas were the allies of these ancient peoples, but within the seas there were evil forces as well as good. Two very destructive demons of the oceans were Aremata-Popoa, whose name means "short wave", and Aremata-Rorua, whose name means "long wave". As implied by their names, these water demons manifest themselves as aspects of the water through which the Polynesians sailed. Aremata-Rorua would send large, often massive, waves against the boats, swamping them, striking them amidships (pooping them), or overwhelming the fragile craft by knocking it on its beam ends. Aremata-Popoa is slyer and uses short, choppy waves to knock the boat back and forth, turning it at right angles to the waves so that it gets pooped or pounded to pieces. Wise sailors try and appease these water demons by singing prayers and spreading offerings of flowers on the water before setting out for any journey into the deep blue sea.

Atakapa: The Atakapa (Attakapa, Attacapa) nation of Native Americans, including the subgroups Akokisas and Deadoses, occupied the coastal and bayou areas of southwestern Louisiana and southeastern Texas until the early 1800s. Atakapa means "eaters of men" in Choctaw, but the question has been raised whether the Atakapas were cannibals for subsistence or ritual. Some legends have it that the Atakapa were not merely cannibalistic humans but some species of supernatural predator, possibly a ghoul or a type of flesh-eating vampire. Unfortunately most of what is known of the Atakapa comes from European accounts which were rarely accurate nor sympathetic to any Native American peoples of the time. One exception is Jack Claude Nezat's self-published book, The Nezat And Allied Families 1630-2007, (Lulu 2007); and in this case the author is a descendant of the Atakapa people.

Atlas Bear: An extinct subspecies of the brown bear that was the only bear native to Africa and which is believed to have become extinct in the late 19th century. However occasional sightings are reported, suggesting that the creature may not have been hunted to extinction.

Ba'a' (also Chequah): Most North Americans think that the Thunderbird is just a sporty muscle car, but for centuries the Comanche of Texas believed in a great bird, similar to an eagle but as large and predatory as a pterodactyl. They called the creature Ba'a', and in their stories this creature brought thunder and rain, and could conjure destructive hurricane-force winds with its wingbeats. Also known as Chequah by the Potawatomi of Michigan and other Native peoples, the thunderbird was believed to have a wingspan of about 20 feet and when standing on the ground towered to eight feet. Its talons could cleave rock and its beak could snap a canoe in half. The Ba'a' was said to be capable of snatching a man or elk off the ground and carrying this meal away with him. In many stories it is described as looking like an eagle but one of enormous size; in other stories it is a kind of hawk, an owl, and some have described it as being composed of fire and lightning.

The most recent sighting of this monstrous bird was by three boys playing in their backyard back in July of 1977. The boys claimed that two gigantic birds swooped down on them, and one of the boys was grabbed by the shoulders and lifted off the ground. Though he was later dropped, he was traumatized for many years by the incident.

If the Ba'a' exists, cryptozoologists speculate that it may either be a surviving subspecies of pterodactyl or, more likely, a surviving teratorn (Teratornis merriami), a gigantic bird supposedly extinct since the Pleistocene age.

Barmanou (Also Barmanu): The Barmanous (literally "big hairy one") is a hominid believed to live in the most remote mountain passes of Pakistan and Afghanistan. The creature is large, hairy and bipedal and is most often spotted by shepherds. At the beginning of the 20th Century serious expeditions have been launched to try and locate the creature. One of the foremost researchers on the subject, Dr. Jordi Magraner, was assassinated in Pakistan in 2002, and since 9/11, all serious investigation into the creature have been shelved due to ongoing war in the region.

Beast of Bodmin Moor: Around the world there are a number of reports of great hunting cats causing trouble in places where they have no reason to be. These ferocious felines are lumped together in the lexicon of cryptozoology under the heading ABCs (Alien Big Cats) –and in this case "alien" refers not to extraterrestrial but from other places on earth, or perhaps other historic eras.

Such is the case with the Beast of Bodmin Moor, a mighty-hunting predator believed to be the culprit in a variety of attacks, including the mass slaughter of livestock in rural areas. In 1995, less than a week after Britain's Ministry of Agriculture released a statement that there was "no verifiable evidence" of hunting cats loose in the U.K., a little boy found the skull of young male leopard on the bank of a stream. And in the late 1990s, large, feline paw prints were examined around Bodmin Moor by officials from the Newquay Zoo.

Beast of Exmoor: A large hunting cat frequently reported in Exmoor, Devon and Somerset in the United Kingdom. In 1983, Eric Ley, a farmer in South Molton claimed that the beast had slaughtered over one hundred of his sheep in just three months -a tally that suggests that the beast hunts for pleasure since it could not possibly have consumed that many sheep in that time. The running theory is that the Beast was a Black Leopard or Cougar released into the countryside following the passing of a law forbidding owning of predatory animals (except for zoos). If so, then the animal is likely to have died decades ago -since cats of that type generally live between twelve and fifteen years. This case is one of a very few of the British big cat stories to yield actual physical evidence: puma hairs were recovered and analyzed by police labs.

Beast of Riber: Another of Britain's mysterious big cat cryptids, this one believed to be hunting livestock in the vicinity of Riber in Derbyshire. The animal was sighted in 2001, and the mauled body of a lamb was found surrounded by unusual animal paw prints. The paw prints measured four inches across, six inches long, and one and a half inches deep. That's no housecat.

Behemoth: The Behemoth is a legendary monster from Biblical legend and was supposed to be so huge that

it could, in one gulp, all the waters that flow from the River Jordan in a whole year. The Behemoth has incalculable strength and can shake the whole world when it moves.

Bergman's Bear: In Kamatchka Penninsula in Russia there have long been legends of a gigantic bear called the God Bear, and the tales were often so outlandish that they have become part of folklore. Then, in 1920 Sten Bergmen, a zoologist from Sweden, discovered a pelt from a bear as of then unknown to science. Unlike the normal bears of that region, this specimen had short hair.

Bessie: (Also South Bay Bessie). A lake snakelike cryptid of approximately 35 to 55 feet in length that has been spotted off and on since 1817 in and around Lake Erie, Pennsylvania. Unlike many of her cousins around the world, sightings of Bessie have increased significantly in recent years, particularly over the last three decades, and in 1992 three people were killed when Bessie allegedly attacked their sailboat.

Big Bird: In a weird example of life imitating art, when a gigantic bird was spotted in the Rio Grande Valley it was given the nickname of Big Bird –after the daffy character from Sesame Street. Unlike the child-friendly yellow bird of TV, the Big Bird of the Rio Grande looks much like a giant bat, standing five feet tall, with great leathery wings, and a face like a night ape. Aside from a few scattered sightings, this particular unidentified flying object has managed to stay off of the radar of cryptozoologists.

Bishop-fish: Sea monsters come in all sizes, from tiny water sprites to leviathan, and their appearance can vary from beautiful mermaids to monsters so hideous that the very sight of them is lethal. Some sea monsters are not so much overtly threatening as simply very strange, as in the case of the Bishop-fish. Also known as a "Sea-Bishop", this creature bears a strange resemblance to a mitered cleric with a shaved head, reminiscent of a Catholic monk, a fishlike body, and a draping of scales that --from a distance—appears to be a cloak, like a cardinal or bishop might wear. Over the centuries a couple of these creatures have been captured, and one was reputedly brought before the King of Poland, who desired to keep it as a pet. However, some bishops in the King's court saw the creature and when it noticed them it gestured to them in a way that suggested an intelligent being pleading for its life. When the bishops appealed to the King for its release, the creature made the sign of the cross, an action later repeated as it was released back into the sea.

Black Tiger: For centuries there have been legends in India of a great black tiger, but zoologists dismissed them as unproven and probably the invention of a romantic writer. Then in October 1992 the hide of a pseudo-melanistic tiger was obtained from a hunter in South Delhi and, when measured, was eight and a half feet long. Just where this hunter (who was also a smuggler and therefore not particularly forthcoming) bagged this specimen is uncertain, but it at least provides proof that the Black Tiger is not just a product of literary whimsy. The hide of this great brute is on display at the National Museum of Natural History in New Delhi.

Blobs (Also Globster): Blobs are the nickname given to any of the several masses of unknown tissue washed up on beaches around the world, and particularly in Bermuda, New Zealand and Tasmania. Scientists often refer to any as-yet unknown beached carcass as a Globster; but the Blobs are a sub-group because of their more unusual nature, and because they have been much more difficult to ultimately classify. These Blobs can range in size from as small as eight feet across to as big as thirty feet; they lack skeletons, and they have very tough and stringy flesh. Some Blobs have a thin coating of hair, and many are roughly cylindrical in shape.

These rare forms of Blobs have become moderately famous in the world of cryptozoology. One such creature, known as Bermuda Blob, was discovered in 1988 by Teddy Tucker. When Tucker attempted to cut the seemingly gelatinous flesh he said it was like "trying to cut a car tire." This Blob also had five stumped appendages that might have been limbs or perhaps foreshortened tentacles. The Tasmanian Globster, discovered by Ben Fenton, Jack Boote, and Ray Anthony near the Interview River in western Tasmania in 1960 was twenty-feet long, eighteen feet wide, and appeared to have a slit-like mouth. Sadly, neither creature lingered long enough for adequate samples to be taken for lab analysis. They either decomposed or were washed away by tidal waters.

Blue Tiger (Also Maltese Tiger): Since 1910 there have been a number of sightings throughout the Fujian Province of China of a great hunting cat whose pelt was a striking Maltese blue in color. American Methodist missionary Harry R. Caldwell saw one and initially thought he was seeing a man wearing unusual blue garments, but then realized that it was indeed an animal. He attempted to shoot the creature, wanting to preserve its hide for scientific posterity, but there were a couple of children playing nearby and he couldn't risk their safety, so he withheld his shot.

Boobrie: In Scotland there are legends of a strange birdlike creature called the Boobrie --a beast with black wings, claws like human hands, black eyes that have a piercing stare capable of driving a man insane, and a large bill as long as a sword. The Boobrie is not a fishing bird, but instead prefers a diet of land animals, and when hungry enough will attack a boat

transporting livestock. Legends tell of them tearing through wooden rails and ripping apart nets and then flapping off into the night with a full-grown hog skewered on its beak. Some tales also tell of the Boobrie tearing apart a sailor or fisherman who tried to stop it from stealing the livestock.

Brosne: A 16-20 foot long lizard-like lake monster with luminous skin living in Lake Brosno frequently reported by residents of Benyok (a few hundred miles from Moscow, Russia). The Brosnie has been reported off and on for over 150 years, but only one photo of Brosnie has been published, but the picture is so badly blurred that it is nearly useless as evidence. And, yes, it's annoying that so many photos of these cryptids are blurry.

Bunyip: The Bunyip is a creature of Aboriginal myth with some of the qualities of a hellhound and is often described as being as big as a moderate sized calf. It lives in ponds and other spots where the waters are calm and for the most part it leaves people alone; but if its home or its territory is disturbed, the Bunyip can turn quite spiteful and savage.

The name "Bunyip" comes from the Aboriginal word for "spirit" and the Bunyip is an immortal and supernatural creature. The creature appears in the Aborigine Dreamtime stories and has been described in a variety of different ways: from a feathered creature not unlike an otter to a beast with flippers and walrus tusks.

Buru: The Buru is a cryptid infrequently spotted in the valleys between the Sub-Himalayas in India that sounds remarkably like a sauropod. According to the Apa Tanis, the people of that region, the Buru was a lizard that

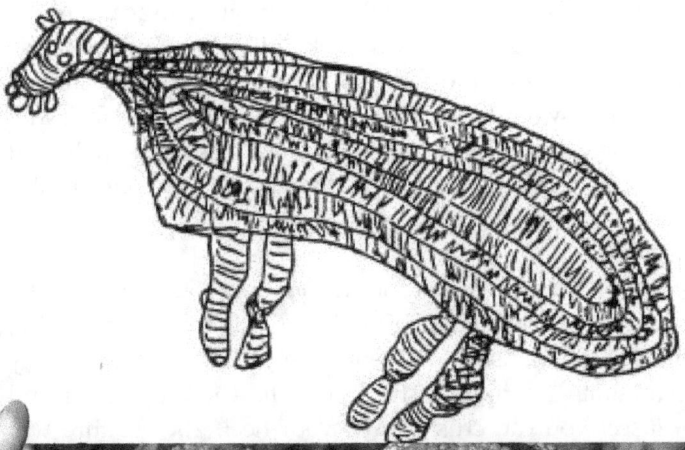

walked on two legs, had vestigial forelegs, a large tail that acted both as support when standing and a counterbalance when running, and had a large head with a big mouth filled with rows of sharp teeth. Its back was covered with shingled rows of armor plating; and its hide was a mottled blue-black in color except for its stomach, which was pale.

Caddy (also The Sea Hag): A giant sea creature spotted in 1920 in the waters of Cadboro Bay, near Vancouver Island, B.C., and seen frequently since. Described as a large serpentine beast 40 to 50 feet in length, with a ridged or knobbed spine and flippers shaped like those of a humpback whale, though not as large. When first spotted, the creature was called "the Sea Hag", a nod to the legends of the Old Hag known to appear in the dreams and folklore of many nations; but over the years the creature has come to be called "Caddy" and, like many lake monsters, is fondly regarded as a kind of local mascot. Caddy bears a striking resemblance to Ogopogo, a cryptid known to haunt nearby Lake Okanogan, and may be of the same species or even the same creature.

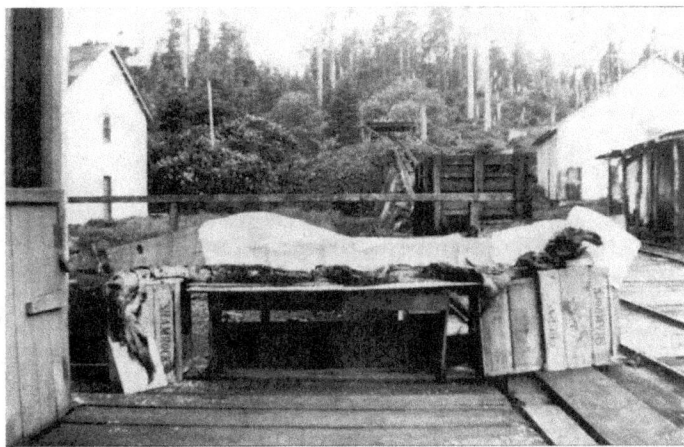

Canvey Island Monster: In August 1954 a man was walking along the beach of Canvey Island when he spotted a large mass covered in seaweed. Under the weed was a creature that, at first look, seemed to be a sea creature, but further examination revealed that it had hind legs like those of a biped. Each leg ended in reptilian feet shaped like a horse's hoof but with five toes and a concave arch. The creature was about thirty inches tall and had reddish-brown skin. Its head was soft, as if either it had no skull or its skull had soften through decomposition; and it had protruding eyes, sharp little teeth, and slits on its throat that appeared to be gills. Despite the presence of legs the creature had no arms or upper-torso fins.

Cartazonon: Folkloric unicorns are often a far cry from the symbols of beauty and innocence we see in Disney movies and fantasy novels. In India and parts Northern Africa, for example, there is a subspecies of unicorn called the Cartazonon that is decidedly aggressive and will kill anyone who tries to capture it, and will even attack humans and animals for no apparent reason. The African variety is particularly aggressive toward lions, and legends tell of the Cartazonon attacking a whole pride of lions and slaughtering them. The Cartazonon has reddish-yellow hair and a long and flowing mane. Its horn is very long and as black and shiny as basalt. No one has ever managed to capture one of these creatures alive and considering how vicious and powerful they are, few have even bothered to try.

Catoblepas: In Greek myth there are many hundreds of creatures, ranging from totally benign to absolutely malevolent. Many creatures are neither and are only threats when provoked, as with the case of the Catoblepas. The creature was described as a bull-like monster with an oversized head, a scaly body over which grew a long mane, and bloodshot eyes that were perpetually cast down. Its name, in fact translates as "that which looks downward".

Champ: Lake Champlain touches on parts of New York, Vermont and Quebec and is the home to "Champ", one of the few lake monsters apparently caught on film and that footage showed a creature with a thick body and a long tapering neck reminiscent of a plesiosaur. Since the plesiosaurs became extinct about 65 millions years ago the footage is a bit startling. The legend of Champ dates back to the Iroquois Indians who lived in that region, though in their tales the creature was a great horned monster. More recent sightings, however, do not describe horns of any kind. Reports of the monster started showing up in newspapers around 1873, when it was spotted by men laying railroad track near the town of Dresden in New York. The workers claim to have seen the head of "enormous serpent" rise up from the water and look at them. The men, wisely, fled. In August of that same year a small tourist ship was reported to have struck the creature and nearly capsized. The reports in the paper following the collision claim that passengers saw the creature on the surface of the water thirty or so yards from the ship. Showman P.T. Barnum put up a $50,000 reward for the "hide of the great Champlain serpent to add to my mammoth World's Fair Show," but never had to pay out the reward.

Chupacabra: Throughout Latin America there have countless reports of a strange creature –or race of creatures-- that viciously attack livestock and drink their blood and other vital fluids. Because goats were among the first victims of this beast the monster earned the nickname El Chupacabra, which translates as "sucker of goats". The Chupacabra is a bizarre being that has three powerful claws on each hand, a ruff of tall spines running from skull to tailbone, mottled skin, and a voracious appetite. The monster's face has been variously described as being like that of a kangaroo, a baboon, or a giant rat. In some reports the creature also has leathery wings, much like the Jersey Devil. There have been Chupacabra sightings and video evidence as recently as August of 2008 when a supposed Chupacaba was caught via the dashboard camera of a Texas lawman. However, this creature that reportedly "ran like no dog I've ever seen" according to the witnesses – and ran like "every dog we've ever seen" to the authors, so it's going to be a difficult call.

The earliest sightings of the Chupacabra were in Puerto Rico beginning in the early 1990s, but there are constant animal slaughters to this day associated with the Chupacabra. From 2000 to 2004 there have been nearly four thousand cases of unexplained animal mutilations in that small island territory. But the Chupacabra is not confined strictly to Puerto Rico. There have been sightings and mutilations all through Latin America. The official explanation in Puerto Rico is that packs of dogs are responsible for the attacks, or perhaps a panther or other big hunting cat illegally owned and released into the woods. As no traces of dogs or hunting cats have been found near the scenes of goat slaughters, this theory holds no more water than the dozens of other explanations floated by various groups. The Chupacabra sightings began shortly after a series of UFO sightings in the region (mostly over Mexico), and some fringe groups insist that aliens have --intentionally or accidentally- released an extraterrestrial predator animal that is now breeding and attacking terrestrial animals. This idea was explored briefly in an episode of the TV series, The X-Files (1993-2002). In UFO circles such creatures are referred to as Anomalous Biological Entities (UBEs).

Another theory is that crocodiles are behind it all, despite the fact that many of the killings are far inland and away from waterways. This idea carries a little weight because of the lurid tales of the "Vampire of Moca", the name given to an unknown "monster" attacking livestock back in 1975. As it turns out the vampire in question was actually a few crocodiles that strayed out of the swamp. But even then, they weren't as far away from the water as many of the Chupacabra have been. It is an interesting coincidence that the Vampire of Moca events also followed a spate of UFO sightings.

Con Rit: In Vietnam and surrounding countries there is a legend of a particularly frightening cryptid called the Con Rit, whose name translates as "centipede", which is unfortunately an accurate description. The Con Rit, however, is not the kind of insect you can crush under your heel. The creature was sighted repeatedly in 1883, and Tran Van Con, a native of Along Bay, Vietnam, claims to have seen the corpse of dead Con Rit washed up on the beach. He measured the carcass and recorded that it was three feet wide and a staggering sixty feet long.

Devil Bird (Also Ulama, Maha Bakamuna): The Devil Bird of Sri Lanka and India is one of the rare cases of a cryptid being moved from the limbo of folklore and onto the solid ground of the verified fossil record. This creature had been frequently sighted in the deepest and most inaccessible jungles of the mountain regions of India.

Dobhar-chú (Also Dobarcu, Doyarchu, and Dhuragoo): Dobhar-chú is the Gaelic name for a lake monster unlike Nessie or the standard saurian cryptids. The Dobhar-Chu earned its name ("water-hound") because it roughly resembles a dog, though it has a longer and sleeker body and teeth like an otter. From tooth to tail it measures about eight feet and is covered in thick white fur. The Dobhar-chú, however, is neither a playful otter nor man's best friend. This cryptid is a man-eater and there is quite a record of it attacking humans without provocation.

~~~~~~

Next time we'll continue with our hunt for Cryptids, UMAs and other beasties of the unknown!

ꙮꙮꙮ

quentin tarantino on django unchained

By Nick Freeman /
The Interview People

"My popularity around the world showed that the American Dream still works."

Quentin, You have Australian accents in the film, how did you come up with that?

Originally I wanted it to be a cool little collection of the Aussie guys from the 70s, like John Jarratt and Steve Bisbee. But the social aspect got cut out of the film. Those Aussies were actually indentured servants themselves. The Australian mining company paid for their trip over and they had to work that off for 3 or 4 years to pay them back. And Django realizes that they are slaves too, but at least he didn't have to pay for the boat ride.

Did the commercial success of Inglorious Basterds change anything for you?

It made me richer, all right. Other than the flush of success and the triumph…

Did it give you more confidence to push it further?

Maybe in my back pocket, without really thinking about it. Maybe if *Inglorious Basterds* hadn't worked, this would have been a harder sell.

How did you come up with the story?

The idea was a two-pronged thing. I wanted to tell a spaghetti western. And about eight years ago I figured out the way I wanted to tell it. I came up with the idea about a black man who was a slave and who became a bounty hunter. His job was to go to plantations looking for outlaws who were hiding there as overseers. That was eight years ago and it just sat sort of in an incubator, growing, waiting for the story to come up. It came to me at the very end of the press tour for Basterds in Japan, in a hotel. I was listening to a spaghetti western soundtrack and had no intention of going into my next project. I was going to take some time off. And suddenly it came to me. I didn't even have a notepad, so I wrote on Hotel stationary. And wrote it out and knew this was going to be my next movie.

And this fascination for the western, does it come from your childhood?

Definitely. I like all westerns, but especially spaghetti westerns. I think the first adult movies I can remember seeing was the Dollars Trilogy because my mother had a crush on Clint Eastwood. I saw all three of them. I remember going to a drive-in and seeing on the lower half of the double bill *A Day of Anger* with Lee Van Cleef and Giuliano Gemma. I have no recollection what the main film was but I've always remembered *A Day of Anger*.

You conceived the movie eight years ago, but at this moment in time there's a new consciousness in this country—with a black president. Is that a comment on American society?

I don't know if it's a comment on society. Consciously or subconsciously. But there's something in the air that connects. I think I would have come up with the story the same way, regardless of whether Obama had won the elections that time or not. But the fact that this is the case right now makes it all the more intriguing and provocative and that there's another movie out with Lincoln that deals with the same topic is even more fascinating.

Is it fair to say that you have a fascination with the underdog?

I guess I do. As far as my success in Hollywood goes I would definitely be an underdog story. My popularity around the world showed that the American Dream still works. I like the idea that in this case, telling this cathartic story with a historical setting, the characters I'm following are always the victims, who make it or not. I want to show that character become a hero, a vanquisher, and an avenger.

Some of the things you are trying to say could be stronger if you hadn't used the humor. Why is he doing target practice with a snow man, for example?

Why, do you want him to shoot at tin cans? Sitting on a log? I've seen that before. Frankly, I didn't just think that's a funny thing, he needs to shoot at a human figure. Actually one of the cleverest moments in the movie is that he figured out to stick

the bottle in the snowman to see if he shot the heart. When I came up with that I was like, wow, this is genius! I don't know if anyone did this before, but they should have.

Is loyalty important to you?

It's probably the most important thing. I'm part Italian but I wasn't really raised around my Italian family here in America, I'm not really into the whole Guido, Mamma Mia thing here in America. However, the one Italian part of me is loyalty. If I'm betrayed that's it. I shut the iron door on you.

Is it hard to find loyalty in this industry?

Not so much. I've had people I've worked with since my first movie. And people letting you down is not necessarily betraying you. Sometimes people do the wrong things for the wrong reasons. You have to have a good sense of self. You have to have compassion about the whole thing. Hollywood is a really good community to work in.

Usually you write very kick-ass women characters but here the girl is a damsel in distress.

I thought it was important, because it's Django's journey. I've not done a film where it's just one person's journey, maybe with the bride in *Kill Bill*. But the chapter's structure stops it from being a complete Odyssey. I thought it was important for her to be a princess in exile trapped in a tower by the evil emperor. I wanted to show Django on a romantic quest. He has his freedom, he's got money in his pocket, he doesn't need to go back for her. But he does to extract her. I thought that was a magnificent quest and shows a black man's love for his woman. She's not passive when we meet her, she's trying to escape on her own, she just can't do it.

Are your sets crazy?

They are not crazy, they are just fun. We're always laughing, playing music. Even when you make a heavy movie like this it can be a lot. The problem with epic filmmaking is the extreme weather conditions, the army, the people moving from one location to the other, etc. It's easy to forget why you wanted to make the movie in the first place. One thing that keeps everyone going is the camaraderie.

Is it usual for you to come up with the opening scene beforehand or do you decide on the set?]

The writing is the writing. Me and a pen and a piece of paper. If I'm happy with a script that's my safety net. Then I get on

THE NEW FILM BY
QUENTIN TARANTINO

DJANGO
UNCHAINED
2013

write characters that I like and then I look for people to fit them. Most people do that but they then look on a list of actors who have been in popular films lately. Even for the smaller parts and character parts. I don't do that. I have a huge long list of people I'd like to consider. All you have to do to be on that list is this: I have to like you and you have to be alive.

You've put a lot of German romanticism in the script like Wagner or Brunhilde.

When I was writing the script, about 50 pages into it, Christoph Waltz came to visit me. They had a big production of Wagner's Ring cycle in Los Angeles and he was inviting me to come see the first Opera. So we were going to see the second one. Before, we were going to dinner, and he's telling me the story of the first one, the story of Siegfried and Wotan and Brunhilde. Then we watched the second Opera and while watching—Kerry Washington's name was already Brunhilde but not in regards to this legend—but while I was watching I noticed the similarities between the two stories. I liked it so much and I found it so apropos. But then I didn't want to see the third Opera not to be influenced too much while writing my script.

So, who came first, Christoph or King?

Christoph, because I can honestly say I didn't consciously come up with a German dentist bounty hunter from Düsseldorf in the Wilde West all by myself. When I came up with that scene, he was just there. He just flowed out of the pen. I must have channeled Christoph.

You were saying how much fun you like to have on set. Do you select people accordingly?

As much as I can. Whenever I hear oh, they are difficult, grumpy, a bit of a jerk but it's ok, they're worth it, I don't buy it. There are enough nice people that are good actors that I'd like to work with. I always want to work with people I like.

The shot party doesn't help.

Every 100 rolls of films we do a shot party.

How about award season? Do you think about that?

We're throwing it in in the middle of the season hoping that we get nominations and win trophies. If not, we would have opened in March or went to Cannes with it in June.

So, do you ever get writer's block?

I've never had writer's block. It might take me a while to come up with a new story. But once I know what I want to write about, it just flows out.

the set and just create. It's always about getting the best out of a scene. I don't do storyboards, I don't do that pre-vis, that's crazy, maybe I do a shot list at the most. But for the most part I show up on set and do rehearsal scenes and that's about it, and I make it up as I go along.

The movie that came to my mind was Blazing Saddles.

I never thought it was that kind of absurd humor going on. That movie is a spoof and I don't think of my film as a spoof.

How come you remembered Don Johnson for a role?

I've always been a big Don Johnson fan. Even in the 70s, 10 or 11 years before *Miami Vice*. I saw him in that hippie movie *The Magic Garden of Stanley Sweetheart*, one of his first leads, or *Zacharia*, the first rock'n'roll western. I saw him in the theater in *The Boy and His Dog* and he had a really cool car movie, *The Return of Macon County* with Nick Nolte. That made me a big fan of his. And I followed him on TV. By the time he became a star in *Miami Vice* I'd already been a fan.

I was wondering what your movie library looks like, now that we're digitally downloading movies…

I don't do digital downloads, I don't like to watch a movie on a computer. I still have my laser disc library, tons of videos, DVDs, I don't have that many blue rays. It takes me a long time to switch formats.

You have resurrected the careers of (John) Travolta and now Don Johnson. Do you get calls from actors who need a career boost?

It doesn't quite work like that. It comes from the fact that I

DJANGO
UNCHAINED

The Holy Hippy Horror of Alejandro Jodorowsky

By Aaron J. French
(with the assistance of Ron and Kristina)

Alejandro Jodorowsky

Psychomagic
The Transformative Power of
Shamanic Psychotherapy

THEL'S MOTTO

Does the Eagle know what is in the pit?
Or wilt thou go ask the Mole?
Can Wisdom be put in a silver rod?
Or Love in a golden bowl?

—The Book of Thel,
William Blake, 1789

"People say I am mad. I am not mad. I am trying to heal my soul."
—Alejandro Jodorowsky

Profound words from film director and counterculture icon Alejandro Jodorowsky, whose autobiographical book *The Spiritual Journey of Alejandro Jodorowsky: The Creator of "El Topo,"* published by Park Street Press in 2008, serves to illustrate that, while healing himself he is doing—still alive at age 84—mad also is he. His seminal work, the film *El Topo*, could easily be described as *Have Gun – Will Travel* on LSD, with its gaudy surrealism and horrendous violence—not to mention it is one of the best cinematic examples of the horror western trope *done right* (this being our current theme, of course).

But behind all the druggy hilarities, Mexican environments, and bloody blown-out kneecaps, there is a message of profound Christian symbolism and Eastern philosophy, reflecting the bizarre and intriguing spiritual journey of the film's director.

In the first scene El Topo (played by Jodorowsky himself) instructs a naked seven-year-old boy to bury his first toy along with a picture of his mother, for because he is seven, the boy is now a man. Moments later, the boy puts a bullet in the chest of a dying villager at the command of El Topo, in a corpse-littered town that has been wiped out by insane bandits. Together, they set out to kill the perpetrators, which they accomplish, however El Topo later abandons his son to missionary monks and rides off with a slave woman whom he christens Mara.

Mara convinces El Topo to defeat the four greatest gunmen in the land, each symbolically representing a particular religion or philosophy. El Topo learns a great deal from each of these gunmen, about life and spirituality, before defeating them separately in a duel, though not through superior skill, but rather through trickery and some good fortune. El Topo is then wounded in highly symbolic fashion, being shot multiple times in the manner of the stigmata, by an unknown woman.

After he is wounded, he is taken underground by a group of mutants and dwarves. The second half of the film depicts El Topo as being worshiped by these dwarf mutants as a godlike figure, similar to Mr. Kurtz in Conrad's *Heart of Darkness*. El Topo, now spiritually reborn and awakened, having survived the stigmata wounds, vows to liberate the mutants from their cavernous underground prison. He even takes a female dwarf as his lover.

Seeking further assistance, El Topo is reunited with his son, who is now a priest in the neighboring town. Together, the three of them—El Topo, priest son, and now-pregnant dwarf lover—manage to free the outcast mutants. But as they enter the town, they are all shot down by the villagers, and El Topo, helplessly forced to witness the massacring of his "people," sets fire to himself with an oil lamp. At the end the son, in his father's clothes, with the female dwarf ride off together after burying El Topo.

The film is a fascinating mix of endless creativity, sex and violence, and esoteric symbolism. Enter the strange and bizarre world of Alejandro Jodorowsky. For those interested in penetrating deeper into the mind that created this iconic film, *The Spiritual Journey of Alejandro Jodorowsky* is the place to begin. The book details the very real, very sincere, and very unconventional path to spiritual enlightenment taken by the ever-adventurous Jodorowsky.

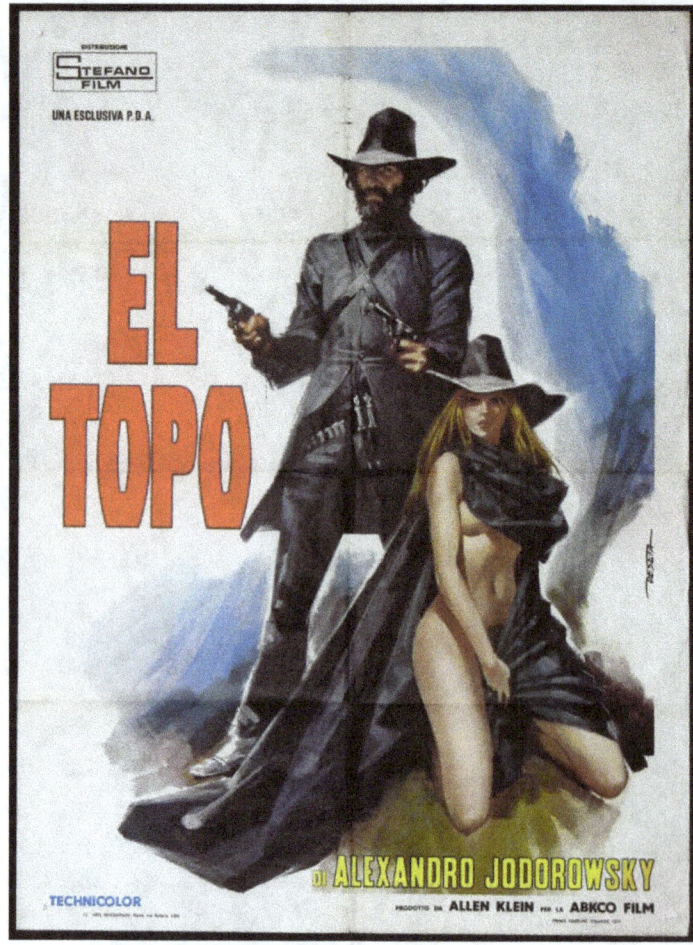

His lifelong quest began with the Japanese master Ejo Takata, the monk who introduced him to the practice of meditation, Zen Buddhism, and the wisdom of koans. Yet Jodorowsky reveals it was a group of four women—synchronistically (Jungian) related to the four master gunmen in El Topo—who initiated him into the practical wisdom of the koans (like Zen mantras) and the secrets of life—and what he would later term Psychomagic (a system that combines art, Eastern philosophies, mysticism and psychotherapy to heal patients with emotional problems).

At the direction of Takata, Jodorowsky went to meet the surrealist painter Leonora Carrington, the first of the four "wisewomen," as well as the most "innocent" of the four spiritual relationships. Next, perhaps the most abrasive of the women, was the powerful Mexican actress and singer Irma Serrano, known as *La Tigresa* (or the Tigress). Serrano had breast implants, hip and butt implants, and even hair implants that made her furry like a tiger. She was meaner than a bed of nails (according to Jodorowsky), dabbling in cannibalism, an episode recounted in the book where she actually *eats* tacos made from male human flesh.

From there he met Dona Magdalena, who taught him "initiatic" or spiritual massage techniques. The story goes that Jodorowsky was walking along the street when several young male prostitutes propositioned him. He responded by calling them derogatory names, and the group of boys attacked him, dragging him into a nearby alley. Magdalena, who had been watching from her upstairs apartment window, came down and interrupted the gangbang already in progress by yelling out, "*Boys!*" After the young prostitutes had scattered, she helped Jodorowsky back to her apartment, where she cared for him and told him that she knew he was on a spiritual journey.

Finally there was Reyna D'Assia, daughter of the famed spiritual teacher G. I. Gurdjieff. D'Assia took Jodorowsky to an old Indian shaman, who gave them both psychedelic mushrooms. During their "trip," which lasted three days, the shaman raped D'Assia while Jodorowsky, helplessly stoned, could only sit by and watch. Maria Sabina, famous priestess of the sacred mushrooms, also played a small but important part in Jodorowsky's development. The experiences he had with these women enabled him to relinquish his emotional armor, and to advance along the path to spiritual enlightenment.

Jodorowsky went on to make many more bizarre and interesting films, including *The Holy Mountain* (1973), *Tusk* (1980), and *Santa Sangre* (1989), as well as numerous nonfiction books on subjects ranging from neo-shamanism to the *Tarot de Marseille*, numerous plays, and even a series of comic books. Yet it is important to remember the source behind the creativity, the endless psychological dramas (and traumas) that Jodorowsky experienced, providing him with the material from which he would sculpt his outré and singular creations.

This lends testimony to the assertion that life is the source of true art, and that everything which is created afterward is only a reflection of experience, recalling Blake's proclamation: "The man who never in his mind and thoughts travel'd to Heaven is no artist." And a great way to see this process in action is to watch Jodorowsky's excellent horror western film, *El Topo*.

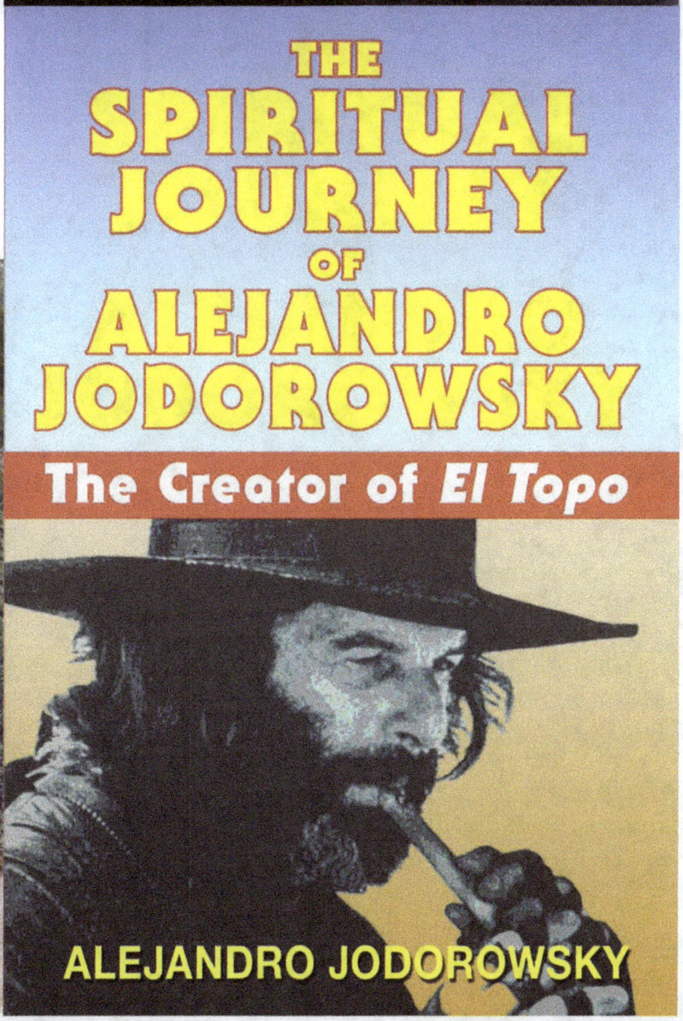

🜂🜂🜂

UNGRATEFUL PLACES

By Gary A. Braunbeck

"Once a fool was soundly thrashed during the night and the next day everyone made fun of him. 'You should thank God,' he said, 'that the night was clear; otherwise I would have played such a trick on you!' 'What trick? Tell us!' 'I would have hidden myself.'"

–17th Century Russian Fable

His name was Edward Something-or-Other and though everyone in the village recognized him on sight no one really knew much about him, except that he was a large and strong young man who was always willing to do odd jobs for reasonable pay, that he never spoke an ill word against anyone, and that he went off to war one cold and foggy September morning where he eventually saved many of his fellow soldiers from certain death, was given many medals, hailed a hero and great warrior, and came home with no face. But by then he had been gone for so long that no one in the village could remember what he'd looked like before war had broken out.

To say he had no face is a bit of an exaggeration; he had eyes for he could see, and he had eardrums because he could hear but no ears to speak of, just bits of dangling, discolored flesh on the sides of his head. The skin which formed his cheeks had been grafted on from flesh the doctors removed from his thighs, and though he was told that everything would heal over and appear normal Some Day Soon, it still hurt him to walk or smile; walking was something he could not avoid, but not so smiling. His nose was gone, as well; his nostrils were two small skeletal caves that were often blocked and forced him to breathe through his mouth, which in turn dried up his throat and made it difficult—sometimes even impossible—for him to swallow; as a result, he was often hoarse and coughed frequently. Gone also were his teeth but his jaw remained intact and his gums were firm, making it possible for him to wear dentures. Sometimes, though, when he talked—which he rarely did, due to his hoarseness, and also because his difficulty in swallowing caused him to drool—the dentures would slip a little and click and whomever he was talking with would make sorry work of hiding their amusement.

And so Edward Something-or-Other, heroic warrior and village handyman, began to speak less and less, until, at last, he spoke not at all... except to the priest.

Everyone in the village took to calling him only "Soldier Boy," and found much humor in it. Edward Something-or-Other merely nodded his head and went about his business. He took to wearing a bandage on the space where his nose used to be. The bandage reached the back of his head and was kept in place with a safety pin. He covered the lower half of his face with a long gray scarf, which he liked to imagine flowed in the wind behind him as he walked, like in the old photos and drawings he'd seen of the aviators in their planes as they flew over the battlefields of Europe. Perhaps, he fantasized, people would see him walking with his flowing scarf and think to themselves, "This is an heroic-looking fellow, and I know he was in the war and was given many medals, perhaps he deserves more respect than we have given to him."

But this never happened.

People left him alone, save for those times when a merchant in the village needed something repaired, or hauled away, or a local farmer needed someone to help spread fertilizer. Edward Something-or-Other was the boy for the job; quiet, a bit disturbing in appearance but seemingly pleasant in nature, no job too hard or too dirty or too undignified.

The odd jobs became sparse, so Edward Something-or-Other, under the name "Soldier Boy," became a fighter with a local carnival. He wore a mask and boxing trunks and was said to be able to knock out any and all challengers before the end of Round One. This he did three times a day, six days a week, throughout the spring and summer. He was always careful never to hit any of his opponents in the face for fear he might leave permanent damage; a good, solid blow to the center of the chest usually did it. "Soldier Boy" was never once knocked down, never lost a fight, and made a great deal of money as a result, though he continued to live as he always had: frugally, in a small and sparse room, continuing to do odd jobs in the village whenever they were offered.

Still, there times, late at night as he lie in his bed trying to remember what his old face had looked like, when he longed to hear the cheering of the crowds as he fought. There, in the ring—even if it was with the carnival—he was, for a little while, admired and cheered as a hero, and no one cared what he looked like.

But like the scarf and his hopes it gave him the air of a hero, it was only something to cheer him a little before he fell into sleep, a little something to help keep the bad dreams away.

The village grew as more children were born and they, in turn, grew to have families of their own. Every summer people came to cheer "Soldier Boy" as he fought his opponents in the ring at the carnival. He was so tall and strong that tiny children would ask to climb on him as if he were a mountain. Edward enjoyed the children, their laughter, the touch of their warm and affectionate hands on his arms, the way they would hug him.

Those who had been alive when he returned from the war grew old and died; only a few remained, and their memories grew dim and fragmented.

"Who is the big fellow who wears the scarf?" younger villagers would ask.

"I don't quite remember," the older ones would reply. "I think he was a hero in the war or something."

"Why does he hide his face?"

Then they would remember: "Because he doesn't have one. That's 'Soldier Boy.' "

Children stopped wanting to play with him after that.

One morning, after cleaning up a local merchant's basement after heavy rains had caused the sewers to back up, Edward Something-or-Other was drinking a glass of water (being careful to hold the rim of the glass under his scarf) when the merchant asked of him: "Did you see many men die during the war?"

Edward Something-or-Other looked at a space in the air as if it contained a window only he could see through, and beyond this window he seemed to see something that haunted him and made him sadder than he was, and instead of answering the merchant with words, he gave a slow nod of his head, but his eyes betrayed that there was much more to his silence and melancholy than this gesture revealed.

What he did not speak of to the merchant that day, what he dared not tell anyone except the priest, was this: he suspected that he was not supposed to have lived, that he somehow had been accidentally passed over by Death that day on the battlefield when the shells were screaming and the mortars exploding and the mines reducing men to chunks of searing meat.

And he suspected this because of the ghosts.

Now, whether they were actual ghosts, he was not at first certain. He only knew that one night, while he sat in his room reading and listening to his tiny radio, a dog began to howl outside his window. The dog sounded frightened, and so Edward Something-or-Other went outside (taking care to first don the scarf so his face would not alarm anyone who might happen by) and lifted the dog in his strong arms. The animal continued to stare down the darkened street and whine, then snarl, and, at last, bury its head in the crook of Edward's arm.

A procession of figures came out of the darkness, walking without sound, all of them carrying burning candles. As they passed by the opened door of Edward's room, he saw that they were all figures of dead soldiers, many of which he had stepped or fallen over on the battlefield. Some were missing arms, others legs, and many, like Edward himself, were missing parts of their faces. It was these figures—those missing facial features—who slowed their step as they passed by his doorway and nodded to him like old friends. They spoke to him, whispering secrets, imparting promises.

At last one of them—an older man, missing forehead and one eye—broke away from the procession and came toward Edward and gave him a lighted candle.

"Keep this nearby," he said to Edward, "and the next time we pass through this ungrateful place, give it back to me."

And with that, he fell back into the procession of dead soldiers and followed them through the streets of the village and into the darkness of eternity.

Edward took both the candle and the dog inside. He allowed the dog to sleep at the foot of his bed. The candle he placed on his nightstand and let it burn through the night as he slept.

He kept hearing the old man's voice calling the village an "ungrateful place," kept seeing the hatred that was in his eyes as he said it, listening as the night carried echoes of the disgust in his voice.

Or perhaps that was all part of his dreams.

***

When he woke the next morning, he saw that sometime during the night the candle had changed into the faceplate of a skull.

The dog at the foot of the bed would not look upon the face. It growled when Edward tried to touch it, then bolted out the door and down the road in the same direction taken by the ghosts.

And it was then Edward Something-or-Other realized that he had been destined to die in battle and not come home with this grotesque remnant of a face.

He went to confession and spoke to the priest. Edward spoke slowly, for his dentures and hoarseness made speech difficult, as did the drooling because he could not swallow at all today. He also spoke in this manner because the priest was now so very old and had trouble hearing.

"Father, they told me that if I were to solve the riddle of the Old Man's Candle, then they would give me back my face."

"Your actual face?" asked the priest.

Edward hesitated a moment before answering. "No, Father, not exactly. One said he would give to me his ears for the sides of my head; another promised me his nose so that I would no longer have to wear this bandage; and yet another said that he would give me his teeth so I wouldn't have to wear these dentures and pretend to not notice when the people laughed at me because sometimes they become loose and click."

"Do you believe them to be ghosts?"

"Yes, Father. I recognized some of them from their bodies on the battlefield."

"This riddle you speak of—"

"The Riddle of the Old Man's Candle."

"—yes. Do you know its solution?"

"No. The candle, Father, it...it changed during the night."

"How did it change?"

"It became... well...." Edward reached into his sack and removed the faceplate and showed it to the priest.

"Lord save us," the priest whispered.

"I know what it is, Father," said Edward. "It is the bone of my face as it will appear when it has been healed and made whole again."

The priest gave the faceplate back to Edward, who, feeling embarrassed and humiliated, slipped it quickly back into his bag.

"Do you read your Bible, Edward?"

"Yes, Father."

"Do you remember what Jesus said to the leper who asked that He heal the sores which covered his body?"

"No, Father, I don't."

"Jesus said: 'Heed not the clay countenance that is the flesh, for bright be the face of the soul.'"

Edward said nothing for several moments.

"Edward?"

"Yes, Father?"

"Do you believe that, if these spirits indeed are real, that they will keep their word?"

"I'm not sure, but I suspect not."

"Ah—you still believe that you were meant to die that day in battle?"

"Yes."

The priest then was silent, deep in thought and seemingly troubled by what he was about to say. At last, he leaned forward and whispered: "This is what you must do, Edward; take a candle from the altar and I shall bless it for you. Take that candle home and light it and then set it upon the face of the skull you have shown to me. Allow the wax to melt so that it covers the entire face, let it dry and harden, and then set three more candles on it—two on the sides, to represent where your ears should be, and one in the center, to show where your nose once was. Do this, and then wait for the spirits to return to you. Only then should you light the three candles and return it to the old man."

Edward did as the priest instructed.

Autumn passed into winter, and then came spring and still the sprits had not returned.

Edward Something-or-Other came to believe deep in his heart that he was not meant to be here, and wondered how many more there might be who were like him, if they too ached for company as they lived out their days in ungrateful places.

Summer arrived, and with it the carnival and the rides and the ring and the return of "Soldier Boy"—only now there were not so many to cheer his battles. He fought well but without the energy of years past. He was knocked down once by a young man from another village, but managed to rise and defeat his opponent.

He looked once into the crowd and saw, sitting among the spectators, those spirits whose faces were as incomplete as his own.

He knew they would be coming for him soon.

Summer passed into autumn and with its passing came the dry, whispering leaves which skittered along the streets during the day and gathered in dark corners at night.

It was on just such a chill and whispering autumn night that the dog returned to Edward's window, howling.

"How are you, old friend?" asked Edward as he came outside and lifted the dog into his arms. He wore neither the scarf tonight nor the bandage; his face was, for the first time in many decades, exposed fully to the world... but no one was there to see it.

The dog buried its face in the crook of Edward's arm as the procession of the dead came out of the darkness, their candles burning bright.

This time, however, they did not pass Edward's

door but began to gather around. The old man who had given Edward the candle stepped forward and smiled, then asked of him: "Do you have the candle which I gave to you?"

"Yes," replied Edward, and produced from behind his back the wax-covered faceplate, now decorated with three burning candles.

The old man smiled and took the burning face from Edward, holding it high for the others to see.

"'Bright be the face of the soul,'" said the old man; then, turning to Edward, said: "You have solved my riddle, Edward Howe. You have offered your soul to save your village as you once risked your life to save your fellow soldiers." He handed the burning face back to Edward.

It had been so long since Edward had heard his true last name spoken by anyone that he did not at first recognize it; nor did the words "...save your village" at first register.

"You shall be rewarded," continued the old man, "in two ways: first, we shall not, as we were supposed to do, take you with us."

"So it's true, then," whispered Edward. "I *was* supposed to die that day?"

"Yes, but no matter now, you shall grow to be a very, very old man, and let us hope that it will be a happy life from this night on. Touch your face, Edward."

He did, and discovered that it was now whole and healed; ears, cheeks, teeth, nose, skin—it was a normal face, one that he would never again have to hide behind masks or scarves.

"I am whole again," he said, startled by the sound of his voice, its fullness, its richness and timbre. For the first time in decades he pulled in a deep breath through his nose; there was no pain.

"Secondly," said the old man, "you shall now be the only true face in your village."

"What do you—?" But before he could complete the question, there came from a nearby window a scream of singular horror, and soon a woman ran into the street clutching her face. She spun around, eyes wide with terror, and pulled away her hands to reveal that she had no nose, only a smooth, flat area of flesh.

Soon other villagers spilled into the street, all of them missing facial features, some who now had no faces at all, merely blank ovals of flesh where their features should have been.

"No!" cried Edward.

"Why?" asked the old man. "Look at us, Edward Howe. Fallen warriors, all of us. Some of us died in battle, but many of us, like yourself, returned home scarred and disfigured, only to find ourselves mocked outcasts. 'Abomination!' they

called us. Well, now, let *them* know how it feels to be the one who is mocked, who is scorned and turned away from, who never again knows the warm touch of a friend, the kiss of a woman's lips upon their own, the feel of a child's loving arms around their necks. We have traveled from village to village to find others just like you, Edward, and they have all accepted our bargain. So many years since the war, and how easily those who never knew battle forget the sacrifices we made for them. Let them know now."

Edward saw the people of his village running, screaming, crying, clutching at their ruined or missing faces, and for a moment, just one moment, a moment he would never forgive himself for, Edward Howe, formerly Edward Something-or-Other and "Soldier Boy," felt a brief, bright satisfaction in their pain; but a moment later he realized just how wrong this was and thrust out the burning face. "No. If this is the price of having a normal face restored to me, I do not want it; and if it means that you take my soul and I come with you now, then so be it. Return everything as it was and you can take my soul. I will not fight you. The wars are over. I have no desire to fight again."

The old man took the burning face and an instant later, the villagers found their faces restored to them. None looked in Edward's direction; even if they had, none would have seen the spirits surrounding him.

"So I come with you now?"

The old man shook his head. "Not now, but soon enough. A season or three. Listen to the wind, and you'll hear our approach in the whisper of leaves across the cobblestones. Good-bye, Edward Howe. Enjoy your isolation and grotesquerie."

They left him there, alone save for the dog, and he watched them vanish up the road toward eternity.

His throat was dry and his nostril cavities were blocked. It was time to take some medicine and try to sleep.

The dog followed Edward into his room and slept at the foot of his new master's bed, where he would sleep for the rest of his days. Years later, upon Edward's death, the dog would be found sleeping at the foot of his master's grave and would refuse to move. It would lay there until it, too, passed away, and would be buried alongside its master.

But that was many years away.

The next morning, everyone in the village was talking about the horror of the previous night, wondering what they could have done to offend God so badly that He would punish them in such a way.

"But He did not make the punishment permanent," said one merchant.

"True," replied a cook. "It was as if he were... warning us."

"Or reminding us," said the priest.

"Reminding us of what?"

The priest said nothing, only glimpsed for a moment toward the doorway where Edward stood, scarf and bandage in their place, his dog at his feet.

Later that day, someone left a fresh-baked apple pie on the sill of Edward's open window.

The next morning, he found a tray with a delicious breakfast waiting outside his door. The odd jobs began to become plentiful again. Sometimes children would stop and ask him about his scarf and bandage.

In their sleep, the villagers would often dream of Edward sacrificing his soul for them so they would never know the loneliness of having a face like his.

They began speaking to him, and, eventually, he began to speak in return. He was invited to attend church socials, to join in a game of cards or come to a village picnic.

Toward the end of his life, he stopped wearing the scarf and bandage. The villagers took to carrying extra handkerchiefs with them so that they might have one should Edward need it on a day when swallowing was difficult for him.

He took his medals out of their box and put them in a case and that case was put on display in the village hall.

He had many friends in the village who grew to love and respect him.

When Edward passed away quietly in his sleep, the village closed all of its schools and shops for the day so that everyone could attend his funeral. The day was pleasant but slightly overcast and warm.

Near his grave, there was found an oddly-shaped candle holder with three candles in it. Attached to it was a note which read: *Some Burn Too Brightly For Us to Take.*

As it was placed on the lid of Edward's coffin, the sun emerged from behind the clouds and the day became as bright as anyone in the village had ever seen.

There were tears, and later there was the business with Edward's poor dog, but, for generations to come, there was also a tale to pass along to the children; some of it based on fact, some on supposition, some of it on dreams, but it, like its subject, would be remembered, if not forever, then for long enough.

It began: *His name was Edward Something-or-Other and though everyone in the village recognized him on sight no one really knew much about him, except that he was a large and strong young man who was always willing to do odd jobs for reasonable pay, that he never spoke an ill word against anyone....*

☠☠☠

ONCE UPON A NIGHTMARE

YA HORROR: WESTERN HORROR

By Amy Shane

In the young adult industry, westerns, as well as horror westerns, are literally something that I haven't found much on the shelves. While doing research for this month's article, it highlighted the fact that there is a lack of westerns in YA literature. This meant I was back to the drawing board on what I was going to write for this issue.

While horror has become a staple in our society, so should western horror. For the Wild West is the history upon which our country is based.

Our roots come from the gun-slinging days of stagecoaches, ghost towns, and gold mines, where their only protection was the law, their horses and a single-action revolver. Which renders the question: How did they protect themselves from the ghosts haunting their dwellings?

I live in one of the most famous areas of the western gold rush. With computer in hand, I went off on a search, looking for haunted ghost towns and legends still remaining from the gold rush days. A few strikes of the keyboard and I was in luck. With more than ten haunted ghost towns in the near vicinity, I had plenty to choose from. However, there was one in particular that stood out in my mind: the legend of the haunted Pioneer Cemetery of Coloma, CA. Not only is it a cemetery, but it is also haunted by the famed ghost named "*The Lady in Burgundy.*" With many shows such as the *Haunted Highway, Gold Rush Ghosts, Haunted Hotels,* and even celebrity psychic Nancy Bradley, researching these phenomena, there had to be some merit behind the ghost.

The Lady in Burgundy is not only a local legend, but a national one as well. She has been seen by many a passerby, as well as many visitors of the cemetery. The best part is that she is not seen only in the twilight hours of the evening, but also in the daytime. She has been described as a woman with dark coal-black hair that has been parted in the middle and pulled back into a tight conservative bun, wearing a simple white collared shirt, dating back to the 1800s, as well as a long burgundy flowing skirt. What's most amazing about this ghost is the fact that those who have seen her remark on the color of her checks, the coal black of her hair, and the vivid illumination of her flowing skirt.

The Lady in Burgundy not only appears to those traveling past the cemetery, she also beckons to them from the roadside, motioning for them to follow her. *The Lady in Burgundy* is a woman with an unknown identity, however what everyone *does* know, is that she faithfully haunts the tombstone of Charles Schieffer as well as his two children William and May. When people follow her up the incline to the cemetery, she walks directly to the headstone of what can only be her former beloved. Leaving those to question her motives and why she always returns to stand beside Charles, what she wants has never been determined, as she disappears before getting her message across.

It appears, through research, that Charles's wife Eliza is buried at the same cemetery, but in another plot with her daughter Catherine, under her remarried name of Taylor. Could this be the ghostly image we see, a wife and mother longing to be laid to rest next to her husband and their children?

This only left me to go and investigate for myself, looking for the sites of famous ghost stories that would make incredible young adult novels. When I arrived at the Pioneer Cemetery, it was a crisp cold afternoon. It only took a few moments to find the tombstone of Charles Schieffer, being one of the largest family plots and headstones therein. While I stood at the graveside, an unsettling air overtook the area, but unfortunately there weren't any sightings of the lady herself. While there were no other disguising factors that stood out, the only thing I noticed was a well-worn path from the roadside directly to the grave. I don't believe a ghost could wear a path in the dirt, so I can only believe that many patrons have been lured from the roadside to the gravesite of Charles.

Just across the street from the cemetery lies the overgrown, crumbling home of the Vineyard House, which — you guessed it! — is also famed to be haunted. Reportedly, one of the spookiest homes in the county, and perhaps one of the saddest. Legend has it that the Vineyard House was built by Robert and Louise Chalmers and became one of the finest hotels in all of Northern Ca., even housing former president Ulysses S. Grant. A successful crop of grapevines were planted and success was theirs.

However, in 1879, just one year after completion, Robert Chalmers went mad, becoming quick-tempered and

frightening, even reportedly being seen lying in freshly dug graves across the street at the Pioneer Cemetery. For his own "protection" his wife Louise built a cell within the cellar in which she chained him, where he eventually starved to death. After his death, the family's livelihood and crop of grapevines mysteriously withered away, leaving Louise no choice but to take on boarders to make a living, as well as rent out the cellar as a jail, and even allow hangings to be conducted in her front yard. Soon, the livelihood of the Inn would vanish, along with the residents and patrons of the hotel. Subsequently they all became so spooked by the shimmering apparitions and the sounds of rattling chains that no one would live or even stay there. According to many websites, apparitions have been seen in the house, as well as voices being heard, and glasses have shattered with no apparent cause. Many believe Robert and Louise, as well as a few fateful guests, are still among those permanently residing within.

With private owners now occupying the house, visitors are not permitted on the grounds. The ill-weathered, paint-chipped, vine-covered home would have to pacify me, as I stood in the driveway contemplating the two local legends situated mere feet from one another. The Vineyard House, a place where you can check in, but surely you can't check out. I was happy to pass on this one.

Instead, I went to check out yet another haunted hotel in Placerville, called the Carey House. Upon entering the Carey House, the old-time vintage charm was apparent. Displays of original room keys, hotel nostalgia lining the display cabinets, and well-polished dark furniture led to an air of richness, giving the feeling of a posh, sophisticated hotel. However, with that being said, the lobby is not what you would expect. It's small, dark, and kept very straightforward, with little more than a few couches and a roped-off piano. While most lobbies are open and welcoming, this one was quite the opposite.

The Carey House exudes an aura that makes it feel more like a place of reverence than an inviting hotel. Even on a bright afternoon, without a cloud in the sky, the lobby was dark and dank, with curtains drawn, lit only by small table lamps, setting the perfect environment for a ghost to wander through. While the manager was hesitant at first, I was eventually allowed the rare opportunity to take one photograph, of one side, of the famed haunted staircase. With its ongoing fame, many stories have surfaced, causing fables to twist the facts of the local legend, making the hesitation understandable. Yet, when asked to confirm the story behind the famous ghost Stan, the manager chose not to comment, which leaves me to report only what has been already published on the Internet.

The Carey House is haunted by a friendly and often mischievous ghost named Stan. A regular stop for stagecoaches, the Carey House was open to many types of travelers, which suited Stan, the desk clerk, just fine. Rumored to be quite flirtatious, this ultimately became his demise, when Stan flirted with the wrong person. This is where the stories collide. There are two about how Stan got himself in a bit of trouble. It is said he made a pass at a woman on the staircase leading up to the rooms, however her husband did not appreciate the advance and stabbed poor Stan right there on the staircase, killing him instantly. However, it is also reported that Stan made a pass at a gentleman traveling up the staircase to his room, where he responded by stabbing poor Stan to death on the staircase.

Whatever story you choose to believe, they both end in the same way, leaving Stan to eternally keep up with his flirtatious ways, where he is reported to "pinch" the bottoms of patrons in the lobby. The Carey House is also rumored to house at least three more ghosts on the grounds. The manager remarked "that all their ghosts were nice," which was a welcome change from the last hotel. Although the manager was not full of details, she did remark that the Carey House will be hosting a paranormal convention in March of 2014, for those of you in the Northern California area who would like to experience the phenomenon for yourselves. However, for me, the picture I took of the staircase is proof enough of Stan's existence. If you look at the top left-hand corner of the staircase (see arrow) you can see an image that was not rendered into the photograph. Could this be Stan? You be the judge.

All these experiences have me thinking, why do we choose the sub-genres we often choose? The one thing that does stay current through it all is, of course, the horror. With that being said, the stories that resonate from the time of the western days would make incredible storylines for young adult books, since YA fiction is often the retelling of old legends. Wild West fables and legends have been passed down for generations, and many have horrific twists. Drawing upon such fables would make westerns all the more delightful in the end.

❧ ❧ ❧

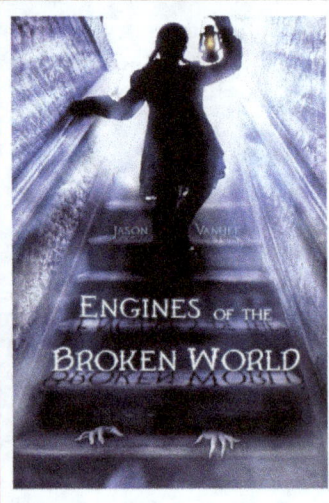

Engines of the Broken World
by Jason Vanhee
Henry Holt & Co.
ISBN-13: 978-0805096293
November 2013; $16.99,

_Wickedly haunting from
the first breath…_

What an ironic place for a beginning… at the end of everything. Merciful and her brother Gospel thought it was just the two of them at the end of their own little world, until the dead rose from the basement to tell them otherwise. In a world that's growing increasing thin and frail, Merciful and Gospel must find a way to remain. Even if that means embracing the words of the animal-like minister and listening to the dead ramblings of the creature living inside their dead mother's body.

Caught in the space between child and adult, Merciful and Gospel must make decisions that affect their lives but also that of the world. When their mother dies, their world seems to die with her. Surrounded by snow, and trapped within their home, the cold creeps in all around them. Quickly, Merciful and Gospel find that they are running out of supplies to survive, other than the old widow who is walking-distance away, they are without a soul to run to.

With the body of their dead mother under the table in the cellar, guilt rises up in Merciful's throat, and slowly begins to choke her, while her dead mother's distant lullaby haunts her. All the while, the one thing they need to fear is the more sinister holy minister, who preaches from his animal form. One who watches with his yellow eyes, leaving discontentment and uneasiness, making sure God's rules are enforced at any extent.

With echoes of the dead haunting them, they soon realize that they are the last ones living in a broken world. One that is so lonely and corrupt, that even God himself has turned his back on it. A world so thin that other worlds can breach the veil and speak through their dead.

A dark fantasy horror, this book has an intrigue that sets it apart from all others, hitting all the points that seemingly form together to create a great horror story. With the dead cached in the cellar, speaking from beyond the grave, and each corpse, with its own motive, wanting to pull you under their own spell. With the only creature left to speak a God-made creature that preaches the Lord's will, you soon realize the end is near for Merciful and Gospel, leaving you fearing it might just be the end of the world.

A story that is wickedly enthralling, as it closes the door on what we know of our world, forcing us into an alternate realm. A world of time that has passed them by, one that is vanishing within a fog, taking with it pieces of their own world along with literal pieces of them.

Jason Vanhee is a fresh voice giving a new perspective to YA horror, with his own unyielding writing style, which grips you and pulls you under its evil spell, haunting you with its lullaby, even after you close the cover.

—Review by Amy Shane

The Glass Casket
by McCormick Templeman
Delacorte Press
ISBN-13:978-0385743457
February 2014; $17.99

In a world where daughters were married off as soon as possible, with no chance of being anything but a helpmate to a husband, Rowan knows she is lucky to have a father who values a girl's mind, seeing her equally as great as any scholarly son.

With dreams of journeying down the mountain pass to see the palace city for her own eyes, Rowan knows her secret longing will one day be fulfilled, as she uses her studies as a key to the palace. So when five palace riders, on horseback, thunder through the village on their way up the mountain, Rowan knows her destiny is about to change. However, destiny can't be pre-determined, and when an enchanting stranger, instead of the riders, emerges from the forest, destiny is about to take shape. Changing Rowan's life in a way that even she can't be prepared for, when the dead bodies of the riders are discovered. Rowan's destiny is about to intertwine with something so vile and sinister, no one is considered safe.

So, when Fiona, a scarlet-hooded beauty, with raven hair and snow-white skin, appears in the village, Rowan starts to lose that of which she holds most dear. She learns that her best friend Tom has been enchanted by the beauty of Fiona, leaving him vulnerable to the allure that befalls her, opening the door to wickedness itself.

Soon, Rowan is plagued with images, as if they were "painted on the back of her eyelids by a wicked hand," as death rips out the throats of those who are close to her. Like two words etched in the snow, "it's starting," death silently ravages the night, like a vile creature creeping over her.

Fear is suddenly awakened with a rumble deep in the woods, of something too large to be any animal. A scream pierces the dead of night, sharp and beyond recognition, ripping a new pain of loss through the village. Where the stench of crimson blood can be tasted in the air.

Bringing with it a sinister beast that comes to rest upon the village, feeding with its insatiable appetite upon the villagers. A beast that can only be described as one that has gaping wounds for eyes, needle-sharp teeth, and rotting breath smelling of dirt and death. Where the forest suddenly becomes a place in which the devil stalks between the trees, leaving Rowan as the only person to discover how to save the village and kill the beast.

In a story where secrets are meant to be kept, _The Glass Casket_ reads like a classic horror straight from the Brothers Grimm. Like a tale that was meant to be told, a door opened and life began. Where secrets resurface in the face of beauty and death lingers in the shadows. Horrific and gruesome at times, McCormick Templeman knows how to deliver in the world of horror.

—Review by Amy Shane

Pearry Teo's Bedlam Stories: The Battle for Oz and Wonderland Begins
by Christine Converse
Dark Häus Press, 2011; Bedlam Stories LLD
978-1492116561
September 2013; $13.99 PB;
eBook, $4.99

Imagine 1922.

Imagine an insane asylum isolated on a dismal gray island; surrounded by a graveyard studded with moldering, canting, illegible headstones; its structures decaying, paint peeling, walls and floors aged to a uniform non-color; its inmates' rooms little more than prison cells with a single hard cot and barred windows. Then square that image.

Image a doctor who, for the best of reasons perhaps, experiments on his helpless victims, using them to try to achieve his heart's desire without any consideration for their pain, their suffering. Then square that image.

Imagine a head nurse who makes Nurse Rachet seem warm and cuddly and Annie Wilkes the epitome of selflessness and nurturing. Then square *that* image.

If you've been able to imagine all of the above, and then transform those into images exceeding the horrific, you have engaged the world of Christine Converse's *Bedlam Stories: The Battle for Oz and Wonderland Begins.*

But that is only the beginning.

Every story of death and darkness needs a protagonist, a voice of reason to resonate with the unreasonable and irrational. In *Bedlam Stories,* that voice belongs to intrepid *New York Examiner* reporter Nellie Bly, who in our world worked for the *New York World* and committed herself to a ten-day stay in Bellevue Hospital to expose the inhumane treatment of its inmates…and died in 1922. In *Bedlam Stories,* she enters Bedlam Asylum for much the same purpose—to research an exposé of how mentally unstable women are treated.

On the ferry trip to the island, she meets a second main character: a young girl named Dorothy Gale, late of Kansas, who has been committed by her Auntie Em and Uncle Henry in the hopes that treatment will cure her of what appear to be dangerous and obsessive powers. A few pages later, inside Bedlam itself, Nellie sees a beautiful mirror on the wall, the only thing in the Asylum that is neither crumbling nor decrepit. As she passes, she glimpses a third character…hidden within the mirror itself: Alice Liddell, the inspiration for Lewis Carroll's *Alice in Wonderland.*

And the stage is set for a phantasmagorical narrative in which worlds—imaginative and 'real'—collide, in which the well-known and well-beloved characters from both Oz and Wonderland have transmuted into horrors…*and* gained the power to move from one fantasy world into the other—and into Nellie Bly's world. Alice and Dorothy possess the power to make their fantasy worlds real, and, for reasons beyond her own understanding, Nellie provides the catalyst for the other two girls.

The result is a mind-numbing panoply of horrors: machines designed to drive the sane insane; imaginary landscapes that are as bleak and inhospitable as Bedlam Asylum itself; characters who inflict physical, mental, and emotional torture on young women, assuring them all of the time that their suffering will eventually "cure" them; and a cataclysmic ending (to this volume at least) that brings to bear all of the evils and terrors of three worlds. The final sentence (not actually a spoiler, since it is implicit in what I've said so far) threatens, "Wonderland will regret the day they ever crossed us, the armies of OZ!"

The next volume will be subtitled: "The Fall of Oz."

Bedlam Stories is a highly intriguing amalgam of historical figures, imaginary landscapes, familiar characters from favorite children's stories; in addition to Dorothy and Alice, there is an enigmatic Wendy. And it is an ideal introduction to what promises to be a complex, multi-volume exploration of the limits of sanity, the powers of imagination, and the metamorphosis of fantasy into horror.

While there are some problems with word choice and sentence structure, *Bedlam Stories* largely overcomes these by the sheer vitality of its storytelling. Like Nellie Bly, once the reader has entered the Asylum, it is difficult to emerge… unscathed.

—**Reviewed by Michael R. Collings**

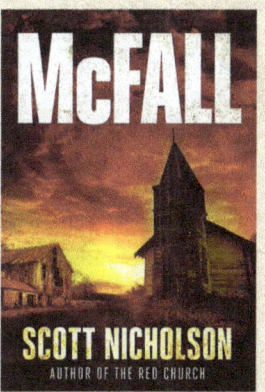

McFall
Scott Nicholson
47North
ISBN: 978-1477849231
February, 2014; $14.95 PB
Reviewed by David A. Riley

This is a sequel to *Drummer Boy* and *The Red Church,* though if, like me, you have not read either you can still enjoy this book.

A member of the villainous family that plagued the previous novels, the McFall of the title, has come to claim the land that belongs to him. But Larkin McFall is different from his predecessors, subtle, suave, a property developer who draws people to him through the promise of work and big profits. The infamous Red Church, in which his predecessor worked so much evil, he has destroyed by fire to make way for a high class development – though what is found within its burned out embers gives a dark glimpse that all is not as he makes it out to be.

Behind all the *bon homie* and the modern aspects of his wealth and power lurks an ancient evil, well hidden by his designer clothes and his apparent desire to help people out. The local sheriff, nearing retirement and still raw from what happened years ago when a different McFall lived locally, is certain about this, even though he can't prove it. But bodies turn up and ghosts from the past are never very far away.

The main protagonists, looking forward to college, are Ronnie Day and Bobby Eldreth, best friends through thick and thin. Ronnie has a reputation for finding dead bodies – a reputation he would rather do without – while Bobby shines as the star baseball player for their high school team with hopes of turning professional if he is lucky enough to be spotted by a scout from a major team. Little by little, Larkin McFall comes into their lives, manipulating them both in what he likes to call a game within a game. Ronnie tries to resist, but he is outclassed. Bobbie, dogged by an over-ambitious father who sees him as a meal ticket to a better life, is easier prey.

This is an engrossing novel, with a fine cast of well developed characters, set within a realistic milleau. The sinister developments are skilfully introduced with cumulative ease as McFall spins his spider's web around the township. Deaths, intrigues, and betrayals, all play their part in a story that quickly sucks you in with consummate ease. A thoroughly modern, thoroughly intriguing horror novel.

—**Reviewed by David A. Riley**

Things Slip Through
By Kevin Lucia
Crystal Lake Publishing
ISBN 978-0992170707; $13.99 PB

Welcome to Clifton Heights. It may be a nice place to visit, but lingering would be a very, very bad idea.

Things Slip Through is an archetypal trickster of a book. The stories in its pages form a dark ride through a town that, though normal enough on the surface, draws its lifeblood from an ominously beating heart. Framed within a wraparound narrative that brings to mind fond memories of the Amicus anthology films, each self-contained story ties into the others, making this essentially a novel in stories, which works admirably well.

But what are the stories about?

Well, a lot of things. Here you'll find pernicious books, nefarious creatures and arcane artifacts. You'll find crazed doctors and crazed gods alike. You'll travel to haunted places and meet haunted people, and to my mind it's these people, more than anything, that really make Things Slip Through shine.

Many of the characters in these stories are on the fringes of society, marginalized or coping with things they can't quite seem to escape from. In writing about their lives, Lucia touches on racism, alcoholism, and abuse both physical and psychological. He does this with a deft and compassionate hand, which makes it that much more horrifying when characters are faced with the encroachment of unnatural, otherworldly things that they will almost certainly never escape from. It's vividly imagined and moves at a brisk pace.

I enjoyed each of the stories, but personal favorites include:

"The Water God of Clarke Street," a coming of age tale about a disillusioned high school girl and her not-so-innocuous imaginary friend.

"A Brother's Keeper," in which an unsuspecting man returns to his homestead to make the ultimate familial sacrifice (with a little help from the friendly family doctor).

"The Sliding," a wonderfully atmospheric piece that invokes a subtle sense of dread and plays with time in an interesting way.

"Mr. Nobody," the final story of the book, a touching and harrowing tale of a mother, a missing son, and a creature borne of dark dreams. Given its brief but poignant sketch of love and loss, and coupled with the conclusion of the wraparound story that follows, this is hands down my favorite of the bunch.

The only qualm I have with the book is some stilted, expositional dialogue, particularly in the wraparound piece. Given the strength of the narrative itself and the characters that people it, however, this becomes a non-issue. Lucia is a gifted storyteller. If you're a fan of the strange and uncanny, and you like the kind of horror that sinks in slowly and hangs around to watch you squirm, you'll be doing yourself a favor by picking this one up.

—**Reviewed by Josh Black**

Demonstra: A Poetry Collection
Bryan Thao Worra
Innsmouth Free Press
ISBN 978-0991675975
December, 2013; $9.99 PB

It took exactly seven lines for me to decide I was onto something special with this new release from Innsmouth Free Press. This book is just that good. In *Demonstra*, Bryan Thao Worra presents an unusual collection of speculative poetry, filled with references to popular horror tropes, traditional Laotian folklore, and Buddhist musings in striking and unexpected combinations. Within, the classic monsters from Universal Pictures and Creature Double Feature rub elbows with Laotian Phi, Rakshasas, and Nyak. The author was adopted as an infant during the Laotian Civil War, and grew up in America, returning to Laos and reuniting with his biological family some 30 years later. The mythology and folklore of both nations intertwine, reflecting the icons of an American youth and the rediscovery of the culture of his family of origin. Poems about Lovecraftian shoggoth and the hungry ghosts of Southeast Asia intermingle with poems about cultural and personal identity. The result is entrancing, delightful, sad, and philosophical.

Horror is consistent throughout, but it is different from much of the conventional gloomy and spooky verse that frequently appears in anthologies and magazines. At times, the work is sublimely ridiculous. A poet asks a monk, "Does a zombie have a Buddha nature?" Later, an aged shaman, speaking through a translator, asks the poet "Who's your favorite wrestler?" and poses like Randy Savage. At other times, the horror is more serious, and there is a darker subtext that permeates the work. Worra speaks of a people haunted not just by monsters, but by war and diaspora. Popular culture is juxtaposed against references to refugee camps and battles from what was, to most of the world, a secret sidebar to the war in Vietnam. The poetry describes the echoes of an ancient culture ripped violently into modern times. Beyond these concerns are universal human stories of meaning and impermanence, set against the black void of space and rampaging kaiju. In a deft balancing act, Worra retains a sense of wonder and humor that complements the darkness. The collection communicates a broad range of emotions. It is a skillfully crafted collection, featuring a fresh and exciting voice.

To supplement the work, the author has provided appendices, including a Lao American Bestiary, describing the many spirits, powers and entities that populate the poems in great detail; a rich bibliography of Laotian culture and history; and translations of Cthulhu Mythos entities in Lao. It isn't necessary to read them to appreciate the poetry, but they do enrich the volume and add layers of meaning. If you know the language and the culture, I imagine it would be a different experience, but wonderful nonetheless. The poetry is also complemented by illustrations by Vongduane Manivong.

Having read it once, I look forward to revisiting it again. The talent that earned Worra a Fellowship from the National Endowment for the Arts and various other awards is on full display here, and I cannot recommend it highly enough. More on the poet and his work can be found at http://thaoworra.blogspot.com/

—**Reviewed by K. H. Vaughan**

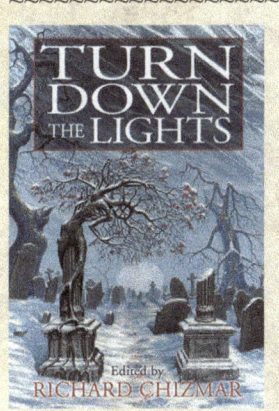

Turn Down The Lights
Richard Chizmar, Editor
Cemetery Dance Publications
February 2014; $35.00 HC

A surprise anniversary anthology from Cemetery Dance is coming out to commemorate 25 years of their magazine. Richard Chizmar launched the debut issue of his publication in December of 1988 and they just published issue #70 recently – as well as a huge amount of books during that time. To celebrate that landmark event, he has put together a collection of all-new stories from many regulars of the magazine and book line.

It's an all-star lineup for this horror anthology and a diverse group of stories too. Stephen King contributes the post-apocalyptic tale "Summer Thunder." A poignant, emotional story in the vein of his novel The Stand that tells of one of the few survivors on earth and his dog. Clive Barker, who hasn't been heard from in a while, tells of the creepy "Dollie." Jack Ketchum gives us a great horror western tale with "The Western Dead." Norman Partridge makes a much welcome return to CD's lineup with his noir-fused monster tale "Incardine." Bentley Little brings us another one of his unique weird tales in "In the Room" and Peter Straub caps it off with a new literary horror story "The Collected Stories of Freddie Prothero: Introduction by Torless Magnussen, Ph.D."

In between there are also great new stories by Ronald Kelly, Ed Gorman, Steve Rasnic Tem and Brian James Freeman. Chizmar kicks it off with an Introduction and popular CD columnist Thomas F. Monteleone does the Afterword. And finally cover art by regular contributor Alan M. Clark. It's a great collection overall, although a bit on the slim side with only 175 pages. Still with the amazing lineup of authors with all new stories, it's definitely worth the $35 price tag in my opinion. (also available in more expensive signed/# and signed/lettered editions). Recommended.

—**Reviewed by Trever Nordgren**

Poe: Nevermore
Rachel M. Martens
BookBaby
ISBN 978-1483500935
June, 2013; $1.99 Kindle

I'm a fan of Edgar Allan Poe's short stories and poems. Apparently Rachel Martens, author of *Poe: Nevermore* is as well: the story is peppered with little bits of trivia about his life and work. This is what brings our main character, Elenora Allison Poe (called "Poe" in this tale) together with Frost, the love interest of the story.

But that doesn't mean the story's tone is lighthearted and romantic. While there are brief moments of true intimacy between the two, Elenora quickly—yet inadvertently—drags Frost into her fear and pain riddled world. But he seems more than willing to come along.

Soon Mr. Poe himself enters the story, bringing Elenora into a "conference room" that can only be entered by the living that are near death, to tell her about a curse that has made her its focus. The curse is based on his works, but he can do little to help her solve the mystery.

Martens has no difficulty in putting her characters through horrible situations—in fact, Elenora is one of the most abused and damaged characters I've read about recently in horror. Yet, she manages to not only survive the traumas inflicted on her by an abusive stepfather, but she begins to cultivate a shaky seed of trust in her heart for Frost. Then a chain reaction happens spreading the world-destroying torture that follows her like a brush fire.

The issues I had with the book were few, but when they happened they took me out of the story. Descriptions, especially the ones of Frost (and his eyes), were repetitive and I found myself wanting variation. However, Martens does a great job of building suspense. Her dialogue is well crafted: full of subterfuge and characters that lie and tap dance around answering questions, making their exchanges and interactions true-to-life. And the "big bad" in the story is completely, yet believably insane, which is something that can be hard to do.

I appreciate when an author isn't hesitant to drag their babies through the mud, sand, and cut glass. A peek at Martens' shows that Nevermore is the first in a series. The concept of using Poe's works as a focus for each story is an interesting one. I look forward to seeing what horrors she dreams up for her next release.

—**Reviewed by Eden Royce**

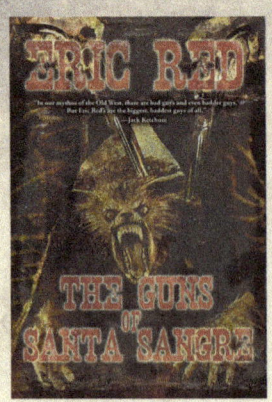

The Guns of Santa Sangre
by Eric Red
Samhain Publishing
ISBN 978-1619215696
November, 2013; $14.00 PB

For connoisseurs of the Old West, Eric Red's *The Guns of Santa Sangre* has all the elements of a classic:

*It opens with a fast-and-furious stagecoach heist;

*It has outlaws who, beneath their coarse exterior, boast hearts of gold;

*It has cruel, corrupt representatives of the law, who deserve everything that happens to them, and more;

*It has touches of Seven Samurai and The Magnificent Seven…with perhaps a tiny wink in the direction of The Three Amigos;

*It has sacrifice and heartbreak;

*It has a beautiful heroine disguised as a boy, even though the disguise isn't exactly perfect;

*It has a town drunk who hides a secret that has kept him alive…and acts as the key to his redemption;

*It has gunplay and horseplay;

*It has a treasure in silver waiting for the taking;

*It ends with the heroes riding off into the sunset, justice…and love…having prevailed.

And…oh yes!…it has WEREWOLVES!

Somehow, though, everything weaves together nicely to create a fun, rapid-paced yarn. The werewolves are given enough background to make their presence entirely logical; and the remaining—human—characters run true-to-type without quite becoming stereotypes. Their actions are at once unique to each and representative of what one would expect in a good Western.

Three gunslingers on the run from an American bounty hunter and the Mexican authorities meet a young Mexican peasant who convinces them to help his small village, now overrun by ruffians who have made their headquarters in the local church. Their reward: the silver statues and other artifacts in the church. All they need to do is kill the ruffians.

Sounds simple enough. Three against a dozen or so… no problem.

Until, of course, one factors in the supernatural. Ruffians killed by day rise again in the night as werewolves, insatiably hungry for human flesh…and they've almost run out of villagers.

Quick, smooth, easily read, *The Guns of Santa Sangre* satisfies on both accounts. It is an almost filmic rendition of the time-honored traditions of the Western, with a deftly handled incursion of the unnatural, with the two blended into a single, intriguing story.

—Reviewed by Michael R. Collings

Absinthe & Arsenic
Raven Dane
Telos Moonrise
ISBN: 978-1-84583-858-4
July, 2013; $18.99 PB

UK-based Raven Dane has had many short stories and poems published in horror and fantasy anthologies and is the author of several novels, including the critically acclaimed Legacy of the Dark Kind series and her award-winning series of steampunk/occult novels featuring Cyrus Darian, the third of which she is currently writing.

Absinthe & Arsenic is a collection of (mostly) ghost stories chosen or specially written for the anthology by Raven Dane. She has selected works ranging from one of the earliest in her writing career (The Attic Nursery) through to very recent short stories, including an excerpt from her award-winning novel Cyrus Darian and the Technomicron.

All of the stories in Dane's outstanding collection are rooted in the late 19th century, and it is evident that she is an enthusiastic student of the era. The terminology and speech patterns she utilizes, along with descriptive passages that swirl like fog from the pages, create wholly believable settings dripping with atmosphere into which she threads effectively chilling ghost stories.

The collection begins with a terrifically bleak pseudo-zombie uprising in The 10.15 to Lealholm and then settles down into traditional Victorian ghost stories that could have been ripped from the spines of the penny dreadfuls of the time, such is their authenticity and Dane's skillful prose. There are no weak entries in this collection, but my personal favorites were In Insomnium Veritas, Worse Things Happen at Sea, A Taste of Almonds, Ghostlight and Heart of Brass – each of the tales being unique despite their shared timeframe.

Although ghost stories are usually things of an intimate, whispered nature, I found the two tales that book-ended the collection, The 10.15 to Lealholm and Heart of Brass, to read like film synopses, the former feeling like a 60's Hammer period piece and the latter like an early Del Toro film by way of Poe, which made the reading of them even more enjoyable.

This accomplished collection of short stories from Raven Dane would be an excellent introduction to readers who have yet to discover her work.

Highly recommended.

—Reviewed by Neil Baker

In the Shadow of Blackbirds
Cat Winters
Abrams
ISBN 978-1419705304
April, 2013; $16.95 HB

Dark, unsettling and atmospherically eerie, *In the Shadow of Blackbirds* is haunting in its own right.

1918, where death was a constant whisper, "I told you I was coming, get ready I am here.

A heart wrenching story highlighting the tragedies of the year 1918, caught between a world devastated by the First World War and emaciated by the Spanish Influenza. A great number of lives were lost and hearts were broken, as everyone feared for their lives. Death was a constant companion, knocking at everyone's door. Between the war and the flu no one was safe, for both of them did not discern between race, rank, or social status, all were subject to be death's companion. Leaving the door open for those who took advantage of the mourner's heart, promising comfort and closure; for them, spirit photographers and séances became the answer.

Mary Shelly Black, an aspiring scientist in a man's world, suddenly gets caught up in the wake of the flu. She is sent to live with her Aunt and abruptly gets thrown in a world that reeked of death and fear. Mary Shelly Black couldn't help but to be slightly mortified by the morbid display of death; stacks of coffins lined the undertaker's yard, and bodies lined the streets. The stench was overwhelming even though everyone roamed the streets with gauze mask covered faces, chewed garlic gum, and ingested onions trying to keep death from knocking on their door.

Just when Mary thinks death has skipped her door the news of her first love dying in battle sends her to question her belief of ghosts and messages from the beyond. Forced to pose for acclaimed, "Spiritualist Photographer" Julius Embers, Mary's life turns upside down as she is thrust into questioning her own beliefs of the spirit realm, when her first love appears to her in spirit form.

Mary soon learns that it is up to her to solve why he has returned and how to solve the mystery of the harrowing corpse eating blackbirds, so that he may finally rest in peace. Introducing you to scenes where Mary's first love returns to her in his bleakest moments; of corpse filled trenches lined with mud, filth and rats, her life soon turns into an empty shell of mystery, murder and death.

The novel is illustrated with eerie and unsettling early twentieth century photographs, which immerse you deeper into the era and transport you to a forgotten time of utter loss and devastation. Helping you picture the setting is a story that was so intensely researched with rich historical accuracy.

Like the plain wooden boxes that line the streets with their death, Cat Winters lays the horror of 1918 before you in a way that can't be ignored. It takes you on a horrifying emotional journey that is equally beautiful as it is haunting. Whether it be the ghosts, the inauspicious photographs, or the horrors of war and the Spanish Influenza, this book is definitely worth reading.

—Reviewed by Amy Shane

*How I Started the Apocalypse,
Book Two: The Hunger War*
**By Brian Pinkerton
Severed Press
October 4, 2013, $9.99**

I read and reviewed Book One of this series a little over a year ago. I enjoyed the story very much, so I was pleased to give Book Two a read.

The story is told from the point-of-view of Chaz Singleton, a man turned zombie by no choice of his own. Unlike other zombies, Chaz is aware of the situation and wants to find the man who put him in this horrific situation. He tries to fight his urges to consume human flesh, but can't; however, he tries to eat only those who he thinks are a detriment to society.

Unfortunately, in an effort to find the doctor in charge of the experiment, he started the zombie plague, first causing an outbreak in Pittsburgh, and then infecting much of New York City. Once Chaz uploads a video confession to the Internet, he becomes hunted by the military. His son tries to help him, but is kidnapped by the doctor as he attempts to flee the city.

Chaz begins to realize he has command over his fellow zombies. They can't talk, but they understand him and obey him. He is also joined by a woman, Dolores, who is in the same predicament. Together, they organize the zombies into an army to fight against the soldiers trying to eradicate the zombies and their plague from New York City.

I enjoyed Book Two as much as Book One. I was actually disappointed to reach the end because I didn't know there is going to be a Book Three, and I was left hanging. This was a fun read, and it was the first time I ever encountered zombie sex. Some things are better left to the imagination.

Gory and action-packed, *The Hunger War* is also funny and touching. One can't help but feel for Chaz and cheer him on in his efforts. Brian Pinkerton has managed to make a sympathetic zombie, impressive in a popular sub-genre where they are an abomination.

I can't wait until Book Three.

—Reviewed by Sheri White

***The Universal and other Terrors.*
Tony Richards
Dark Renaissance Books
$40 HB**

The Universal and Other Terrors is a solid collection of unsettling stories highlighted by atmospheric artwork by M. Wayne Miller. The dozen stories range from overt horror to subtle evocations, allowing readers to complete the narratives for themselves.

The headnote story, *The Universal,* sets the standard. A character discovers a notebook abandoned in a long-deserted testing center. Among intriguing equations and ominous sketches, he finds: "*This is generally acknowledged to be one of the great Universal Laws. Events that are impossible are never allowed to happen within our sphere of existence. If that were not the case, then reality would be under constant threat of breaking up in places or even collapsing entirely.*" None of the subsequent stories precisely act as *sequels,* but each explores the impossible intruding into everyday life.

In "The Universal," evidences of collapse are small, relegated to seemingly neglected buildings near a normal seacoast town. Little happens…except that the narrator sees things that cannot be. And they slowly increase.

"Aegea" is a story of perception. Matt discovers a secluded beach with several sunbathers, each facing in the same direction, each wearing the same swimwear and the same style dark sunglasses. Aware of a oddity about the beach and the bathers, Matt swims out until his feet no longer touch bottom. Then he turns toward the beach…and sees just how odd—how *impossible*—things there are.

"The Visitors in Marvell Wood" explores on the perilous interface between childhood and adulthood and on the consequences when something *impossible* alters that interface.

In "Covered Mirrors," following a death in a household, all mirrors are covered as mourning. Though young Jody does not quite understand why, he knows that the tradition causes a breach between his unbelieving mother and his father. Eventually, he understands that there are consequences—*impossible* consequences—to looking beneath the shrouds.

In "The Crows," nothing horrific happens. Howard's wife, Marjorie, notices crows in the garden. He returns to the evening paper with its news of increased glacial melt and out-of-control global events. Later, a neighbor's dog is killed by a car…and Howard notices more crows. Life happens. And there are more crows. And more. And more.

"By a Dark Canal," 'unofficial' prequel to one of the most famous horror novels, Bram Stoker's *Dracula,* introduces an atheistic, opinionated, sexually-charged, brilliant medical student named…Abraham Van Helsing. Believing that a man's health and sanity depend upon his going "through the motions of breeding" weekly, he visits part of the city along a pitch-black canal and he meets a lady of the evening who transforms him and everything he believes possible.

"Sense" demonstrates how gradually yet inevitably the impossible-to-contemplate becomes not only possible but everyday reality, a horror version of Martin Niemöller's famous poem beginning: "First they came for the communists,/and I didn't speak out because I wasn't a communist." It shows the inevitable encroachment on human rights and liberties—even human life—when small exceptions are made to standards of decency and humanity.

The final story, "A Town Called Youngesville," suggests Levin's *Rosemary's Baby,* cross-fertilized with classic episodes of *The Twilight Zone,* and a hint of Levin's *The Stepford Wives.* Youngesville is a perfect planned community. Yet…yet several things do not seem right. Determined to find out what is going on, Frank begins searching…and discovers truth, leading to confrontation, understanding, and horror as the *impossible* imposes itself upon everyday reality.

And the reader returns to "The Universal," having traveled through twelve variations on the basic premise: *if reality begins to unravel, what horrors might be released.*

Highly recommended.

—Reviewed by Michael R. Collings

❦ ❦ ❦

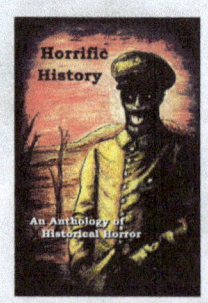

The Beast Within (Blu-ray; Rated R)
Director: Philippe Mora
Cast: Ronny Cox, Bibi Besch, Paul Clemens
Shout! Factory
December, 2013

The Beast Within is a weird one. Let's get that right out of the way. It's about a woman down in Mississippi who one night is raped by some…thing. It's not clearly shown, but it is obvious not human. Seventeen years later and the horrible assault has produced a normal looking teenage son named Michael who is having some…problems. Poor Michael is having nightmares, pain, and is going through some…changes. And by changes, I mean normal teenage boy things. You know, like killing and eating people! Yes, there is some sort of beast within Michael that's just now starting to come to the surface.

Now don't worry, that's not really a spoiler, as that tidbit is given away early on in the movie. There is an interesting, if somewhat outlandish, mystery as to who or what was Michael's real daddy and what horrible *Beast* lurks *Within* the young man. There is also something out there killing people, other than Michael, in horribly violet ways. Could it be the unseen, spooky-sounding thing that's been locked away under an old, abandoned barn that Michael is inexplicably drawn to? Then there is the question as to why Michael goes crazy whenever he hear the cricket-like chirping of the cicadas.

Damn it, I can't keep it to myself, it's just so weird and awesome, so SPOLIERS for a 30+ year old movie if you have yet to see it.

You see, Mike's mommy was raped by a bug-man-thing that's sort of a big cicada. And just like cicadas' seventeen-year-long lifecycle, now that Michael is seventeen, it's time for him to answer nature's unnatural call. Yes, this poor kid is a werecicada! Or at least, someone turning into a mutant man-bug thanks to some state of the art (circa 1982) special effects that are at once both cheesy and awesome. Hey, I'll still take effects like these over CGI any day of the week.

So in *The Beast Within* you get an original, albeit implausible as hell, story that's well told thanks to the efforts of screenwriter Tom (*Fright Night, Child's Play, Psycho II*) Holland. The direction by Philippe Mora is solid, or at least miles better than what he did for *The Howling II & III.* All the actors deliver their A-games here despite the silly premise, with special nods of approval go out to longtime genre vets Ronny Cox, R.G. Armstrong, and L.Q. Jones. And did I mention the groovy special effects?

As usual, the always amazing Scream Factory has put a lot of work in making this old, mostly fright flick look incredible. Simply put, you have never seen bugman rape look this good. As for the extras, they are both a hit and a miss. The hits are twofold; being a pair of pretty good audio commentary tracks. The first one is with director Philippe Mora and actor Paul Clemens who plays the unfortunate werecicada in the movie. The other is with screenwriter Tom Holland. Sadly the miss is everything else, as there are no featurettes, interviews, behind the scenes bits, or anything. There is just a theatrical trailer and some radio spots. That's it.

The Beast Within is a weird but cool monster movie with an admittedly silly premise. If you can overlook that, you'll likely have a lot fun with this one. If you're a fan of the type of early 80s horror that they just don't make anymore, then you'll love this movie. As I am a huge fan of that, I can highly recommend this crazy little flick to anyone with similar tastes.

—Reviewed by Brian M. Sammons

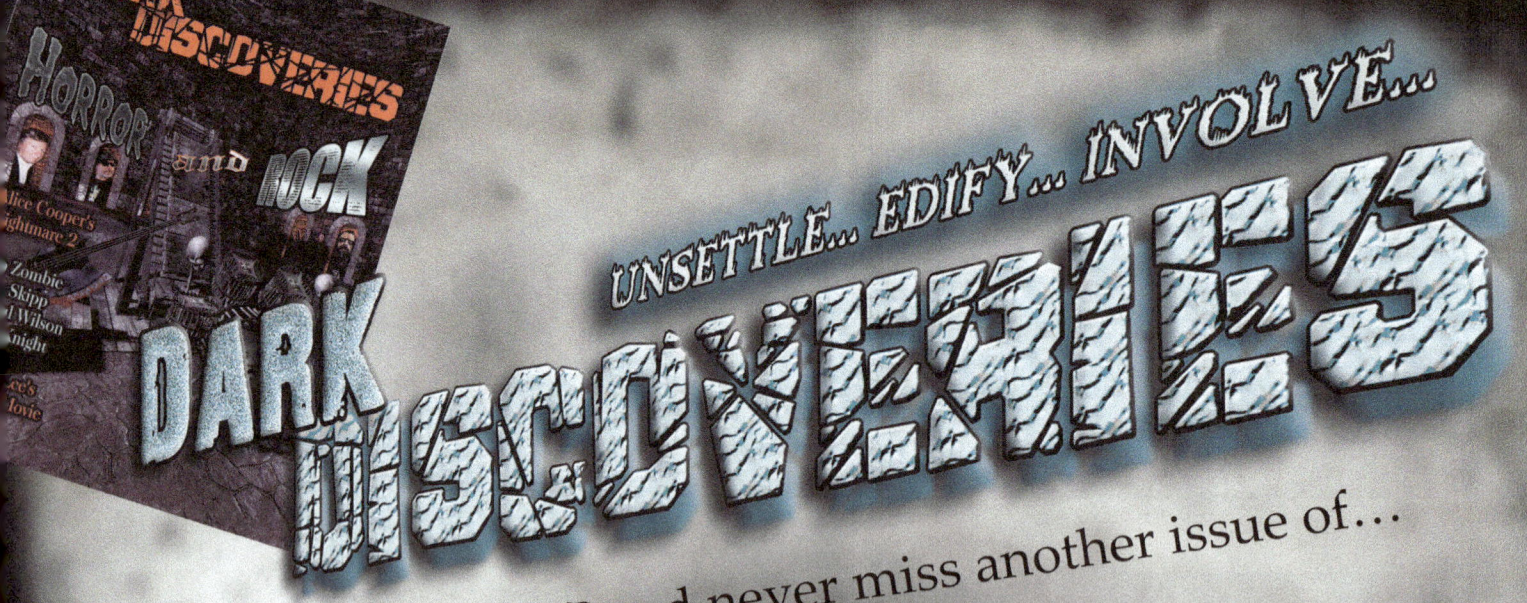

UNSETTLE... EDIFY... INVOLVE...

DARK DISCOVERIES

SUBSCRIBE and never miss another issue of…

www.darkdiscoveries.com

FEATURES:

Weird Fiction & Film, Extreme Horror, Comics & Pulps, New Blood, Dark SciFi, Twilight Zone, H.P. Lovecraft, Horror in Rock, Forgotten Horror & SF TV…

INTERVIEWS:

Ray Bradbury, Bruce Campbell, Christopher Lee, Joe R. Lansdale, William F. Nolan, EC Comics Al Feldstein, Brian Keene, Jack Ketchum, David Cronenberg…

FICTION:

Richard Matheson, Ray Bradbury, Thomas Ligotti, Richard Laymon, John Shirley, William F. Nolan, Ramsey Campbell, Joe R. Lansdale, Lisa Morton, Edward Lee…

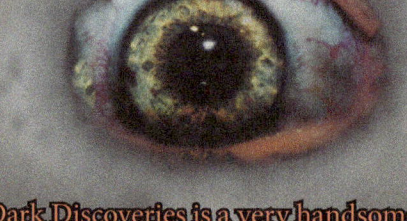

"Dark Discoveries is a very handsome publication..."

--Dean Koontz

"A bright new force in Dark Fantasy."

--William F. Nolan

"Dark Discoveries is a high quality mag... and it keeps getting better..."

--Horror Fiction Review

PRINT SUBSCRIPTIONS

4 issues (1 year): US ($37.95) Canada ($46.95) Overseas ($69.95)

8 issues (2 years): US ($74.95) Canada ($92.95) Overseas ($139.95)

(*Shipping is included on print subs)

ADVERTISERS!

Inquire via E-mail for rates!

Please Note: Future content subject to change without notice. All rights reserved.

DIGITAL SUBSCRIPTIONS

4 issues (1 year): $19.95
8 issues (2 years): $39.95
Payment accepted via PayPal:
christophercpayne@journalstone.com
Also by Check/M.O. (Payable to)

JournalStone Publications, 1261 Peachwood Court, San Bruno, CA 94066, USA

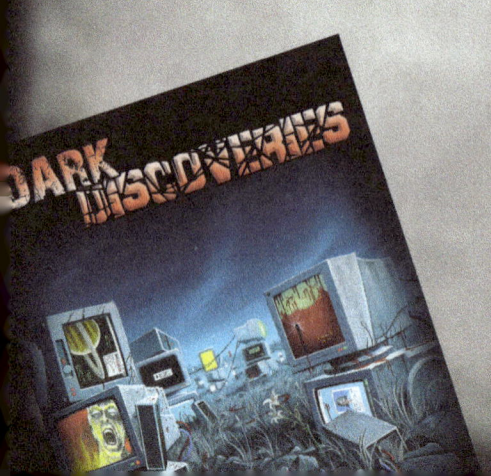

JOURNALSTONE
YOUR LINK TO ARTISTIC TALENT